MW00437424

REASONABLE FEAR

REASONABLE FEAR

By

SCOTT PRATT

ISBN: 1481215663
ISBN 13: 9781481215664

This book, along with every book I've written and every book I'll write, is dedicated to my darling Kristy, to her unconquerable spirit and to her inspirational courage. I loved her before I was born and I'll love her after I'm long gone.

Reasonable Force – That degree of force which is not excessive and is appropriate in protecting oneself or one's property. When such force is used, a person is justified and is not criminally liable.
– Black's Law Dictionary

PART I

CHAPTER ONE

A ten-year-old boy, fishing along the bank of Boone Lake with his father, was the first to spot the body. She was floating about ten feet from shore in the gray light of dawn, slightly submerged in the still, green water. I arrived around 6:30 a.m., shortly after the emergency medical people. The sheriff had called me as soon as he was notified.

It was the end of summer, the "dog days" as they're known in northeast Tennessee, the time of year when the heat is sweltering and the humidity stifling, when the first of the leaves separate from the branches that have sustained them through spring and summer. They float briefly, silently, on the breeze until they drop to the earth, signaling the beginning of the season of death.

Normally, the district attorney wouldn't show up at the scene of an apparent drowning, but the sheriff said the boy's father told the emergency dispatcher that the woman in the water was naked. Maybe she was skinny-dipping and drowned. Maybe she was drunk and fell from a boat. Maybe she committed suicide. Or maybe she didn't go into the water voluntarily. If she was murdered, I'd ultimately be responsible for seeing to it that whoever killed her was prosecuted, and I liked to be in on the investigation from the beginning whenever possible.

My name is Joe Dillard, a name bestowed upon me when Lyndon Johnson controlled the White House and Robert McNamara and "the hawks" controlled U.S. foreign policy. My father, the son of a Unicoi County cattle and tobacco farmer, was a casualty of those hawks. He'd been drafted and sent to Vietnam. He'd visited my mother and infant sister in Hawaii while on leave from the war six weeks before he was killed. It was during that visit to Hawaii that I was conceived. I never met my father, but from the photos I've seen of him, there's no doubt in my mind about my paternity. The last photograph ever taken of him—two days before he died—showed a tall, strapping young man, tawny and shirtless beneath the afternoon sun on a mountainside, both his arms draped over the shoulders of his buddies. His hair, like mine, was dark; his eyes, like mine, were green; his shoulders and chest wide and thickly muscled, his waist lean and rippled. He was grinning widely, an innocent, boyish grin that belied the fear that must have resided in his belly.

At the age of forty-three, I found myself occupying the office of district attorney general over four counties in northeast Tennessee. I wasn't elected. I was appointed by the governor of Tennessee after the previous district attorney was accused of a terrible crime. My temples were flecked with gray, and my joints ached occasionally, but all in all, I'd managed to remain relatively robust as I entered middle age.

A young sheriff's deputy and his stocky partner were dragging the dead woman onto the grass as I walked down the bank from the road. Two other deputies were searching for evidence while yet another was standing in the road talking to a man—who I assumed made the initial call—and a boy. It was Sunday morning, the day before Labor Day. In two days, the Tennessee Valley Authority would begin the yearly process of steadily drawing down Boone Lake. By October, the lake would be twenty to thirty feet below full pool and would look like a giant mud puddle. It would stay that way until February, when the TVA would begin using the system of dams constructed during Roosevelt's New Deal era to gradually fill it again. Each year, on the Saturday before Labor Day, the lake is covered with house boats, pontoon boats, deck boats, ski boats, and jet skis as the locals take advantage of their last opportunity of the summer to enjoy the water at full pool. They come early and stay late, many of them drink like Irish Catholics at a wake, and nearly every year, someone dies.

The rising sun was hot against my face and a purple haze enveloped the surrounding mountains like a giant shroud. The sky was pale and blue, the air thick and moist. I could already feel sweat running down the side of my face from my temples. I stopped about ten feet from the body and watched while a paramedic efficiently but unenthusiastically attempted to revive her. After a few minutes, he looked at his partner and simply shook his head.

"How long you reckon she's been in the water?" a voice behind me said.

I turned and saw Sheriff Leon Bates, mid-forties, tall, lean and tan, clad in his khaki uniform, cowboy hat and boots, striding toward us. Bates was an immensely popular sheriff who was in the last year of his first four-year term, although I had no doubt he would be around for as many terms as he desired. He was a consummate Southern sheriff, mixing a congenial brand of back-woods lingo with a sharp mind for law enforcement, and over the past three years, he'd earned both my respect and my friendship.

"I'm not an expert," the EMT said, "but it doesn't look like she's been in long. Her lips are purple, but I don't see any signs of lividity. She isn't even in rigor yet."

I moved closer and looked down at the woman. I guessed her age at mid- to late-twenties. She was pretty, even in death. Her face was angular, her nose petite. Her open eyes were turquoise, and her hair was long and blonde. Her breasts were ample and her body lean. Her pubic area was shaved clean. She was wearing a thin, gold chain around her neck and rings of various types on all of her fingers.

"Any wounds or marks that you can see?" Bates said.

The EMT shook his head. "Just a tattoo."

I'd noticed the tattoo when I walked up, but I hadn't looked closely. When the EMT mentioned it, I stepped over and crouched down next to her. It was on the inside of her right forearm, a single, pink petal clinging to the stem of a dying rose. Beneath the rose were several withered petals lying in green grass. Above the stem and petal was the word "Hope."

Bates removed his cowboy hat and began scratching his head.

"How does a young beauty like this wind up drowned in the lake on the busiest night of the year without a soul seeing it?" he said to no one in particular. "Nobody's reported a girl missing. Nobody's called in and said she fell in or went swimming and went under. Nobody's said a word."

"She didn't drown," the EMT said.

"Excuse me?"

"I said she didn't drown. There isn't any water in her lungs."

"That's an important tidbit," Bates said. "I appreciate you getting around to sharing it with me."

Bates walked over next to me and hooked his thumbs in his belt.

"No water in her lungs means she was dead when she went in," he said. "Not a mark on her. How do you reckon she died, Brother Dillard?"

I shrugged my shoulders. "You're the sleuth. I'm just the lowly lawyer."

Bates looked around, scanning the tree-covered hills that surrounded the water. He raised his head skyward, and I followed his gaze. A half-dozen turkey vultures, black against the sky with wing spans of at least six feet, were circling ominously above.

"Amazing," he said. "How do you reckon they figure it out so fast?"

"They smell it," I said.

"Is it true they don't make any sound?"

"They hiss. Like a snake."

Bates sighed and resumed his survey of the surrounding area. "No houses in sight," he said. "Maybe a few campers scattered here and there, but we'll play hell finding anybody who saw anything. I guess we do what we always do when we run across a body with no witnesses."

"What's that?" I said.

"We start at the end and go backward."

CHAPTER TWO

I left a short time later and drove my truck along the narrow back roads that wound through the gently rolling hills of the Gray and Boones Creek communities. I rolled the windows down and let the smell of the morning swirl through the cab of my truck. Cattle were lying in the pale-yellow shade of the elms, locusts, poplars, and oaks that grew along the fringes of the pastures, and the rectangular tobacco patches were golden against the hillsides. Along the way, I started thinking about how hardened I'd become, how the sight of a dead young girl no longer moved me. It troubled me to think that I'd come to accept violence and cruelty as a part of everyday life.

Other attitudes had changed as well. I'd long ago rearranged the idealistic beliefs of my youth when it came to understanding or rehabilitating violent criminals. Whether the traits that caused them to commit their terrible transgressions were created by genetics, environment, or substance abuse was no longer of concern to me. My single purpose was getting them off the streets, into a secure warehouse, and keeping them there for as long as possible so they couldn't injure, maim, or kill again.

I pulled into a convenience store in Boones Creek and was just starting to fill up the tank in my truck when I heard someone call my name. The voice was vaguely familiar. I turned and saw a woman walking out of the store toward me. She was as vaguely familiar as the voice. Then it hit me.

"Leah? Leah Turner?"

The woman walked quickly to me and threw her arms around my neck.

"I heard you were here," she said into my ear. "It's so good to see you."

She stepped back, and I looked at her. Leah Turner was a classmate of mine at the University of Tennessee College of Law. I hadn't seen her in close to twenty years, but she'd changed very little. She had light brown hair that fell in ringlets around her dimpled cheeks, the clearest, prettiest, blue eyes I'd ever seen, and a smile that could melt the iciest heart.

"What are you doing here?" I asked.

"I've been transferred," she said. "Just this week. I can't believe I ran into you like this. Tell me you're not still married."

I smiled. As much as I hated to admit it, there had been something between us in law school. It was an attraction that was deep and physical, and it took every bit of control I could muster to resist her. Not that she made it easy. She hit on me openly and shamelessly. She even hit on me in front of my wife, Caroline, a couple times; I remember it was all I could do to keep Caroline from punching her in the nose.

"Still married," I said. "It's been good."

"How many kids did you end up with?"

"Just the two. They're both out of the house now. What about you? Are you married?"

"I'm Leah McCoy now," she said. "I got married five years after we graduated. His name is Carmack McCoy. Everybody calls him Mack. Great guy."

"Kids?"

"One. Robert. He's fifteen years old, and he's not happy about moving here. He's not happy about much of anything, really. If you want to know the truth, he's a pain in the butt."

"Teenager," I said. "It'll get better."

She squeezed both of my hands.

"You look good, Joe," she said.

"Thanks, so do you."

She was tall, just under six feet, lean and leggy. She was wearing running gear—skimpy shorts and a light blue, sleeveless top—and still had a sheen of sweat on her tanned face.

"Would you be interested in having an affair?" she asked. "I'm so bored."

"Who ... ah, who transferred you here? Who are you working for?"

"I was kidding, Joe. My husband is a super-human. There isn't a boring bone in his body. And I work for Uncle Sam himself. I'm an FBI agent, believe it or not. So is Mack."

"No kidding? How long have you been with the FBI?"

"Fifteen years. I worked for an insurance defense firm in Nashville after law school, but I hated it. I met Mack at a bar on Printer's Alley. We started dating and got married a year later. He was already an agent, and one day when I was complaining about work he suggested that I apply to the bureau, so I did. They hired me, and Mack and I have been with them ever since. It's been an interesting life. We've lived in a bunch of places, most recently Miami. I loved the work there, but I hated the climate. We both put in for transfers to Tennessee about a year ago, and a couple jobs came open. They gave us twenty-four hours to make up our minds. It didn't take me twenty-four seconds."

"So you're working in the Johnson City office?"

"No, I'm in Greeneville. Mack's in Johnson City."

"Only thirty miles apart. That's not so bad. What kind of cases are you going to be working?"

"I'm going to be doing crimes against children: kidnappings, pornography, stuff like that. Mack worked drugs in Miami, but he's going to work public corruption here."

"I'm sure there's plenty of work for both of you."

"Yeah, it's a shame, but it's true."

The handle on the gas pump popped, indicating the tank was full and breaking the momentum of the conversation.

"We should get together," Leah said, "the four of us."

"Definitely. Where are you living?"

"Just down the road. Big brick house. The corner of Highway 36 and Boring Chapel Road."

"I know exactly the house you're talking about. Been for sale for about a year."

"Not anymore." She kissed me lightly on the cheek. "I'll see you around, big boy."

She turned and I watched her walk away toward her car. She knew I was watching because halfway across the lot she blew a kiss over her shoulder and started swaying her hips back and forth like a fashion model on a runway. She climbed into a charcoal gray Infiniti and pulled away.

I got back into the truck thinking about what she'd said: *"We should get together, the four of us."*

Caroline would be thrilled.

CHAPTER THREE

Seeing Leah tripped another emotional trigger, and as I drove toward home, I found myself wondering about the choices I'd made and the stark contrast between my professional life and my personal life. When I walked out the door each morning, it was as though I stepped into a different plane of existence. Everywhere I turned, there were battles to be fought: battles with defense lawyers, battles with trial judges and appellate judges, battles with defendants and victims and victims' families, battles with employees, and worst of all, battles with my own conscience. There were days I'd return home feeling like I'd been abandoned by my own soul, like it had been ripped from my very being and had crawled off to hide, wounded and bleeding, until it had healed enough to rejoin the fight.

But at home, things were different. Caroline and I had been together since high school and were still deeply in love. She'd been battling breast cancer for more than two years and had been deeply scarred, both physically and emotionally. There was now a long, pink ridge across Caroline's lower abdomen and two more that ran from her scapulas to the small of her back, each a result and a painful reminder of the three failed attempts to reconstruct her amputated breast. Her surgeon had decided that replacing the breast with a "flap," or slab of transplanted tissue, was the best course of action. He took the first flap from her abdomen and it seemed to do well until she underwent radiation therapy. The radiation caused the blood vessels in both the flap and the surrounding tissue to shrink to less than half their normal size, and most of the flap died, liquefied, and exited her body through wounds that opened like large blisters and took months to heal.

Six months after the first failure, the surgeon decided to try again. This time the flap came from muscle and tissue in Caroline's back, but because the radiated blood vessels couldn't handle the amount of blood being carried to the site by the healthy vessels, most of that flap died too, leaving her with another bloody mess that seemed as though it would never heal.

A year later, over my strenuous objection, Caroline consented to a third attempt at reconstruction. The surgeon, assuring us all the while that the third time would be the charm, "harvested" yet another flap from the other side of her back and transplanted it to the same site. Less than a week later, the transplanted flap began to turn black. The surgery failed so miserably that the surgeon had to remove it. So after more than two years and nearly a dozen surgeries, Caroline now had what looked like a large shark bite where her breast used to be. I dressed the wound every day, and Caroline went about her life as though it wasn't there. I could no longer accompany her on visits to the surgeon, however. His arrogance had caused Caroline untold amounts of pain, heartache, and worry, and I wanted to snap his neck like a dry twig.

But I'd grown accustomed to the wounds and the scars that marked Caroline's body like bomb craters on a battlefield. To me, she was still the same beautiful creature I'd fallen in love with so many years ago. I think I loved her even more, if that was possible. Through it all—the chemotherapy, the radiation, the sickness, the fatigue, the surgeries—she'd remained unfailingly upbeat and positive. On the extremely rare occasions that her resolve would begin to flag, she would pull herself out of it immediately and would even go so far as to apologize to me for being weak. She'd shown such courage and such strength during her illness that it left me in awe, and whenever I began to feel sorry for myself because of what I did for a living, all I had to do was think about Caroline and what she'd been through. My problems paled in comparison.

Our eldest child, Jack, had been drafted by the Detroit Tigers after his junior year of college and was finishing up his first season in the minors down in Florida. Our daughter, Lilly, was just beginning her junior year at the University of Tennessee in Knoxville and was enjoying her life away from home. Caroline and I shared the house with a couple dogs, a German shepherd named Rio and a teacup poodle named Chico.

We'd saved plenty of money and Caroline had invested it judiciously, primarily by staying away from the wolves on Wall Street. I should have enjoyed life more, but just beneath the surface of my psyche, a bubbling pool of turmoil churned like magma inside a volcano. I struggled constantly to contain this nagging sense of doom and inner rage that seemed to intensify as I grew older. I thought I knew its origins, believed I had a fundamental understanding of the events that had nurtured it over the course of my life, and I'd attempted to take steps—many steps—in a sustained and determined effort to diffuse it, but still it remained. Most often, the rage manifested itself in the form of nightmares—vivid, violent scenes that would cause me to wake up screaming and sweating. Worst of all, they caused me to fear sleep, to avoid it at both a conscious and subconscious level, and the resulting deprivation would inevitably result in exhaustion, followed by restless, involuntary sleep, and even more nightmares. Occasionally, if enough pressure was brought to bear, the psychic magma would spill over the sides of my inner volcano into molten lava and I would lash out, sometimes verbally, sometimes physically. It was as if I would suddenly become some type of feral being, undomesticated and violent, and I would focus my rage upon whatever, or whoever, had caused the internal pressure to rise to the boiling point.

Whenever it happened, whenever I allowed the demons from the past to gain the upper hand, I would turn, inevitably, to Caroline. She was my Athena, my Great Ameliorator. She knew how to soothe me, how to convince me that the world was not as dangerous as I might believe it to be. She reminded me always that love is most important in this world, that I was loved, and that despite my psychological torments I retained a far greater capacity for love than for violence. She would patiently reassure me that the path I'd chosen was the right path, that I wasn't wasting my life, that not only was I relevant, I was *necessary*. I suspected at some level that she was placating me, but she always managed to do it in a manner that convinced me, at least for awhile, that what she was saying was true and that, as the cliché goes, everything would be all right.

The sun was well above the horizon as I pulled into the driveway. A red Mustang that belonged to my sister, Sarah, was parked to the right of the garage. Sarah was a year older than me, a dark-haired, green-eyed, hard-bodied woman who was living proof of the power of genetics. She'd spent most of her adult life abusing herself with drugs and alcohol and had spent a fair amount of time in jail, but you'd never have guessed it by looking at her. With the exception of tiny crow's-feet at the corners of her eyes, she appeared the picture of health and clean living.

I hadn't seen Sarah in over a month, which was always a bad sign. So was the fact that she'd apparently come over unannounced on a Sunday morning.

I knew something was wrong as soon as I walked in the door. Sarah and Caroline were standing next to the kitchen table. Caroline's arms were around Sarah's neck, and Sarah, who wasn't given to displays of emotion other than anger, was sobbing. Rio, our German shepherd, was lying next to the wall to their left. He must have sensed the sadness in the room because he always greeted me enthusiastically. His ears perked up and he looked at me, but he didn't move. I walked across the kitchen and caught Caroline's eye. She was stroking the back of Sarah's head, and I could see that she, too, was crying.

"What's going on?" I asked quietly.

"Some bad news," Caroline said. Her wavy, auburn hair had grown back to the length it had been before she lost it to chemotherapy, and her dark eyes were glistening with tears.

"Is Gracie all right?" Gracie was my niece, Sarah's eighteen-month-old daughter.

"Gracie's fine. She went to church with one of Sarah's friends."

Sarah pulled away from Caroline and ran both her hands through her hair.

"Sorry," she said. She was wearing a wrinkled, pink sweat suit and looked like she hadn't slept.

"Should I go back to the bedroom?" I asked, half-hoping Sarah would say yes and the two of them would work out whatever the problem was without me.

"It's okay, just give me a sec," Sarah said.

I sat down on one of the stools near the counter, feeling awkward. Caroline pulled a couple napkins out of a drawer in the kitchen and handed one to Sarah. The two of them sat down at the round table in the dining area, just a few feet away.

"Roy and Sarah are splitting up," Caroline said. "She and Gracie are moving back into your mother's old place."

The news stunned me. Roy Walker, who was known by his nickname, Mountain, was a Washington County sheriff's deputy who had worked undercover drug cases for Sheriff Bates for several years. He and Sarah had met at a biker bar two years ago and had been together ever since, by far the longest relationship Sarah had ever maintained. She'd moved in with him just a few months after they met, and Gracie came along shortly thereafter. I knew Roy's work occasionally required him to be away from home more than Sarah liked, but my impression had been that the two of them were getting along well.

"What happened?" I asked Sarah. "I thought you guys were doing great."

"I've tried everything I can think of to make it work, but he took an assignment with the DEA in Memphis without even asking me about it. He could be down there for two years, maybe more."

"Why don't you go with him?"

"I don't want to move to Memphis. It's too big, it's too hot, and it's too dangerous. I don't want to quit my job, and I don't want to raise Gracie there. Oh, and there's one other thing. He doesn't love me anymore, if he ever did."

"What makes you say that?"

"He told me. He said the words, 'I made a mistake. I don't love you, and I never will.'"

She started to tear up again, which made me uncomfortable. I could count on one hand the number of times I'd seen her cry during our lifetime.

"I can't really blame him," she continued. "I'm ten years older than he is and I'm not exactly a prize. My track record alone would make most men run as fast as they could in the other direction."

"Don't talk that way," I said. "You've been through a lot."

"Yeah, and most of it has been of my own making."

"Do you want me to talk to him?"

"No, Joe, I don't want you to talk to him. You can't fix this. Besides, he's already gone. He left this morning."

"This morning?"

"They offered him the assignment a month ago. We've been arguing about it ever since, but I knew he'd go. He barely speaks to me, and he treats Gracie like she's somebody else's child."

I'd seen the pain in her eyes many times before, and it caused me to think about how arbitrary and cruel fate can be. Sarah's life had always been star-crossed, like some tragic figure in Greek mythology, tormented by the gods for their pleasure and amusement. It started when she was only nine years old on a Friday evening in June. I was eight years old. ...

My mother and grandparents had gone out and left Sarah and me at our grandparents' small home in rural Unicoi County with our uncle, a sixteen-year-old named Raymond. I was watching a baseball game on TV and dozed off on the couch. When I woke up, it was dark. The only light in the house was the light from the television. I remember sitting up and rubbing my eyes, and then I heard a noise. It scared me because it sounded like a cry for help. I got up off the couch and started tiptoeing toward the noise, growing more frightened with every step.

As I got closer to the sound, I could make out words, "No! Stop! Don't!"

I knew it was Sarah's voice, and it was coming from Uncle Raymond's bedroom. I pushed the door open just a little. In the lamplight I could make out Raymond. He was on the bed on his knees, naked, with his back to me. Sarah's voice was coming from underneath him. She was saying, "It hurts. Stop it."

I didn't know what was going on. I was too young and too sheltered to know anything about sex. But there was so much pain, so much fear in Sarah's voice that I knew whatever was happening was bad. I finally managed to say, "What's going on?" from where I was standing in the doorway. I remember being surprised that my voice worked.

Raymond's head snapped around, and he looked at me like he was going to kill me.

"Get out of here, you little twerp," he said.

"What are you doing to her?" I asked.

At that moment, Sarah said something in a tiny voice, something that haunts me to this day. She said, "Get him off me, Joey. He's hurting me." I would hear that phrase thousands of times, later, in my dreams.

I stood there mute for a few seconds trying to figure out what I should do, but Raymond didn't give me a chance. He jumped off the bed and grabbed me by the throat. He slammed my head so hard against the wall that it nearly knocked me unconscious. He grabbed me by the collar of my shirt and by the waistband of my pants and pitched me like a bale of straw out into the hallway. I skidded a couple times on my stomach, and he slammed the door. I thought about going out to the garage to get a baseball bat or a shovel, an axe, anything. I could hear Sarah crying on the other side of the door, but I was frozen with fear. My arms and legs wouldn't work. I was too scared to move.

Finally, after what seemed like forever, they came out of the room. Sarah was sniffling and wiping her nose with the back of her hand. Raymond grabbed both of us by the back of the neck, dragged us into the living room, and pushed us onto the couch. He bent down close to us and pointed his finger within an inch of my nose.

"If you say one word about this to anybody, I'll kill your sister," he hissed. Then he turned to Sarah. "And if you say anything, I'll kill your brother. You got it?"

Neither of us ever said a word. We'd never even mentioned the rape to each other until a few years ago, just before I stopped practicing criminal defense law. It was a breakthrough that seemed to help temporarily, but I knew neither of us would ever put the incident behind us completely. I'd carried the guilt I felt for not being able to stop Raymond around like a yoke for almost four decades, and I couldn't even begin to imagine the terrible violation, degradation, and humiliation Sarah felt.

We'd dealt with our emotions in different ways, but at the heart of it, I believed Sarah was more honest. I acted like it never happened. She acted like she couldn't forget. Through it all, though, through the drinking and the drugs and the abusive relationships and the petty thefts and the incarcerations, I'd always remembered the innocent, smiling face that was hers before Raymond took her into the room that night, and I'd tried never to judge her. She was my sister and I loved her—a simple ideal that had endured through a lifetime of complexity.

And now the gods were at it again, leaving her a single mother in her mid-forties, feeling as though she'd failed her mate, her child, and herself. And once again, I felt helpless. There was nothing I could do except try and help her deal with the fallout.

"So are you going to be okay?" I asked her.

"If you're asking if I'm planning on getting plastered, the answer is no. I admit I've thought about it, but whenever I do, I look at Gracie and the urge goes away."

"Good. I'm glad to hear that, Sarah."

"Can we talk about something else?" she said. "I vented for an hour before you got here. Caroline has probably heard enough."

"You can vent all day if you want," Caroline said. "I'll even let you cuss at Joe if you think it'll make you feel better."

Sarah's lips turned up slightly. Sarah's mouth could rival General George Patton. There'd been times in the past when she'd cursed me the way an old farmer would curse a disobedient mule.

"Thanks," she said. "I'll keep that in mind."

Caroline turned to me. "What was going on at the lake?" she asked. "Was it bad?"

"It was a young woman," I said. "We don't have any idea who she is yet."

"Drowned?"

"I don't think so. There wasn't any water in her lungs. Looks like a murder."

She winked at me. "You'll catch 'em," she said. "You always do."

The thought crossed my mind that Caroline had evolved to the same place that I had. I'd just gone to view a dead body, I'd just told her there'd been a murder, and it was as though I'd casually mentioned that the price of gas had dropped two cents a gallon.

"Joe and I were planning to drive up to Grandfather Mountain this afternoon," she said to Sarah. "It's so beautiful up there, and it'll be a lot cooler than it is here. Why don't you and Gracie come with us?"

My cell phone, which I'd laid on the counter, started to buzz. I picked it up and looked at the ID. It was Bates. I seriously considered ignoring it, but after a few seconds, I answered.

"Hope you ain't got settled in yet, Brother Dillard," he said, "'cause I'm afraid I've got some bad news."

"I'm waiting."

"There're two more floaters. Both women. Both too young to die."

CHAPTER FOUR

I arrived at the office early the morning after the bodies were discovered. Sitting across from me was a young lady named Cathi Lingart, a thirty-year-old Wisconsin native who had followed her husband to northeast Tennessee several years earlier and had somehow managed to get hired on as a secretary at the DA's office in Unicoi County long before I took over. She was wearing a flowered, yellow summer dress, and her hands were folded primly in her lap. Cathi was a couple inches shy of five feet tall. She wore her wispy, brown hair cut short, with the exception of long, straight bangs that fell nearly to her eyebrows. With her heavy jowls, she looked like a cross between an English bulldog and a page boy, and when she spoke, she did so with her eyes closed.

"He rolls his eyes at me all the time," Cathi said with her eyes tightly shut, her eyebrows quivering as if she were trying to blink. She was speaking of Landon Burke, the assistant district attorney who ran the Unicoi County office. Burke was in his mid-fifties, a cantankerous sort, and the oldest lawyer on the staff. He was yet another employee of the district attorney's office who was hired before I came along. I knew him only casually.

"And he's always telling me to open my eyes," she continued.

Cathi had made the appointment with me two weeks earlier, and despite the fact that we suddenly had what appeared to be a triple homicide on our hands and I knew she was coming to me with some sort of petty grievance, I didn't cancel. Since taking over the office, I'd tried to treat all the employees equally and tried to make myself available to them whenever possible. But as time passed, I was beginning to think I'd have to put some restrictions on the open-door policy.

I was now responsible for supervising fifty lawyers and support people in four counties, each of whom dragged a large pile of personal baggage to the job. The office had approximately five thousand cases pending in fourteen different courts at any given time, and if anything went wrong in any of those cases, the blame inevitably fell on me. I was also responsible for creating and maintaining a budget; managing the vast amounts of paperwork required by the courts, the legislature, and the feds; hiring and firing employees; maintaining good relationships with the law enforcement community, the judges, the defense bar, and the public; and overseeing a child support division that enforced the laws against deadbeat parents. I didn't realize it at the time, but the day the governor appointed me to the district attorney general's job, I was involuntarily converted from a hard-driving lawyer who investigated and tried violent criminal cases to an unfamiliar and uncomfortable mixture of politician, bureaucrat, and babysitter.

"Is he abusive?" I said to Cathi.

"I don't know. Well, no, I wouldn't say he's *abusive*. He's just mean sometimes."

"That's his nature, isn't it? You're not the only person he's mean to, are you?"

"He's mean to everybody, but he's meanest to me."

"What do you want me to do, Cathi?"

"Can't you fire him?"

I felt the beginnings of a headache coming on, and I leaned back in my chair and started massaging my forehead with my fingers.

"Landon has three kids in college," I said. "He's a good lawyer. He handles his case load and hasn't done anything particularly stupid that I'm aware of. I can't fire him because he's sometimes unpleasant to work with."

"Couldn't you just transfer him then?"

"I tell you what. I'll make it a point to take him to lunch next week and I'll talk to him. I'm afraid that's the best I can do right now."

The telephone on my desk buzzed, and I picked it up.

"There's a woman here to see you," Rita Jones, my secretary and paralegal, said. "She doesn't have an appointment but she says she's an old friend."

"What's her name?"

"Barlowe. Erlene Barlowe." Rita lowered her voice to a whisper. "She's crying."

"Tell her I'll be right out."

I stood, a signal to Cathi that the meeting was over. I walked her to the door, hovering a full foot and a half above her, assuring her once again that I'd speak to Landon as soon as possible.

I hadn't seen Erlene Barlowe in nearly four years. She owned a strip club outside Johnson City called the Mouse's Tail, and before I quit practicing criminal defense, she'd hired me to defend a young girl who was accused of murdering a preacher. We took the case to trial, and after the girl was found not guilty, the police charged Erlene with the murder. She asked me to represent her too, and despite what was probably a conflict of interest, I wound up getting the case dismissed. I hadn't seen her since, but I still held fond memories. Erlene was smart, funny, tough, and easy to look at, despite the fact that she was in her early fifties and she dressed like a street walker. She'd also paid me more than a quarter of a million dollars in cash to defend her and the girl, money that Caroline had turned into a great deal more.

Erlene was sitting on a small couch in the reception area of my office, sniffling and dabbing her eyes with a tissue. When she saw me, she immediately sprang to her feet, walked across the room, and wrapped her arms around my neck. Her hair was the same unique color of red that I remembered, a strange, sanguine shade somewhere between a roan horse and a carrot. She was wearing tight, black leather pants, spiked heels, and a tiger-striped orange-and-black top with a neckline that was cut a little below indecent.

"Oh, Mr. Dillard, I think something terrible has happened," she whispered in my ear. "And it's all my fault."

"Come in and we'll talk about it."

I put my arm around her shoulders as I turned to go back in the office and caught a glimpse of Rita Jones, who was gaping at me wide-eyed and open-mouthed.

"Hold the calls, please," I said to Rita, and I shut the door behind us.

"Three of my girls are missing," Erlene blurted as soon as she sat down. I sat in the chair next to her and offered my hand, which she took immediately. Her eyes were red and puffy, and tears had nearly washed away the makeup she wore on her cheeks. "I'm afraid they might be the girls y'all found in the lake."

"Start at the beginning." I patted the back of her hand. "Take your time."

"There's this man," she said through a sniffle, "this man who's been coming to the club every year at this time since Gus and I opened the place. He always wants three girls. He takes them out on a boat with two other men on the Saturday night before Labor Day, and they stay out all night."

"So three of your girls went out on the lake Saturday night?"

She nodded. "I heard about them finding the bodies on the news late yesterday afternoon. As soon as I heard it, I got this awful feeling in the pit of my stomach. I started trying to get a hold of the girls, but none of them would answer their cell phones. I called the other girls. Nobody had seen them or heard from them, so last night I drove by their places. None of them were home. I kept hoping they'd show up. I kept calling. I didn't sleep a wink last night, and then early this morning, I thought about you. Please, Mr. Dillard, you have to help me."

The Erlene Barlowe I'd known before was flirty, manipulative, and confident. She called everyone "sugar" and "honey" and "sweetie pie" and could talk the pope himself out of his clothes and into her bed. But this woman was different. The tone of her voice reflected deep sorrow, regret, and perhaps fear. She'd barely looked at me since I first saw her in the reception area, and her shoulders were slumped forward, giving her a demeanor of defeatism.

"Maybe they aren't your girls, Erlene. You said the man has been coming around for a long time. Have you or any of your girls ever had any trouble with him before?"

She shook her head. "Did you see them, Mr. Dillard? When they came out of the lake?"

"All blondes," I said quietly. Her hand tightened around mine. "All young, probably in their twenties. All pretty. One of them had a tattoo on the inside of her right forearm. It was a dying rose with only one petal left on the stem. The word 'Hope' was written above it."

Erlene shuddered and let out a sound I'd never heard, a guttural, primeval wail that could have originated only from the depths of her soul. She pulled her hand away from me, curled into a fetal position on the chair, and began to sob uncontrollably. I tried to comfort her initially, but it was like she was no longer in the room with me. She'd traveled to a place of pure sorrow, a place where only the aggrieved could enter. I sat there helplessly for several minutes, then went to a drawer in my desk and took out a box of tissues. I sat back down next to her and looked up to see Rita standing in the doorway, her arms spread and her palms facing upward, silently asking me what was going on. I motioned her away and waited for Erlene to regain at least some of her composure.

The sobbing began to subside after about fifteen of the longest minutes of my life. When she finally pulled her hands away from her face and looked at me, she was almost unrecognizable.

"You have to get them, Mr. Dillard," she said in a menacing tone, her grief suddenly turning to anger. "You have to make them pay for what they did."

"First things first," I said, taking her hand again. "We need to identify the bodies. If you're up to it, I'll take you to the medical examiner's office."

She pulled a wad of tissues from the box and began to wipe her face. When she was finished, she stood, straightened her back, and took a deep breath.

"Anything," she said. "Anything for my girls."

CHAPTER FIVE

Erlene insisted on driving, so she followed me to the medical examiner's office in her red Mercedes convertible. The office was located at the Quillen College of Medicine, attached to the Veterans Administration in Johnson City, about six miles from the courthouse. Along the way, I called Sheriff Bates and told him I thought I was about to get a positive identification on the women. He said he'd meet us there. I tried to call the medical examiner to let him know we were coming, but got no answer.

Erlene and I walked in to find Hobie Stanton, the acting medical examiner, sleeping on a gurney in the examination room. Hobie was in his mid-seventies. He'd been a forensic pathologist for thirty years when he retired at the age of sixty-five, but he had been asked to fill in temporarily two weeks earlier after the previous medical examiner packed his bags unexpectedly and moved to Florida. I knew Hobie was supposed to be performing the autopsies on the three dead girls, but he hadn't called me or faxed me any preliminary results, and now I wondered whether he'd even started.

I walked over and tapped him on the shoulder. His liver-spotted hands were crossed over his chest like he was lying in a coffin; his glasses were perched on the tip of his nose. He was wearing a white lab coat, and what little white hair he had left was sticking straight out from his head. The tapping didn't do any good, so I leaned over him and listened. He was breathing, so I began shaking him.

Hobie's eyes suddenly flew open and he bolted straight up from the waist. He glared at me for a second, obviously confused, and then threw his legs over the side of the gurney.

"You scared me," he growled. "I nearly peed my pants."

"Don't you have a secretary?" I said. "An assistant? An intern or resident or something?"

"My predecessor took the secretary with him when he left," he said. "He failed to take his wife and child along, however. The conditions in this office must be conducive to romance."

He pushed his glasses up with an index finger. "I suppose you're here about the bodies. I've been working all night. I finished the last one about an hour ago."

"This is Erlene Barlowe," I said. "She might be able to identify them. Erlene, this is Dr. Hobie Stanton."

Hobie grunted and nodded his head. "They're in the cooler."

He led us down a short hallway into a refrigerated room with stainless steel walls. There were four gurneys sitting against the wall to our right. One of them was empty, but the other three were occupied by sheet-covered bodies with tags on their toes.

Hobie walked to the first gurney, then turned and looked at me with raised eyebrows as if to say, "Well?"

"Are you ready?" I said to Erlene.

She nodded and raised trembling fingers to her lips. Hobie lifted the sheet, revealing the face of the first girl, the one with the tattoo. Her skin was now the color of cold ashes. Erlene gasped.

"Oh no, that's her," she said. "That's Lisa." She began to cry softly as Hobie moved to the next one.

"Kerrie," Erlene whispered, her voice barely audible. A moment later, she identified the third girl as Krystal, and I put my arm around her shoulders and led her out of the room.

"Is there an office we can use for a little while?" I said to Hobie. "We're going to need some privacy."

"You can use mine," he said. "I'm going to get some coffee."

"Go in and have a seat," I said to Erlene as we walked by Hobie's office. "I need to talk to the doctor for a minute."

I followed Hobie out the front door into a hot, overcast morning. It had rained up until about an hour ago, and the steamy water evaporating from the streets rose toward the sky like an opaque curtain. Hobie pulled a pipe out of his pocket and lit it.

"What killed them?" I said.

"The one she called Lisa died of heart failure, apparently too much high-quality cocaine," he said, the pipe clenched tightly between teeth stained by nicotine. "The other two were strangled. Both of them had fractured hyoid bones and tears in the cartilage around the neck."

I noticed Bates pulling into a parking spot about twenty feet away.

"How long were they in the water?" I said.

"Not long. I'd guess an hour, maybe a little more. They went in within five or ten minutes of each other."

"I don't suppose you found anything that will help us prove who did it."

"Sorry, no calling cards. I can testify to cause of death, but that's it."

Hobie shuffled off toward the cafeteria just as Bates stepped onto the curb.

"Got your teeth in, Hobie?" Bates called.

"Go kiss a rat's patoot," Hobie hollered over his shoulder as he kept shuffling in the opposite direction.

"Hold still a minute and I'll bend over and pucker up."

Bates stood on the sidewalk, hands on his hips, grinning and watching Hobie walk away.

"I take it you know him," I said.

"Me and Hobie are kin, Brother Dillard. He's my momma's cousin on her daddy's side. I see him every year at the family reunion."

I filled Bates in on the identifications and the causes of death, and he and I walked back inside to talk to Erlene. Her eyes were still red and puffy when I introduced her to Bates, but she wasn't crying.

"Are you okay?" I said as I took a seat next to her. Bates sat down in Hobie's chair on the other side of the desk.

"I want to help you find out who did this," she said. "I'll cry later."

She took a deep breath, folded her arms beneath her huge breasts, and began to rock back and forth in her chair.

"He called himself Mr. Smith," she said. "Every year it was the same. He'd call the week before Labor Day and tell me he wanted three blonde-headed girls for the whole night on the Saturday before Labor Day. He paid three thousand dollars apiece for the girls. He'd come by the club the day after he called, come into my office, and pay me in cash. Always hundred-dollar bills. The girls would go, they'd party, and they'd come back. Never a single problem. And now this ...."

She dropped her head and began biting her lip, fighting back the tears again.

"What does he look like, Erlene?" I said.

"He's not very tall, shorter than both of you," she said. "Stocky. Black, curly hair and dark eyes. Probably in his early thirties. He's a rooster—I can tell you that. Cocky. Talks like he's a gangster or something. Wears his pants real low on his hips, a lot of jewelry."

"Did he talk like he was from around here?" I said.

She nodded. "He talked like a black man, but I'm guessing he's local."

"Any tattoos or scars?" Bates said.

"Not that I can recall."

"Did the girls drive out to meet him or did he pick them up?" I said.

"He always picked them up in front of the club and brought them back the next morning."

"Any idea what he was driving?"

"I saw him pick them up in a Ford Expedition a couple years ago, but I was in my office the other night. I didn't see him."

"You said they went out on a boat," I said. "Any idea whether they went to someone's house or to a marina?"

"The girls always told me the boat was huge. One of those great big houseboats that looks like a giant birthday cake when it's floating down the lake at night."

"Marina," Bates said. "People don't keep those things at their house."

"That narrows it down some," I said. "There are only three marinas on the lake."

"I remember the name of the boat," Erlene said. "It's *Laura Mae*. Several of the girls have told me that over the years. *Laura Mae*."

Bates smiled. "That'll narrow it down even more, ma'am. I doubt we're going to find many houseboats named *Laura Mae* on the lake."

"Anything else you can remember about Mr. Smith or the boat?" I said.

"The girls always made fun of Mr. Smith. They called him 'gofer' because all he did was run around and wait on the other two men on the boat. He was the one who got the boat ready to go, drove it, and when they'd stop, he'd bring them drinks or food or change the music, whatever they told him to do."

"So there were two men on the boat besides Mr. Smith?" Bates said. "Is it the same two men every year?"

"I don't know," Erlene said. "I didn't ask for descriptions or anything. All I know is the girls said they wore expensive jewelry and clothes and they liked to party."

I stood up and looked at Bates.

"Why don't you start looking for the boat?" I said. "I'll stay here with Erlene and have her tell me everything she knows about the girls."

CHAPTER SIX

It was almost noon as I wound my pickup through the curves of the narrow, two-lane road toward Ray's Marina. Bates had called my cell phone while I was talking to Erlene. He said we needed to talk to a man named Turtle. Turtle apparently ran the day-to-day operations at the marina, and Bates said if anyone knew what was happening on the lake, it would be him.

The clouds had cleared and the sun was high in the sky, beating down relentlessly, almost oppressively. The temperature had climbed to ninety degrees, the humidity was at least 80 percent, and the wind was absolutely still. I tried to focus on how Bates and I would approach the witness, but I couldn't get my mind off Erlene and the pain that had radiated from her soul like a radio signal. The girls' names were Lisa Kay Burns, Kerri Elizabeth Runion, and Krystal Dawn Nickels.

Lisa, twenty-five, the girl with the "Hope" tattoo, had grown up in Austin, Texas, the daughter of an accountant and a nurse. Both her parents were killed in a car accident when Lisa was fourteen years old. She was shipped off to Midland to live with an aunt, became depressed, got into drugs, and wound up stripping. She'd made the rounds through Dallas, Atlanta, Charlotte, and Knoxville and started working for Erlene a little over three years ago. She'd been a passenger on the boat each of those three years. Erlene had helped her kick her cocaine addiction ten months ago, and Lisa had given up stripping, earned her GED, gotten a job as a reception-ist in an accountant's office, and enrolled part-time at a local community college. When Erlene told Mr. Smith that Lisa wasn't available, he said he'd double the usual offer from three thousand to six thousand. Erlene passed the information along, and Lisa agreed to go one last time. Mr. Smith had asked for her by her stage name, "Chastity."

Kerrie, also known as "Gypsy," was a twenty-three-year-old from Columbus, Ohio. Her parents divorced when she was sixteen. After a year of bouncing back and forth between them and listening to them bicker, she decided she'd had enough. She got on a bus one day and never looked back. She'd made porn films in New York and worked for a high-dollar escort service in Washington, DC, before one of her colleagues told her about this little strip club in east Tennessee. Erlene described her as a "sweet little ol' thing" who loved ani-mals and Rice Krispies Treats.

Krystal, twenty-one, was from Memphis. She was a junior at East Tennessee State University, studying pre-medicine. Erlene said she came from a poor family; both her parents were deaf and lived off Social Security dis-ability checks. She'd been sexually abused by a neighbor when she was young and, as a result, didn't have much use for men. She'd earned an academic scholarship to college and had decided to maximize her earning potential in her spare time by taking advantage of her best asset—her body. Erlene told me that Krystal didn't drink, smoke, or use drugs. She showed up for work on time, left when her shift was over, and stayed away from the usual hanky-panky the girls tended to get into. She'd worked hard to improve her dance skills, and because of the combination of her beauty, her act, and her aloof nature, she'd developed a large following at the club and was making more money than any of the other girls.

I was struck by the tenderness in Erlene's voice when she spoke of them. In northeast Tennessee, which was often referred to as the buckle of the Bible Belt, most people would regard three strippers who moonlighted occasionally as hookers the same way they would regard a crackhead or a burglar. But Erlene spoke of them as though they were her children. She was proud of Krystal, fond of Lisa, sometimes frustrated by Kerrie. It took almost two hours to get basic information from her because she broke down and sobbed time and time again. The guilt she felt was palpable, almost visceral. It was obvious that she blamed herself for their deaths.

When I pulled into the parking lot at the marina, I saw Bates leaning against the black BMW he'd confiscated from a drug dealer a little over a year ago. His cowboy hat was perched atop his head at a slight angle, and he was talking on his cell phone. I parked, got out of the truck, and looked out over the marina. There were at least a hundred and fifty watercraft tied to the docks, everything from jet skis to huge houseboats. A small, pale-blue building with an attached deck housed a grill and a bait shop, and there were two gasoline pumps on a dock below the deck. A short, heavyset man wearing cutoff jeans, a wide-brimmed straw hat, and a loud Hawaiian shirt was pumping gas into a ski boat that was filled with young men that looked to be about my son's age.

I knew neither Bates nor I could board the boat if it was there. We'd have to have a search warrant for that, but there was nothing preventing us from taking a look around the outside. If we saw something that might be of evidentiary value to us, the "plain view" doctrine would apply, and we'd be able to get a search warrant. I knew we might be able to get a warrant based solely on an affidavit from Erlene, but I preferred to have more evidence before I went to a judge.

"That's got to be him," Bates said as he came off the car and stuck his cell phone into his shirt pocket. "A couple of my investigators do a lot of fishing out here. They said if it happens on the lake, Turtle knows about it. Said he's a chubby guy who always wears a straw hat."

Bates and I stepped onto the dock just as the man was hanging the nozzle back on the gas pump. He turned to face us and grinned.

"Well, I'll be," he said. "If it ain't the two most famous law men in the county. You're both uglier in person than you are on TV."

He offered a meaty hand, and I took it.

"Joe Dillard," I said, "and this is Leon Bates."

"Jasper T. Yates," he said. "Folks call me Turtle on account of I don't move too fast."

Turtle's face was covered with dark stubble, and the bridge of his nose bent sharply to the right. He peered out from under the straw hat with bright eyes. In his jaw was a wad of chewing tobacco about the size of a golf ball.

"We're looking for a boat," Bates said.

"Which one?" Turtle said.

"It's called the *Laura Mae*. I believe it's one of the big houseboats."

"Be happy to show her to you if she was here, but she ain't. She's gone."

"Gone?"

"As in adios, sayonara, bye-bye. Somebody took her out late yesterday evening, and I ain't seen her since."

"Who took her out?"

"Some young feller. Never seen him before."

"Any idea where he went?"

"One of the fishermen told me he saw her being pulled out of the water over at the Winged Deer Park ramp."

"Does that happen often?" I said.

"It happens once a year. They take her out and store her until springtime, but they don't usually come get her until mid-September. Follow me, fellers. I need to get outta this heat and back into the air conditioning."

We started walking, very slowly, back up the dock toward the building. Turtle wasn't joking about not moving too fast. The steps he took were less than a foot long.

"Were you working Saturday night?" Bates asked.

"Of course I was working Saturday night," he said over his shoulder. "It's our busiest night of the year."

"Did you happen to see whether the *Laura Mae* went out?"

"I filled her up with gas around five that afternoon. She went out around nine that night. I didn't see her come back in though. I was out here 'til almost two in the morning, but even ol' Turtle has to get a little shut-eye now and then."

"Any idea who was on the boat Saturday night?" Bates said.

"I saw three young ladies get out of a white limo just before dark. They got on the boat with Nelson Lipscomb. I'm guessing they're the three y'all fished out of the lake the next morning."

"What makes you say that?" Bates said.

"You're here, ain't ya?"

"Did you get a good look at the girls?"

"Yeah, but I wasn't looking at their faces. They was all blondes, though, 'cause when I saw 'em, I started singing, 'Three blonde mice, three blonde mice, see how they bounce, see how they bounce.'"

"Say they were with somebody named Nelson Lipscomb?" Bates said.

"That's right."

"How well do you know him?"

"Well enough to know that he's an uppity, rich punk who ain't got sense enough to get in outta the rain. What do y'all know about him?"

Bates looked at me, and I shrugged my shoulders. "Never heard of him," I said.

"Me either," Bates said. He looked back at Turtle. "Should we have heard of him?"

Turtle began to laugh, a high-pitched *hee hee hee* that sounded like a bird in distress. He spat a long stream of tobacco juice toward the water and wiped his mouth with the back of his hand.

"You boys ain't got a clue what you're getting yourselves into. I'm sure you've heard of John Jacob Lipscomb, ain't you?"

Bates and I both stopped cold. John Jacob Lipscomb was a legend in the community. He was born and raised in Johnson City and had started an investment company in Nashville called Equicorp back in the late eighties. Equicorp grew quickly and went public a short time later, making Lipscomb an extremely wealthy man in the process. The rumors around town were that he was worth more than half a billion dollars, and judging by the amount of money he gave away, I tended to believe it. John J. Lipscomb had funded two libraries, a cancer research center, a prenatal clinic, a Little League complex, a Pop Warner football field, and dozens of college scholarships. He was the university's most important benefactor and donated liberally to every politician in northeast Tennessee.

"What does he have to do with this?" I said.

"Maybe nothing. Maybe everything," Turtle said. "It's his boat."

"Was he on it Saturday night?" Bates said.

"Couldn't say, but I've heard it told that he comes up here every year at Labor Day and goes out for a little rest and relaxation with a few young ladies. Recharging the batteries, I reckon. Pretty sleazy, though, if you ask me, since he named the boat after his wife."

We finally made it to the building. Turtle stopped just outside the door and began wiping the sweat from his neck and face with a bandana he'd pulled from his pocket.

"Anything else I can do for you boys?" he said.

"You're absolutely certain you saw Nelson Lipscomb get on that boat with three blonde girls?" Bates said.

Turtle put his hand over his heart. "God as my witness, it was him." He began wringing the sweat out of the bandana. "Y'all be careful out there, ya hear?" He turned and disappeared through the door.

As Bates and I walked back toward our vehicles, I felt the breeze pick up. It was coming out of the north, no doubt bringing a cold front along with it. A break in the temperature would be nice, but along with the cool air would come the violent storms of early September.

"I got a bad feeling about this one," Bates said as I opened the door of my pickup.

"It's just another murder case," I said. "We get our proof together and send somebody to prison."

"It ain't gonna be that simple." He took his cowboy hat off and began rubbing his fingers through his hair. "We better put together an airtight case, and we better do it quick because as soon as we start sniffing around John Lipscomb, there'll be hell to pay. I reckon you better get me some help from the TBI."

My cell phone rang and I looked at the ID.

"It's Rita calling from the office," I said. "Probably a matter of some grave importance. I'll bet you a hundred bucks it's about somebody who wants me to help their grandson or nephew or brother get out of a DUI, or maybe one of the toilets in the office has stopped up."

"Getting a little cynical, are we?" Bates said.

"Where are you going right now?"

"Thought I'd get me a search warrant and pay a visit to Nelson Lipscomb. We've got enough for a warrant, don't we?"

"We need signed affidavits from Erlene and Turtle, but that should be enough."

"I reckon you're headed back to the office to do some administrating."

Bates gave me a wry smile. I turned the cell phone off. It felt good to be out, doing some real work for a change.

"To hell with the toilets and the DUIs," I said. "I'm going with you."

PART II

CHAPTER SEVEN

I reluctantly punched the number of the Tennessee Bureau of Investigation's local special agent in charge into my cell phone as I drove to Bates's office. Over the years, I'd come to regard Tennessee's most respected law enforcement agency with a sense of trepidation. The agents were largely well trained and committed, but many of them were egotistical and competitive. They regarded local cops with an air of disdain, and the upper echelon of the TBI seemed to be more interested in political standing than law enforcement.

Ralph Harmon, the SAIC at the Johnson City field office, was *not* my idea of a good cop, let alone a cop who should be serving in a supervisory capacity. Harmon was abrasive and cocky around his agents, but I'd also seen his brown-nosing act when the TBI brass came to town. He was a potbellied bully whose office walls were covered with photos of a much younger version of himself in various military garb, which was something that grated on my nerves. I'd served in the army as a Ranger, had killed men in Grenada, and had seen one of my buddies killed by a rocket-propelled grenade. The memories had haunted me for more than two decades, to the point that

I'd gotten rid of every object or photograph that might remind me of my military service. I wasn't ashamed of it; I just didn't want to relive it, and the fact that Harmon surrounded himself with his own military memorabilia told me that he'd never seen what I'd seen. He simply wanted visitors to his office to admire him because he'd been a soldier, which was fine until I asked him about the photos one day.

I learned that Harmon's father had been a helicopter pilot in Vietnam and had taught Ralph to fly when Ralph was a just a teenager. At the age of eighteen, he joined the army reserves, became a warrant officer, and spent four years as a weekend warrior. He'd never seen active duty, although the photographs would lead one—especially the unindoctrinated—to conclude otherwise. When I mentioned that the photos might tend to present a false impression, he became angry and ordered me out of his office. As a result, Harmon and I weren't exactly close. But as the district attorney general, I was responsible for "requesting" the TBI's assistance when a city or county police force needed help with an investigation.

"I figured you'd be calling," Harmon said in his clipped tenor when he answered the phone. "I suppose you need some help with your homicides."

"Yeah, we do."

"Bates can't handle it?"

"It might be a little different than he's used to."

"Different? What do you mean?"

"The suspects are wealthy. Extremely wealthy. They're also pretty well connected from what I understand."

"You mean mob-connected or politically connected?"

"Politically connected."

"Who are they?"

"Ever heard of John J. Lipscomb?"

There was a long pause, which meant Harmon had, indeed, heard of Lipscomb. I knew Harmon was considering his options, trying to decide how he might best manage the situation either to benefit himself or ensure that, if there was future political fallout, it would be directed at someone besides him.

"You're sure he's involved?" Harmon said when he finally spoke.

"Not positive, but it looks that way."

"How solid is your case?"

"We don't have a case yet. That's why I'm calling you."

"How many people do you need?"

"As many as you can spare."

"When do you need them?"

"Yesterday."

"We're pretty busy, but I'll see what I can do. Somebody will get back to you within the hour."

I started to reply, but the line went dead. *We're pretty busy? Somebody will get back to you?* I'd never before heard of, let alone experienced, a TBI supervisor telling a district attorney that the agency might be too busy to help with a homicide investigation. My first thought was to start making phone calls to Nashville and go over Harmon's head, but the more I considered it, the more the idea struck me as juvenile. It would be like tattling, and it would certainly do more harm than good. I closed the phone, dropped it on the seat next to me, and drove to Bates's office. When I arrived, the place looked like a beehive.

"Called in the cavalry," Bates said from behind his desk when I walked in. "I've got danged near every cop in the department working. The overtime's gonna bust my budget."

As the evening progressed, we were able to establish without any doubt that Nelson Lipscomb had been seen with the girls before their deaths. Erlene didn't actually witness Lipscomb picking the girls up at the club, but one of her bouncers, a thick-necked country boy named Henry Willis, saw them walk out the front door of the Mouse's Tail and get into a white limo a little before 9:00 p.m. with a stocky, dark-haired man. Bates found a booking photo of Nelson Lipscomb on the computer, and Erlene and Willis both positively identified him as "Mr. Smith," the man who had paid Erlene for the girls' services. Turtle signed an affidavit saying that he saw Lipscomb and three blondes get out of a white limo at the marina about 9:15 p.m. and all four of them boarded the *Laura Mae.* The boat pulled out shortly thereafter and didn't return until sometime early the next morning. A few hours after the girls were found, a young man Turtle didn't recognize came to the marina and drove the boat away. It hadn't been seen since. We still couldn't prove that Nelson had killed anyone, but it was enough to get a search warrant for his condo.

While I was working on the affidavits for the warrant in Bates's office, he and his people set about finding out everything they could about Nelson Lipscomb.

Nelson was forty years old. His parents were Dr. Jonathan David Lipscomb, a vascular surgeon, and Gloria Ann Pickens-Lipscomb, a housewife who was also the president of the local Monday Club and the arts council. He had one brother, the ultra-wealthy John Jacob Lipscomb.

Nelson was a ne'er-do-well. He'd dropped out of University High School at the age of seventeen, had never filed a tax return, and apparently had never held a job. He'd been arrested twice for public intoxication, once for misdemeanor drug possession, and once for punching a girlfriend, but each charge had been dismissed. After his first arrest, he'd asked a Sessions Court judge to appoint a public defender to represent him, but when the judge asked him how he supported himself, Nelson confessed that he lived off a trust fund—five thousand a month— that had been set up for him by his grandparents. His request for a public defender was denied. He'd been sued twice for child support, apparently having fathered two illegitimate children.

It was almost six o'clock when Bates and I, along with two investigators from the sheriff's department and two patrol deputies, pulled into the Lakeview Terrace condominium complex and knocked on Lipscomb's door. It took a full five minutes before Lipscomb, wearing only a pair of boxer shorts and looking haggard, answered.

"Nelson Lipscomb?" Bates said, holding his badge and ID in front of Lipscomb's face.

"Yeah."

"We have a search warrant. Step aside."

Bates handed Lipscomb a copy of the warrant and started moving forward. The rest of us followed him inside. Lipscomb, surprised and bewildered, stepped away from the door and let us pass.

Lipscomb was around five feet six and looked to weigh in the neighborhood of a hundred and eighty pounds or so. He was thick, but he looked soft. The prominent ridge across his eyebrows reminded me of a Neanderthal, and his chest and abdomen were covered in dark hair. His brown eyes were small and close set, and his black hair rose from his scalp in tight curls. Around his neck were three thick, gold chains of varying lengths.

"Late night?" Bates said. It was obvious that Lipscomb had been asleep.

"What're y'all doin' up in here?" Lipscomb said. As soon as he opened his mouth, I knew what Turtle and Erlene had been talking about. Lipscomb, a white man from a rich family in the hills of Tennessee, talked like a black gangster.

"Ain't you got a robe or something?" Bates said. "I can't stand looking at all that fur."

Lipscomb grunted and walked off through the den into a bedroom with Bates right behind him. I looked around the condo. It could have been a nice place, but it was filthy. Dishes were piled in the kitchen sink and flies were buzzing around a plastic trash container that was overflowing. Empty beer bottles were scattered all over the place, along with pizza boxes and ashtrays full of cigarette butts. It smelled as bad as it looked—a putrid mixture of stale cigarette smoke, spilled beer, and rotting food. The malaise reflected in the condition of the apartment told me as much about Nelson Lipscomb as any of the information Bates had gathered that afternoon.

"Ain't much of a housekeeper, are you, Nelson?" Bates said as they reappeared. Lipscomb was now wearing a pair of basketball shorts, a LeBron James jersey, and a cap that he'd plopped sideways onto his head. He looked ridiculous. "Have a seat on the couch and stay there."

Lipscomb sat down, crossed his arms, and stared at the floor. Bates told his guys to go ahead and start the search. He and I stayed in the den with Lipscomb.

"Mind telling me where you were Saturday night?" Bates said, standing over Lipscomb with his hands on his hips.

Lipscomb remained mute.

"It's a simple question," Bates said. "Any chance you were out on the lake Saturday night? In a big houseboat maybe? With three girls you picked up at the Mouse's Tail?"

"Man, I ain't gotta tell you nothing," Lipscomb said.

Bates took a couple steps closer to Lipscomb. He put his hands behind his back and leaned forward from the waist.

"That's right, smart guy, you don't have to tell me anything. But if you don't, then I'm gonna think you committed three murders. You see, those girls you picked up at the strip club Saturday wound up floating in the lake, deader than John Dillinger. So I'm afraid I'm gonna need an explanation from you. Otherwise, you're in up to your eyeballs."

"Get off me, man," Lipscomb said. He looked Bates in the eye briefly, trying to act brave, but his lower lip was quivering. "You can't be comin' up in my crib and gettin' all up in my grill and talkin' some kinda nonsense. I know my rights. So just take your flunkies and get outta here. You want to talk to me, call my lawyer."

Bates shook his head, but didn't give any ground.

"That's the wrong way to play this, Nelson, or should I call you Mr. Smith? I'm trying to help you out here. We already know you were on the boat with the girls. People saw you. You know why they saw you? Because you like to be flashy. Limos, strippers, great big ol' boats. You see, in the law enforcement business we have these things called witnesses, and these witnesses say you paid twelve grand for the three girls, you picked them up at the strip club around nine, you rode in a limo over to the marina, you and the girls got on the boat, and you didn't come back that night. The problem, Mr. Smith, is that the girls are dead and you're still kicking. And now the boat is gone, jerked out of the water the very next day.

"I checked your record before we came over here. You're pretty much of a scumbag, but I don't figure you for a killer. Something bad happened on that boat, Nelson. I got three dead girls on my hands, and somebody's going to pay for it. You can help yourself out by telling us what happened, or you can keep walking down this road you seem to be choosing. But if you do that, you might just wind up eating the whole enchilada. Three murders. Heinous crime. Strangled and dumped naked into the water like so many bags of trash."

Bates nodded toward me.

"You see this gentleman here? His name's Mr. Dillard. He's the district attorney general. He's the man who's gonna decide whether this is a death-penalty case. What do you think, Mr. Dillard? Is ol' Nelson here looking at a needle in his arm?"

The truth was that it was a borderline death-penalty case. Recent rulings from both the Tennessee and United States Supreme Courts required a killing to be particularly heinous, atrocious, or cruel in order to qualify, and depending upon what really happened that night, this case probably didn't meet the criteria. But Bates expected me to play along, and I had no intention of disappointing him.

"It's like the sheriff says. Triple homicide, death by strangulation, bodies dumped naked into the lake. No question about it. Death penalty."

"Look at this." The voice came from behind me and I turned. It was one of Bates's investigators, Rudy Lane, a skinny guy who looked like a middle-aged Peter Sellers. He'd walked in from Lipscomb's bedroom and was dangling a baggie from his fingertips.

"Oh my," Bates said dramatically. "Say it ain't so, Nelson. Is that cocaine? It sure looks like cocaine. Tell me that ain't cocaine."

The baggie contained a white powder. It appeared to be at least a half an ounce.

Bates took the baggie and held it gingerly in front of Lipscomb's face.

"That's resale weight, brother," he said. "Class B felony. Eight-year minimum sentence. What do you think,

Brother Dillard? Do you think you can convince a judge to send him away for eight years?"

"Absolutely," I said, "maybe longer."

"Unless, of course, he wants to tell us what happened on that boat Saturday night," Bates said.

Lipscomb responded by burying his face in his hands. He began to rock back and forth on the couch. Bates turned and looked at Rudy Lane.

"Detective Lane, would you kindly cuff Mr. Smith and take him out to Deputy Barnes's cruiser? He can wait out there while we finish our business."

Lane started to cuff Lipscomb's hands behind his back.

"No need for that," Bates said. "You can cuff him in front."

Lane did as Bates asked and led Lipscomb out the door.

"Deputy Barnes!" Bates called.

A young deputy hurried in from the bedroom. "Yes, sir."

"Are we good to go outside?"

"Yes, sir."

"Good man. Keep searching."

"I can't wait to see who he calls," Bates said after the deputy had left the room. A sly grin crossed his face.

"From the cruiser?" I said.

"Yeah, he picked his cell phone up off the dresser and stuck it in his pocket when we were in the bedroom. He thought I wasn't looking, and I didn't say a word. I was hoping we'd find a reason to send him outside so he could have a little privacy."

I shook my head. Behind the good-ol'-boy front, Bates was as wily as a raccoon after midnight.

"C'mon and sit down," Bates said as he pulled a laptop from the briefcase he'd carried in. "Let's see if ol' Nelson will take the rope I gave him and hang himself."

CHAPTER EIGHT

The laptop booted up, and in less than a minute, we were watching Nelson Lipscomb in real time in the backseat of the cruiser. He'd slid down in the seat, and his knees were pulled up close to his chest. It was obvious he was trying to retrieve his cell phone from his pocket.

"Hot damn," Bates said, "I love this newfangled, techno-spy stuff."

After a few desperate moments, Lipscomb finally dug the phone out. He slid back up in the seat and held the iPhone in his trembling fingers. The temperature outside had cooled off quite a bit since earlier in the day, but sweat had formed on Lipscomb's forehead and was dripping from the end of his nose. He pushed the buttons feverishly and waited.

"Hey Rudy!" Bates called. "Pretty rude of you to leave that boy out there with the windows rolled up."

"Answer the phone!" Lipscomb yelled. He disconnected and pushed the button again, apparently redialing the same number.

"Yo, it's me," Lipscomb said. "The poh-lice are up in my crib with a warrant. They searching the whole place.

They already found some blow that don't belong to me, but they gonna try to hang it on me. You need to hit me back like *now*. You know what I'm sayin'?"

"He's leaving a message," Bates said. "I'm guessing it's for big brother."

Lipscomb immediately dialed another number.

"Yo, yo, yo, thank God, Momma. Listen, Momma, I'm in a lot of trouble. No, no, nothing like that. I was just chillin' at my crib and these poh-lice came in on me. Yeah, they just barged in like a bunch of Nazis. One of my boys left some stuff in a drawer in my bedroom and they found it. Nah, nah, Momma, I swear it ain't mine. I swear on my babies' lives. It must have been some kind of setup. Yeah, you know me, you *know* me. I wouldn't swear it if it ain't true. You got to help me, Momma. They talkin' about eight years in prison. Eight years, and I didn't do nothin'. Can you bail me out and get me that lawyer? Nah, Momma, you don't even need to say nothin' to Pops about it. Yo, yo, wait just one second. I'm gettin' a beep. I gotta take this, Momma. They'll take me to the Jonesborough jail. Call a bondsman and get me out as soon as you can."

Lipscomb disconnected from his mother and answered the second call.

"'Bout time you calling me back."

There was silence while Nelson listened to the voice on the other end. Suddenly, his forehead wrinkled and his eyes tightened.

"I ain't in no mood to be putting up with none of your bullshit. I got poh-lice so far up my ass they tickling the back of my throat and you sitting down there in your fancy office drinking champagne and chasing booty."

There was another long silence.

"What seems to be the *problem*?" Nelson yelled. "The *problem* is that they say they got witnesses that saw me with them three shorties that wound up dead Saturday night. They say their witnesses saw me pick them up and then get on a boat with them. The *problem* is they come up in my crib with a search warrant and found some blow and now they saying I'm looking at eight years for the blow plus they talking about pinning three murders on me and giving me the death penalty. *That's* the *problem*. Now what you gonna do about it? Damn straight you'll take care of it. This is your fault anyway. You need to start throwing some cash my way. A lot of it."

The voice on the other end must have asked Lipscomb where he was.

"I'm in the back of a poh-lice car. Nah, man, they don't know I got my phone. Nah, they ain't nobody around. I done told you they all up in my crib tearing the place apart. ... What? What did you call me?"

A look of confusion came over Lipscomb's face. He held the phone out in front of him, and his expression changed to one of pure hatred.

"Nah, you didn't just hang up on me. Ah-ight, we'll see who's the idiot. I ain't the one killed three shorties."

Lipscomb stared at the phone for a few seconds longer, then shoved it back into his pocket.

"Gotcha," Bates said, and he closed the laptop with an exaggerated flourish.

CHAPTER NINE

We finished the search less than three hours later. Bates's people found another quarter-ounce of cocaine, nearly an ounce of marijuana, fifty-four Xanax tablets, thirty-five hundred dollars in cash, and an unregistered .357-magnum pistol. Everything was tagged, bagged, and the inventory written out. We then drove back down to Bates's office, which was connected to the jail in Jonesborough. Bates opened his laptop and took notes while the two of us watched and listened to Lipscomb's conversations again. We couldn't hear the people on the other end, but one was obviously his mother and the other was probably his brother. We'd know for certain as soon as we got a subpoena for his phone records.

"How long you reckon he's been practicing his gangster routine?" Bates said, a look of amusement on his face.

"Too long," I said.

"Why do these white boys want to sound black? Are they ashamed that they're white?"

"They think if they sound like a gangster and act like a gangster, it makes them tough."

"I think it makes them stupid. Let's go talk to Nelson."

We made our way through the maze of gray-walled hallways and gray, steel doors to the booking room. Supper had already been served at the jail, and the place smelled like hot dogs and corn. Nelson Lipscomb was in one of the holding cells that lined the wall across from the booking counter. He was lying on his back on the concrete platform that served as a bunk. His right arm was across his eyes. He didn't move when we walked in.

"Still got your cell phone?" Bates said. "I reckon not. These boys down here are pretty strict about that stuff. So who'd you call from the backseat of the cruiser besides your momma, Nelson?"

Lipscomb's knee jerked involuntarily. He had to be wondering how Bates knew who he'd called, or maybe he realized that he'd been duped.

"You said, 'This is your fault anyway.' Whose fault *is* it, Nelson? And you said, 'I ain't the one that killed three shorties.' Who *is* the one that killed three shorties?"

Nelson slowly removed his arm from his face and turned his head toward Bates.

"I want a lawyer," he said, and he put his arm back over his face.

Just then, the cell door opened and a man in a suit walked in. I assumed immediately that he was an attorney, but I'd never laid eyes on him. He was about six feet tall and looked like he belonged on the cover of the *American Bar Association Journal*. Silver-gray hair, perfectly groomed, sky-blue eyes, tanned and fit. Angular jaw, dimpled chin, perfect nose. The quintessential Aryan WASP. He was wearing a navy blue suit, a white, button-down shirt, and a navy blue and yellow striped tie. He stopped just inside the door and eyed Bates and me like we were peasants.

"Niles D. Brubaker," he said in a syrupy Southern drawl. "I represent Mr. Lipscomb, and I demand that all questioning cease this instant."

His tone angered me immediately.

"You don't have to demand," I said. "Asking will suffice."

"Leave us alone. I'd like to confer with my client."

"Do you have some identification?"

He looked shocked. "You don't know who I am?"

"Sure don't."

"I'm the president of the Tennessee Bar Association."

"Good for you. I don't associate with the Tennessee Bar Association. Do you have some identification?"

Niles D. Brubaker reached into an inside jacket pocket and produced a wallet. He removed his bar card and handed it to me.

"Photo ID?" I asked. He was so pretentious I couldn't help jerking him around a little.

He took a deep breath and handed me his driver's license. I scrutinized it for entirely too long.

"Where are you from?" I asked.

"Nashville."

"Nashville? How'd you get here so fast?"

"Are you familiar with modern aviation?"

I held his license out, but just before he took it, I dropped it on the floor.

"Sorry about that," I said as he bent over to pick it up. "Your client is going to be charged with felony drug possession and a weapons violation. We also suspect him in a triple homicide. Have a nice chat."

As Bates and I were walking out the door, Brubaker cleared his throat.

"And who might you gentlemen be?" he said.

I stopped and turned to face him.

"This might be Sheriff Leon Bates," I said, "and I might be Joe Dillard."

"Are you an investigator?"

"No. I'm the district attorney. I'm the one who'll be sending your client to death row."

I turned my back on Brubaker, and Bates and I walked out of the booking area toward his office.

"I was hoping we'd have time to sweat him some more," Bates said. "We don't have near enough to charge him with murder."

"I know, but we can pressure him with the drug charges. The phone calls he made are circumstantial, but they'll be useful somewhere down the line."

"What kind of person gets the president of the Tennessee Bar Association to drop what he's doing and fly all the way up here on a moment's notice this time of night?"

"A rich one."

"He'll make bond in an hour," Bates said. "We need to find that boat, and we need to figure out who was on it Saturday night."

Bates's cell phone rang as we walked down the hallway. He talked for a few minutes, hung up, and looked at me.

"My boys have been working," he said. "We've already run down the limo driver and taken a statement from him. He confirms that he picked up Nelson and three women from the club Saturday night and dropped them at the marina. He also says he was supposed to pick them up at six the next morning, but Nelson called him around five thirty and canceled. The boat is registered to John Lipscomb's corporation, and we're in the process of contacting all the places around here that normally store boats that size. One of my guys went down to the courthouse to look at the tax records, and he found out that Lipscomb owns a big house on the lake. He's checking to see if there's a gardener or caretaker or somebody who can tell us whether Lipscomb was around over the weekend. He's also going to go out to the airport to see whether Lipscomb might have come in by private jet or helicopter."

"Not bad," I said, "but even if we can put Lipscomb in the area that night, we still can't put him on the boat, and even if we do put him on the boat, we can't prove he had anything to do with the murders."

"Maybe not, but if he had something to do with it, one thing will happen just as sure as I'm standing here with my teeth in my mouth and my elbow halfway down my arm."

"What's that?"

"He'll lie, Brother Dillard. He'll lie like a politician. And when he does, we'll know it."

CHAPTER TEN

I didn't get home until after ten that night. The moon was rising above the mountains to the west, casting a pale, yellow glow that framed the peaks like a halo. Caroline had fixed dinner and kept it warm, and after I changed into a pair of old sweat pants and a T-shirt, we ate silently by candlelight on the deck. I was sure Caroline was curious about the day's events, but I was content just looking at her face in the soft glow, watching the flickering shadows play across her face. She looked up once to find me staring at her, but all she did was smile and wink, a simple gesture that conveyed what I already knew.

When we were finished, I helped her gather the dishes and clean up the kitchen. Rio followed me every step of the way with his ragged tennis ball in his mouth. Chico, the mischievous little teacup poodle I'd bought for Caroline after her last surgery, was right beside him with a rubber frog hanging from his teeth. They were an unlikely pair—a hundred-pound German shepherd and a five-pound poodle—but they'd become inseparable. I was surprised at how gently Rio treated the puppy. Chico tormented him constantly, jumping up and biting at his face, chewing on his tail, running around him in circles, and barking incessantly. If Rio made the mistake of lying on the floor, Chico immediately crawled up on his back and went to work on his ears. For the first several weeks Chico was around, Rio learned that he could escape by climbing onto a couch. But Chico was athletic; he could now jump onto the couch himself, and Rio's refuge was no more.

As soon as I finished wiping down the stovetop, I looked down at the dogs and said, "All right, give 'em up."

Rio dropped the ball next to my feet, and Chico did the same with his frog. I bent over, picked them up, and walked out to the deck. Rio whined in anticipation, and I threw the tennis ball into the darkness. He bolted for the steps that led to the backyard, stopped for a second to listen for the ball landing, and disappeared. Chico looked like he was riding a pogo stick, jumping up and down and nipping at my knee. I tossed the rubber frog across the deck, and he scrambled furiously after it.

I heard the phone ring inside the house and hoped Caroline would ignore it. I'd worked more than fifteen hours that day, and as far as I was concerned, that was enough. But less than a minute later, I saw her walking through the kitchen toward me. She motioned for me to come inside.

"I think you want to take this," she said, covering the receiver with her hand.

"Who is it?"

"Trust me. You want to take it."

I took the phone from Caroline and looked at the number on the caller ID display. I didn't recognize it although I did recognize the area code: Nashville.

Caroline sat down at the kitchen table, and I took a seat across from her.

"Joe Dillard," I said into the phone.

"Please hold for the governor," a female voice replied.

The governor? There was no doubt in my mind what the topic of conversation would be.

"Joe! Linc Donner here."

James Lincoln Donner III was the man who had appointed me to the district attorney general's job at the behest of Leon Bates. He was a wealthy Democrat, a silver-spooner who had inherited his family's vast real estate development fortune and had risen steadily through the ranks of the state Democratic Party. I remembered being surprised by his stature when I met him aboard his private jet, in which he'd flown to Johnson City to deliver the news of my appointment in person. In his television ads, he appeared to be tall and substantial. But Donner was a small, thin, hollow-cheeked man. He had politician-length chestnut-brown hair and gray eyes. His voice was a peculiar, throaty bass that reminded me of a bullfrog.

"This is quite a surprise," I said into the phone.

"Do you remember when I flew up there and signed your appointment? You were just about to leave the plane, and I stopped you and said something to you. Do you remember what it was?"

"I think you said, 'Don't make me regret this,' or something to that effect."

"Exactly. Don't make me regret this. I'm afraid you're beginning to make me question my decision."

"And why is that?"

"I was made aware of some information today that genuinely shocked me. Is it true that John Lipscomb is the target of a murder investigation?"

I cursed Ralph Harmon under my breath. The leak had to have come from him.

"With all due respect, Governor, I don't think that's an appropriate question for you to ask me."

"With all due respect to you, sir, I'm the governor and the head of the executive branch. And frankly, I'm not interested in what you think. John Lipscomb is a close friend of mine and one of the leading citizens of this state. He's poured more money into your community than any man living or dead. The very idea that he would somehow be involved in a murder is preposterous. Do you really think he would associate with strippers and whores?"

"Strippers and whores to you, Governor. Citizens of the district to me. Besides, I don't know Mr. Lipscomb. I don't know who he might associate with."

"If news that you're even considering him as a suspect gets out, it could do irreparable damage to his reputation. Now I asked you a simple question, but since you didn't seem to understand the first time, I'll ask you again. Yes or no, is John Lipscomb the target of a murder investigation in your jurisdiction?"

The tone of his voice was accusatory, almost threatening, and I felt anger beginning to boil inside me. Caroline must have noticed because she immediately reached across the table and took my free hand.

"There is more than one ongoing murder investigation in my jurisdiction," I said. "The key word being *ongoing.* As such, I'm not at liberty to discuss any of them with you."

"Dammit, man, I'm not a reporter. I'm the governor."

"Yeah, I think you mentioned that."

"How dare you take that insolent tone with me! If you want to keep your job, you'll treat me with the respect I deserve."

"Respect is something that's earned, Governor. It seems to me that you're calling and trying to intervene in a murder investigation on behalf of one of your rich friends. That doesn't earn you much respect in my book. And as far as my job goes, unless I break a law or fall over dead, you're stuck with me for at least another three years. And as long as I'm here, I'll do the job the way I think it should be done. Discussing ongoing investigations with politicians isn't my idea of the way things should be done. But it's good to talk to you, Governor. Feel free to call anytime."

I pushed the button on the receiver and set the phone down on the table in front of me. Caroline was staring at me wide-eyed.

"Did you just do what I think you did?" she asked, a smile beginning to form at the edges of her lips. "Did you just hang up on the governor of Tennessee?"

"I think maybe I did."

"You're insane—do you know that? You're certifiable."

"That's a matter of opinion."

"You were also right, for what it's worth."

"Thank you."

"Do you think there'll be any repercussions?"

I nodded my head. "Probably."

"What kind?"

"I don't know. I've never crossed a governor before. I guess we just wait and see."

CHAPTER ELEVEN

That night I dreamed of my mother. She was sitting at her sewing machine in the small house she shared with my sister and me, half-watching the black-and-white television that cast an eerie glow across the tiny den. Our den was always cloaked in darkness, as was the rest of the house, because my mother had put blinds on every window, and she kept all of them drawn. She didn't want to see the world outside, and she didn't want it to see her.

Her black hair was pulled tightly into a bun, and her face, which could have been pretty, was tight and stern. She was wearing a full-length, long-sleeved, black dress with a wide, black belt around her waist. The dress was buttoned to her throat, and as I looked at her hands, I noticed her fingernails were painted black.

I was very young in the dream, and I was apprehensive. I rarely approached her because her mood was always dark and her comments often sarcastic, but on this particular afternoon my young mind, or perhaps my heart, was looking for some answers. The annual field-day festivities had been held at school that day, and the parents of nearly all the children in my class had attended. I won several events, but my parents were absent, as always. I'd never asked her why she didn't attend any of the functions that other parents attended, and I'd never asked her about my father. My grandparents had told me that he was in heaven with Jesus, but my mother had never offered any information, and I'd never broached the subject. I stood next to her chair, staring at my feet, waiting for her to acknowledge me. She didn't. Finally, I spoke.

"Momma, can I ask you a question?"

"Don't you think you're a little old to be calling me 'Momma'? It makes you sound like a little sissy boy," she said without looking at me.

Her words surprised me, and I took a minute to gather my courage. She'd never hit me, so I wasn't afraid of physical abuse, but up to that point, just a word from her, uttered in her razor-sharp tone, could reduce me to tears.

"What do you want me to call you?" I asked.

She looked up from her sewing and raised her pencil-thin eyebrows. Her eyes flashed with a familiar anger.

"Don't get smart with me."

"I'm not being smart. I'm just asking what you want me to call you. If you don't want me to call you 'Momma,' then what? Mother?"

"Don't call me 'Mother.' I don't like it."

"Ma?"

"Fine. I don't care."

"Can I ask you a question, Ma?"

"Can't you see I'm busy?"

"What happened to my dad?"

She stiffened, but her eyes stayed on the needle that pumped up and down, up and down, like a drill bit driving into the earth in search of oil.

"He's dead," she said matter-of-factly.

"How did he die?"

She hesitated slightly before saying, "He was murdered."

"Who killed him?"

Her foot came off the pedal, and the sewing machine went silent. Her right hand slowly lifted away from the piece of material she'd been holding, her index finger extended, and she pointed at the television.

"They did," she said. "Those men right there. They murdered your father."

I turned and looked at the television. A row of men in suits were talking to a man sitting alone at a table.

"Who are they?"

"Politicians," she said. "Worthless, gutless politicians. Do you know what they're doing right now? They're talking to a man who works for the president of the United States. Do you know who the president of the United States is?"

"Nixon."

"That's right. Those men there are going to try to impeach Nixon for doing something every one of them does every day."

"What's that?"

"They're going to impeach him for lying. But they all lie. They're all hypocrites."

"Is that how they killed my dad? By lying?"

"They lied to all of us. They made him go to a place he'd never heard of and fight in a war he had no business fighting. They wanted him to kill Viet Cong and North Vietnamese soldiers."

"Why did those men want him to fight?"

"Because it's what they do. It's what they've always done, and it's what they'll always do."

"Will they make me fight too?"

"I can't believe I have to raise you and your sister in a world like this," she said. "There's murder and corruption everywhere. It's hopeless."

Looking back on that conversation with my mother, I believe now that my soul, as young as it was, began to form a callus. It was a conversation I'd dreamed about many times, but this night, the dream took an ominous turn.

My mother rose from her sewing and glided silently across the den, disappearing briefly into the back of the house. When she returned, she was carrying Sarah, who was fast asleep, in her arms. She laid Sarah on the couch and motioned for me to come and sit. When I was seated, she knelt in front of me.

"There is no God, you know," she said. "There is no good in this world. There is only evil and deception and murder. The best thing I can do for you is spare you from it. You shouldn't have to live in this world. No one should."

She reached behind her back and pulled something from her belt. I looked into her face. It was blank, as devoid of emotion as a sand dune. Suddenly, I felt the cool steel of a gun barrel against my forehead.

"This is the best thing I can do for you and your sister," she said, and I heard the hammer click.

CHAPTER TWELVE

The phone on my desk rang at seven the next morning. I'd been in the office for more than an hour, having quit the idea of sleep following the nightmare. I looked at the phone curiously before I picked it up, wondering who would be calling so early.

"Joe Dillard."

"Uh, Dillard? Ralph Harmon here." The SAIC of the local TBI office was supposed to have gotten back to me the day before. "I didn't expect anyone to be in the office so early."

"So why did you call? Planning to leave a message?"

"Actually, I was," Harmon said, sounding flustered.

"A message for me or for someone else?"

"Ah, listen, Dillard, about the homicide investigation. I'm afraid we're not going to be able to help out on this one."

I nearly dropped the phone. I'd never heard of the TBI refusing a district attorney's request for assistance. "It's a little early in the morning to be jerking my chain, Ralph."

"I'm serious. We're going to pass."

"Since when do you have that option?"

"Since my boss talked to his boss, who went straight to the director. The director called the state attorney general for an opinion. The attorney general looked at the statute and says we don't have to get involved if we don't want to. The statute says you can make a request. It doesn't say we have to honor it. Oh, and by the way, I don't think I have to tell you who the state attorney general answers to."

"The governor."

"That's right, the governor. The man you hung up on last night."

"I appreciate you leaking information about our murder investigation, Ralph. You're a real peach."

"Listen, Dillard, this isn't my call. The governor thinks you're trying to make a name for yourself at the expense of one of his friends. He thinks you're off on some kind of witch hunt, and you didn't help matters any by blowing him off the way you did. Bottom line, it looks like you're going to wind up on your own if you stay on this Lipscomb guy. I wouldn't be surprised if Bates jumps ship on you next."

"Bates isn't going anywhere."

"We'll see about that."

"We've got three dead girls at the morgue, Ralph. We need some help."

"Three dead *strippers*. Good luck with your case."

The line went dead and I sat there stunned, trying to comprehend the meaning of what had just occurred. The TBI refusing a request from a district attorney to join a multiple-homicide investigation? Unheard of. Unprecedented. Impossible. I pulled the Tennessee Code

Annotated up on my computer screen and spent the next half hour tracking the law. When I was finished, I clicked the computer off in disgust. It appeared that the state attorney general was correct; the statute that outlines the powers of the district attorney general says he or she can "request" the assistance of the TBI. It doesn't say anything about whether the TBI has to comply. The legislators obviously left them a loophole.

I pulled Bates's number up on my cell phone and hit send. No answer. I left him a simple message. "Call me as soon as you get this."

I walked down the hallway to the bathroom and splashed some cold water on my face, seething at the efficiency of this particular part of the political machine. They were attempting to stop the investigation before it got started, they were doing it from the top down, and they were doing so effectively. Governor Donner was manipulating people as though they were marionettes and he a skillful puppeteer. He was selling the idea that I was trying to make a name for myself at the expense of John Lipscomb, and I was certain his stooges and cronies were buying without questioning. What had *I* ever done for them, after all? How much money had *I* donated to their reelection campaigns or PAC funds? What kind of beneficial influence could *I*—a hick prosecutor from the hills who'd never even been through an election—bring on their behalf if the need ever arose?

I finished wiping my face and walked out of the bathroom to my office. Bates was leaning back in one of the chairs in front of my desk with his legs stretched out and his cowboy boots propped on the corner of the desk.

"How's this for a quick call back?" he said without turning around.

"Do you know what's going on? Do you know they're trying to shut us down before we get started?"

"Didn't your mama ever teach you anything about phone etiquette?" Bates asked. He was running the fingers of his right hand around the edge of the cowboy hat he held in his left.

"He was out of line," I said as I walked around the desk and sat down.

"He was out of line when he called me too, but I didn't spit in his face."

"What'd you tell him?"

"I told him yes, Governor, sir, Mr. Lipscomb's name has come up in connection with our murder investigation but no, Governor, sir, we don't have any evidence that places him at the scene, and it doesn't appear that we'll be taking the investigation any farther in that direction. And yes, Governor, sir, you can rest assured that no one from my department or Mr. Dillard's office will mention Mr. Lipscomb's name in the same breath as this nasty affair and by all means, Governor, sir, I will keep you abreast of anything that may develop in the future that involves Mr. Lipscomb."

"So are you folding the tent or did you lie to him?"

"I told him what he wanted to hear. That's the way this game is played. And no, I'm not planning on folding the tent just yet."

"Which means you lied to him."

"I have no doubt that under similar circumstances, he'd do the same."

"The TBI's out, you know. I just got a call from Harmon. He says the governor thinks I'm trying to make a name for myself. They're refusing my request for assistance. That's never happened, at least not to my knowledge."

"Don't worry about it. The TBI guys are a bunch of prima donnas anyway."

"What's next, Leon? Where do we go from here?"

Bates pulled his feet from the desk, leaned forward, put his hat back on his head, and took a deep breath.

"What say you and me take a little trip over to the jail? There's somebody I want you to meet."

CHAPTER THIRTEEN

udy Lane, the Peter Sellers look-alike who'd led
Nelson Lipscomb out to the cruiser during the
search of Nelson's condo, found the caretaker. Rudy
was one of Bates's best investigators, partly because, like
Bates, he was able to pull off the disarming, country-boy-
charm routine while possessing the instincts of a blood-
hound. He was also determined and tenacious, and when
he was given an assignment, its successful completion
became a matter of personal pride.

At five in the morning—two hours before I received
the telephone call from Ralph Harmon telling me the TBI
was blowing us off—Rudy saw headlights, and a pickup
truck rolled up to a gated mansion on Boone Lake. It was
also Rudy who'd checked the county tax assessor's office
to see whether John J. Lipscomb owned any property in
Washington County.

"Five-hour energy drinks and diet Pepsi," Rudy
would later tell me when I asked how he'd managed to
stay awake all night. I knew he'd barely slept since the
girls were found nearly seventy-two hours earlier.

A security light came on, and Rudy saw a man
hold a card in front of an electronic eye. The black,

wrought-iron gate began to swing open. Rudy turned on
his emergency lights and pulled in behind the pickup.
He got out of his unmarked cruiser and walked up to
the driver's side window. He shined his flashlight over
the interior of the cab, then directly into the driver's face.

"Morning," Rudy said. "Can I see your license and
registration, please? And some proof of insurance?"

"Have I done something wrong?"

The man inside the cab appeared to be Latino. His
face was chubby and pock-marked, his eyes dark, and
black hair curled from beneath a Los Angeles Dodgers
baseball cap. A black goatee encircled his mouth.

"What are you doing out here at this time of the
morning?" Rudy said.

"I could ask you the same thing," the man said. He
produced a driver's license. "I have to open the glove
compartment to get the registration and the insurance
card. Don't shoot me."

"Do it slow," Rudy said, taking a step back and plac-
ing his right hand on the butt of his nine-millimeter.
"Keep your left hand on the steering wheel."

The man did as instructed and handed the docu-
mentation out the window.

"Step out of the car, please."

"What have I done?"

"Listen, friend," Rudy said, "it's dark out here. I'm
alone. I don't know you, and I don't know what you
might have in the truck. Don't make this difficult. Get
out, put your hands on the front fender there, and spread
your feet."

Rudy pulled the door open and stepped back.

"I'm not a criminal," the man said as he climbed out and assumed the position.

"Good. Then you and me will get along just fine."

Rudy patted him down thoroughly. He wasn't carrying any contraband or weapons. Rudy reached behind his back for his handcuffs. "I'm going to cuff you now, for your safety and mine. Then I'm going to ask you to sit on the ground right here next to the truck. If everything checks out, I'll take the cuffs off in a few minutes. Do you mind if I look around inside the vehicle?"

"This is harassment," the man said.

"So sue me. Do I have your permission to look through the vehicle?"

"Go ahead. I'm not hiding anything."

The name on both the driver's license and the registration was Hector Arturo Mejia. A check with dispatch revealed no wants or warrants, and the cab of the truck was clean.

"Sorry, Mr. Mejia," Rudy said as he helped the man up and unlocked the handcuffs. He smiled and patted Mejia on the back. "It's a dangerous world. We've had a couple reports of prowlers in this area, so we're staking it out. I'm assuming there are some valuable goods in a place like this. Now, back to the original question. What are you doing here at five in the morning?"

"I work for Mr. Lipscomb," Mejia said, rubbing his wrists. "I take care of the place."

"Which Mr. Lipscomb do you work for? John or Nelson?"

Mejia shook his head in disgust. "I don't work for Nelson. The only time Nelson comes around is when he wants to act like a big shot. But I guess he doesn't have many people he wants to impress because he isn't here much."

"What are you taking care of at five in the morning?"

"The pool. Mr. Lipscomb is very fussy about the pool. He wants it clean at all times. I come out here and clean it in the morning before I go to work. It's cool and it's quiet. I like it here early in the morning. Then I come back in the evening and do whatever else needs to be done. I take care of the gardens, mow the lawn, maintain the place."

"Where do you work besides here?"

"I work for Stengard. I'm a shift foreman."

Stengard was a manufacturer in Johnson City that built water heaters, a plant that was infamous for low wages and hot, difficult, dangerous working conditions.

"Are you a U.S. citizen, Mr. Mejia?"

"All my life. I was born in Telford and graduated from Crockett high school."

"Who pays you for keeping the pool clean and keeping the place up?" Rudy said.

"Equicorp. Mr. Lipscomb's company. I email my hours to his secretary, and they send me a check every other week."

"How long have you been working for him?"

"About eight years. My father worked here before me. Can I go now? I need to get started so I'm not late for my other job."

Rudy ignored Mejia and kept talking in his polite, Southern drawl. "So I reckon you know Mr. Lipscomb pretty well, do you?"

"Why are you so interested in Mr. Lipscomb?"

"Hells bells, Mr. Mejia, he's a celebrity around here. You might as well be working for Elvis. I mean, I've heard he's got more money than the Almighty and that the inside of this place looks like the Taj Mahal or something. It must be pretty neat working for somebody so rich and famous. Now me, I haven't even ever *seen* Mr. Lipscomb. Never laid eyes on the man except for pictures in the newspaper. Does he ever come around?"

"Yeah," Mejia said, "but only once a year."

"Really? When does he come? Maybe I'll drop by and say howdy. I could introduce myself, maybe tell him if he ever needs any private security work done, I'm the man for the job."

"You'll have to wait a year. He was here over the weekend, but he's already gone. But you won't get to see him even then. He doesn't see visitors when he's here."

Rudy felt his heart accelerate slightly. "Well, that's just my luck. Say he was here this past weekend? Maybe that's why we've been getting calls. Maybe somebody drove by and thought *he* was the prowler."

"I doubt it," Mejia said. "You can't see the house from the road."

"Does he come the same time every year?"

"Labor Day weekend. Him and his lawyer, just the two of them. They come up Saturday afternoon and leave Sunday afternoon."

"His lawyer? Do you know his name?"

"Pinzon. Andres Pinzon. He's a nice guy, which is more than I can say for Mr. Lipscomb."

"Why you reckon they come up on Labor Day?"

"I've heard them bragging about it. The Friday before Labor Day is the anniversary of Mr. Lipscomb taking over some insurance company. He says it made him richer than he ever dreamed."

"Tell me something," Rudy said, lowering his voice and taking on a conspiratorial tone. "How does a guy like that travel? I mean I doubt he gets in his car and drives up here from Nashville, right? And I doubt he wants to fly into Tri-Cities airport with the common folks. Does he have a private jet or something?"

"Helicopter," Mejia said, now relishing his role as the local authority on John J. Lipscomb. "There's a helipad next to the house. He just flies in and flies out. He's a pilot."

"Must be nice to be rich. I'll bet he's got a garage full of nice cars too."

"Nah, just a Lexus. But he never drives it. I take it out once a month or so, just a few miles, to make sure it's running okay."

"Do you drive him around when he's here?"

"He never goes out. I spend the night in the guest house out back every year in case they need anything. They just stay in the house and drink and tell each other how great they are. If they want food, I go get it and bring it back to them. I don't think anybody else even knows he's here except for Nelson because Nelson takes them out in the boat on Saturday night every year. They stay out all night. I clean up the mess."

"I've heard rumors about those boat trips," Rudy said. He winked slyly at Mejia. "I hear they like the ladies."

Rudy shook his head and spat on the ground. "I've warned them. I've told them you can't keep secrets in this town, especially with someone like Nelson running around."

"Did you see them? The girls?"

"Yeah, I saw them, just for a second when Mr. Lipscomb and Mr. Pinzon were getting on the boat."

"How many girls?"

"Three. I saw three."

"Did all three of them have blonde hair?"

Mejia's head jerked quickly around. He stared hard into Rudy's face.

"Wait a minute," Mejia said. "Is that what this is about? Those three girls that were found in the lake?"

"You tell me," Rudy said. "*Is* it?"

"I don't know anything about that. I think you should go now."

"Can't do it," Rudy said. "You see, this little chat we've been having makes me believe that you're either a material witness or you're an accessory to a triple homicide. Either way, I'm afraid I'm going to have to arrest you."

Rudy dangled his handcuffs in front of Mejia's face.

"Sorry, Mr. Mejia," he said, "but I reckon you're gonna have to put these back on."

CHAPTER FOURTEEN

hree hours later, after we'd talked to Hector Mejia at
the jail and made some hasty arrangements, Bates and
I were headed to Nashville. I'd asked Tanner Jarrett,
a young assistant in the office whom I trusted, to help
Rita keep things running smoothly while I was away. The
trip was perhaps a bit premature, but the circumstances
were such that Bates thought—and I agreed—we should
attempt to confront Lipscomb and, at the very least, get
him to commit to a story. After talking to Mejia, we knew
that Lipscomb and Andres Pinzon had been at Lipscomb's
house on the lake over the weekend. Mejia actually *saw*
Lipscomb and Pinzon board the *Laura Mae* on Saturday
night, but rather than sleep in the next day and leave for
Nashville in the early afternoon as they usually did, Mejia
said the helicopter woke him up as it lifted off from the
pad sometime after five the next morning. Lipscomb and
Pinzon left no note and no explanation for the early depar-
ture, and when Mejia drove to the marina later in the day to
clean the boat, it was gone. He called Nelson to ask where
the boat was and was told that the engine gave them problems on Saturday night, so Mr. Lipscomb hired somebody
to remove it from the water and was having it overhauled.

So as we drove west along I-40 in Bates's black BMW, we felt confident that we were on the right track. Nelson had paid for the girls, picked them up, and escorted them to the boat the night they were killed. He was seen getting on the boat with them and driving the boat away from the marina. Mejia could put John Lipscomb and Pinzon on the boat the same night, and he said they left in a hurry. Mejia was still being held at the jail. I didn't think he had anything to do with the murders, but I didn't want him contacting John Lipscomb either, so I told Rudy Lane to hold him for twenty-four hours and then cut him loose.

Bates parked the BMW in a garage just off the interstate about five miles east of downtown Nashville, and we took the elevator to the ground floor. As we walked out of the garage, the Equicorp corporate headquarters building rose from the ground like the Tower of Babel against a darkening sky. The building was eight stories, constructed of steel and glass, and the interior lights shining through the tinted windows glowed eerily. The area surrounding the building was surprisingly desolate. Apart from the parking garage that obviously served only Equicorp, there was nothing but vacant lots within hundreds of yards on all sides of the building. I noticed a sharp, grinding sound and looked to the west. Beyond the vacant lots in that direction was a faded yellow sign with black letters: "A-1 Salvage." It was a scrap yard, and the sound I heard was metal being crushed.

A north wind was howling as we approached the building, blowing so fiercely that Bates had to hold his cowboy hat down with his hand. I'd suggested that he wear something besides his uniform, but the idea had been dismissed outright. "The only time I take the uniform off is when I go to bed and when I go to church," he'd said. "I'd feel naked without it."

The foyer on the first floor was opulent. The walls and ceiling were covered in cedar and trimmed in brass, the floor was granite tile, and a crystal chandelier the size of a compact car shimmered twenty feet above our heads. A bank of elevators was directly in front of us, and on the wall a directory of the building. There were only two offices on the eighth floor—John J. Lipscomb, president and CEO, and Andres L. Pinzon, vice-president and general counsel. Bates and I got on the elevator and pushed the button.

"Not exactly what I'd call a secure facility," Bates said as the elevator began to climb.

"I guess they don't have any reason to be afraid," I said.

"That's about to change."

The elevator opened onto yet another glimmering example of wealth and excess, nearly a carbon copy of the foyer downstairs. An attractive brunette dressed in a sharp, navy-blue business suit was walking across the floor to a circular desk in the center of the room. She was obviously the gatekeeper, the first obstacle we would have to negotiate before we could get an audience with the king. She smiled sweetly as Bates and I approached. I noticed the nameplate on her desk: Monica Bell.

"My goodness, am I in trouble?" she said, looking at Bates. She had milk-chocolate-colored eyes and a smile that shined like the chandelier above.

"Sheriff Leon Bates, ma'am," he said, extending his hand. "Mighty pleased to make the acquaintance of such a lovely young lady. And this is Joe Dillard, attorney general of the First Judicial District of Tennessee. We're both from the same neck of the woods as Mr. Lipscomb. Any chance we could visit with him for just a couple minutes?"

"Are you a personal friend, Sheriff?"

"I met Mr. Lipscomb at a political function a few years ago, but I'm sorry to say I can't claim we're friends. It's an important matter though. We drove over three hundred miles just to see him."

She picked up the phone on her desk but changed her mind and set it back down.

"Will you gentlemen excuse me for just a moment? Please wait here."

Monica got up from her desk, walked across the tile floor, and disappeared behind a cedar door to our right.

"Watching her walk away was worth the trip down here," Bates said.

"I don't think he's going to want to see us voluntarily," I said.

"Me neither, let's go."

We headed for the same door Monica had gone through. Bates pulled it open, and we walked into another office, this one occupied by an older, but no less attractive, woman. Her strawberry-blonde hair was pulled into a bun, and with her reading glasses resting halfway up on her nose, she looked the model of corporate efficiency. She scowled at us over the glasses.

"You can't come in here without an appointment," she said.

I saw a broad door with a nameplate: John J. Lipscomb, President and CEO, and hurried toward it.

"This is an important police matter, ma'am," I heard Bates say behind me.

Monica was standing in front of Lipscomb's desk. The look she gave me when she heard the commotion and turned around was anything but attractive.

"I told you to wait outside!" Her nostrils flared, and her face suddenly took on the look of a viper. For a moment, I thought she might actually strike and sink her fangs into my neck.

Lipscomb, whom I recognized from photographs and television news stories, stood behind his desk.

"It's all right, Monica," he said calmly. "Please ask Andres to come in."

Lipscomb had the same dark features as his brother, Nelson, and was about the same height, but he had become, to put it mildly, obese. I'd seen newspaper photographs of him presenting checks to the beneficiaries of his philanthropic endeavors, but it had been years earlier. He was heavy even then, but he'd easily gained another fifty pounds. His head had taken on the shape of a jack-o-lantern, and the sheer volume of his girth made his arms and legs look disproportionately short. With his slightly upturned nose, he looked piggish. His hair was black and cut short; it looked like a shoe brush. He was wearing a maroon, silk shirt with an open collar, and he regarded me through dull brown eyes with a smirk. From the research Bates and I had done, I knew both Lipscomb and Pinzon were forty-five years old.

"I reckon you know who we are," Bates said.

"Yes, I *reckon* I do," Lipscomb said in a tone heavy with sarcasm. "You are the good ol' boy county sheriff, Leon Bates, and your friend here is Joe Dillard, the incorruptible district attorney general."

"We'd like to talk to you, Mr. Lipscomb," I said.

"That's obvious. The question, though, is whether I'd like to talk to you, isn't it? And in light of the fact that you've barged into my office uninvited and unannounced, I don't believe I'm inclined."

"I'm sorry you feel that way," I said, "because based on the telephone calls the sheriff and I have received from the governor, you know we're conducting a murder investigation, and you know your name has come up. We thought the most discreet way to handle the situation was by coming directly to you."

"How considerate of you. Do you plan to arrest me on some trumped-up charge the way you did my brother?"

"Where were you Saturday night, Mr. Lipscomb?"

"I was banging your wife. Didn't she mention it? I have to admit it wasn't as good as I'd hoped though. All that nastiness around the breast. Quite distracting. Not sexy at all."

My mouth went dry immediately, and I could feel myself beginning to tremble with rage. No one had ever spoken of Caroline in such a manner, and I didn't intend to let him get away with it or do it again. I took a step toward him and felt Bates's hand wrap around my forearm.

"Easy, Brother Dillard," he said. "He's just baiting you." His voice was distant, as though he was speaking from another room.

"Mention my wife again and I'll rip your tongue out," I said to Lipscomb. I took another step, trying to get away from Bates. He stepped between us, pressing his chest against me, talking in a calm voice.

"You don't want to go to jail in Nashville," Bates said. "Just breathe easy."

"My, my, aren't we excitable?" Lipscomb said. His expression had changed, however, and I noticed he was backing away slightly. The smirk was gone, replaced by a look of fear. He must have been accustomed to saying whatever came into his mind without fear of repercussion.

"You have no idea how excitable I can be," I said, my voice quivering with anger.

I was peripherally aware of the door opening and a man walking in. Lipscomb saw him too and walked around to the other side of his desk. He moved quickly behind the man.

"This is my lawyer," Lipscomb said. "Anything you have to say to me goes through him." He turned and waddled out of the room.

The lawyer was a tall, impressive-looking man wearing a black suit and tie over a wine colored shirt. He had a full, black, impeccably trimmed beard that covered his angular face, black hair that fell to his shoulders, olive-colored skin, and eyes as dark as a moonless night. He carried himself confidently, shoulders back, chin up, arms hanging loosely at his sides. He walked straight to me and offered his hand.

"I'm Andres Pinzon, general counsel for Equicorp."

I shook his hand robotically, still staring after Lipscomb.

"Have I missed something?" Pinzon said to Bates.

"I'm afraid your client insulted Mr. Dillard's wife. He's none too happy about it."

"I apologize on Mr. Lipscomb's behalf," he said. "He sometimes speaks before he thinks."

Pinzon spoke with a bit of an accent, most likely Spanish, but his tone wasn't confrontational or sarcastic like Lipscomb's. He looked me directly in the eye. "Perhaps Mr. Dillard and I should speak alone. Lawyer to lawyer. No police, no target."

"Who said he was a target?" Bates said.

"We know you arrested Mr. Lipscomb's brother, and we know the general nature of the questions you asked him. So please, if you would kindly wait outside, Mr. Dillard and I can talk here."

"Brother Dillard?" Bates said. By this time, he'd let go of me, and my breathing was beginning to slow.

"Sure," I said. "Fine."

"I'll just walk on back outside and see if I can patch things up with Miss Monica," Bates said. He sauntered out the door, and Pinzon motioned to a chair in front of Lipscomb's desk.

"Let's sit."

The few short moments inside Lipscomb's office had been so intense that I'd failed to notice my surroundings. Two of the walls were windows from floor to ceiling, offering expansive views to the south and east. The other two walls, both cedar trimmed in brass, were covered with oil paintings and tapestries. The floor was a gleaming, dark hardwood, the furnishings modern and expensive.

"I take it your foul-mouthed client likes cedar," I said as I sat down in an overstuffed chair that probably cost as much as I made in a month.

"It's Lebanese," Pinzon said. "Very rare. Very expensive."

"I didn't think we did much business with the Lebanese."

"People are always willing to do business if the price is right, but surely you didn't travel all this way to discuss cedar. What exactly can I do for you, Mr. Dillard?"

"You can tell me where you and Mr. Lipscomb were on Saturday night."

"And why would I want to do that?"

"Because I already know where you were. I just want to see whether you're going to lie."

"How could you possibly know where I was on Saturday?"

"We have three dead women in my district, Mr. Pinzon."

"Yes, I heard. Such a tragedy."

"The women were seen boarding a boat owned by Mr. Lipscomb's corporation just before dark. They were in the company of Mr. Lipscomb's brother. I have information that leads me to believe that you and Mr. Lipscomb boarded the same boat a short time later. The women wound up floating in the lake. You and Mr. Lipscomb left in a hurry and the boat has disappeared. Given those facts, what conclusion would you draw?"

"What kind of information would lead you to believe that Mr. Lipscomb and I were on the boat?"

"The kind that comes from a reliable source. Stop playing games with me. Where were you and Mr. Lipscomb on Saturday night?"

"Mr. Dillard," Pinzon said, rising from his chair. "It's been a pleasure meeting you, but I'm afraid this conversation is over."

"Short and sweet," I said. I stood and faced him, looking into his eyes. "This is your last chance to tell me what happened on that boat, Mr. Pinzon. If you tell me now, we can try to make the best of a bad situation. If you don't—"

"I don't know any more about what happened on the boat than you do," he interrupted. "What I do know is that you're playing a very dangerous game. It would be best for all concerned if you would turn your attention away from Mr. Lipscomb and focus on what you can prove."

"We'll be back," I said, turning toward the door, "with arrest warrants and handcuffs."

"That would be an extremely bad idea," I heard him say behind me. The tone of his voice had changed; the pitch was slightly higher and the words came out much more quickly. Could it have been desperation? "Please," he said as I started to pull the door closed behind me, "just let it go."

CHAPTER FIFTEEN

Over the course of the investigation, I would come to know a great deal about John J. Lipscomb and his lawyer, Andres Pinzon. Initially, most of the information came from people Bates and his deputies spoke with—family, friends, enemies, business associates, former employees. Later, I learned much from Pinzon himself. He told me this about how he and John Lipscomb met:

Andres Pinzon was thirteen years old, standing at a middle-school urinal when he heard the door open behind him and the sound of laughter.

"Clear out," a voice said, and the other students began to scramble.

Andres finished his business, zipped his fly, and turned toward the door. Standing in front of him were three boys, all larger than him. Andres recognized the boy in the middle as John Lipscomb. He lived directly across the street from Andres.

"That's the new kid," Lipscomb said. He was an inch or two taller than Andres, with dark hair and a ruddy complexion. His eyes were intense as he stared at Andres disdainfully. The other two boys, both blond-headed and green-eyed, looked to be twin brothers. Both of them were a good five inches taller than Andres, and both were built like athletes with wide shoulders and narrow waists.

"He looks like a monkey," the blond to Andres's left said.

Andres felt the fear in his stomach. It was his first day in an American school. Andres's father, a pediatric endocrinologist who had received his medical training in the United States, had moved his family to Tennessee earlier that summer, fearing the escalating violence in his native Colombia. He also feared the influence that the *Nadaistas*, or "nothingists," as they called themselves, might have on his children. *Nadaismo*, a philosophy espoused by a Colombian intellectual named Fernando Gonzalez, mirrored the hippie movement in the United States and was sweeping Colombia. Its central theme was "the right to disobey," and the youth of Colombia were expressing their disdain for the ruling class in much the same way their American predecessors had done: they grew their hair long, they dressed and acted outrageously, they lampooned their elders in their music, and they smoked dope—lots of dope.

Andres had spent much time listening to his father trumpet the virtues of America: the democratic principles, the educational and economic opportunities, the rule of law. He had not, however, been prepared to deal with bigotry on his first day in school.

"You're right," Lipscomb said. "He looks like a monkey. Where you from, boy? The jungle?"

"My name is Andres Luis Pinzon," Andres said as steadily as he could. "I am from Envigado, Colombia."

"That's some accent you got there, monkey boy. You know what we do to monkey boys who talk like you?"

Lipscomb took a step closer and began to unzip his fly. Before Andres realized what was happening, Lipscomb was urinating on Andres's pants leg.

Andres reacted instinctively. He heard himself mutter something in Spanish and launched himself at his aggressors. For the next thirty seconds, it was as though he had fallen into a dream. Everything was in slow motion. He didn't feel his fist connect with Lipscomb's nose, didn't feel himself being grabbed from behind, thrown to the ground, and kicked repeatedly in the ribs. He didn't hear the teachers, who, after being summoned by the students that had been ordered to leave the bathroom, had rushed in to break up the fight.

Ten minutes later, after the adrenaline rush had subsided, Andres found himself sitting on a bench outside the principal's office. Across from him were Lipscomb and one of the blond boys who had attacked him. Both boys wore smirks on their faces. The second blond was on the other side of the door. They could hear the principal yelling.

"You got balls, monkey boy, I'll give you that," Lipscomb said, holding a wad of toilet paper to his nose.

Andres looked at him fiercely. "If you keep calling me monkey boy, I'm going to punch you in the face again."

"What did you say to me?"

"I said if you call me monkey boy again, I'm going to punch you in the face."

"No, back in the bathroom, before you went all crazy, you said something about *punta*. Isn't *punta* some kind of Spanish cuss word?"

"It means whore," Andres said.

"You called me a whore?"

"No. I called you a son of a whore."

Lipscomb smiled and looked at his friend, then turned back to Andres.

"You know something, Colombia?" he said. "I think you and me are gonna get along just fine."

CHAPTER SIXTEEN

The day after Bates and I returned from Nashville, I stopped at a grocery on the west side of town on my way home. Caroline had asked me to pick up some fresh vegetables and some dog food, and as I walked around the corner of one of the aisles, I saw a familiar figure leaning over in the beer section. I froze momentarily, shocked to see her in that particular section of the store. She was wearing khaki shorts, a black T-shirt with "AAA Bail Bonds" emblazoned in white letters across the back, and a pair of flip flops. She picked up a case of beer and loaded it into a shopping cart. Sitting atop the cart was my niece, Gracie, who was only eighteen months old. Sarah staggered momentarily, and my heart sank.

She was drunk. I turned around and walked back through the store and out into the parking lot, feeling a mixture of anger and sadness, hoping I'd find someone sitting behind the wheel of her car. I hadn't talked to her since Sunday morning—I just hadn't had time—and a familiar pang of guilt ran through me, the kind of guilt I knew I shouldn't be heaping on myself. Short of tying her up, there wasn't anything I could do when she decided to binge.

I knew I had to confront her, but I didn't want to make a scene in the store. Sarah was belligerent when she was drunk, and I knew I was in for a fight. But I couldn't let her drive away. I located her Mustang in the parking lot and stood several feet away, waiting for her to emerge from the store. She did so a few minutes later and began, with a great deal of difficulty, loading the beer and the baby into the backseat.

"Hey there," I said, walking up behind her.

She jerked, startled, and banged the back of her head against the roof.

"Dammit!" She rubbed the spot and looked at me angrily. "What're you doing here?"

"Just stopped by for some dog food. I saw you coming out and thought I'd say hello."

"Well, you said it. Goodbye." Her words were slurred and her eyes reddened.

"Why the rush?" I stepped closer to her, and the smell of beer assaulted me.

"Gotta go ... cookin' supper."

She slid in behind the steering wheel and started fumbling with her keys, trying to get them in the ignition.

"Hold up there, Sarah. Can't I at least say hi to Gracie?"

"She needsa eat. Gotta go."

I reached into the car, snatched the keys from Sarah's hand, and backed up toward the rear bumper.

"What the hell are you doing?" she yelled. "Gimme my keys!"

"How much have you had to drink?"

"What are you? A cop?"

"I can smell it all over you."

"Gimme the keys."

"Sarah, there's no way I'm going to let you drive this car drunk, especially with Gracie in the back."

"Gracie's fine. I'm fine. Lemme alone."

"C'mon, I'll drive you home. We'll pick up the car in the morning."

"I'm not leaving my car here! Now gimme the damn keys!"

At that moment, I noticed a Johnson City police cruiser coming slowly toward us. He pulled up behind Sarah's car, stopped, and rolled down the window. He was a young guy, typical of the police officers today, with a thick neck and a shaved head. He peered at me with dark, steady eyes as I walked to his car.

"Evening, officer," I said.

"Evening. Everything all right here?"

"Everything's fine."

"Gimme back my keys!"

I turned to see Sarah climbing out of the Mustang. The officer put his car in park and got out. He was about my size, roughly six three and two hundred pounds. He put his hat on and pointed at Sarah.

"Miss, I'm going to need you to stop right there," he said. She was leaning against the car with one hand, using it to balance herself. She ignored his command and grabbed me by the arm.

"My keys! Now!"

"You two know each other?" the cop said.

"She's my sister."

I saw a young woman approaching from my left. She was wearing a smock and a baseball cap with the store's insignia.

"That's her, Officer," she called, pointing at Sarah. "She's the one. She has a baby in the car."

Sarah turned and glared at the girl, suddenly even more enraged.

"Shut your mouth, you fat pig!" she bellowed. "Go back inside and mind your own business!"

She still had a hold of my arm with her right hand, and she continued to use her other hand to steady herself against the roof of the car. The situation was quickly deteriorating. The police officer keyed his microphone and spoke quietly into it as I tugged on Sarah, trying to get her attention off the store employee. A small crowd was beginning to gather, and thirty seconds later, two more cruisers pulled into the parking lot.

"This is great, Sarah," I said. "This is just great. Now you're going to wind up in jail."

"Get your hands offa me."

She was tugging and twisting, trying to break loose. She even tried to kick me in the shin. I looked over at the newly arrived cops and was relieved to see that I recognized one of them, a stocky, mid-thirties shift supervisor named Bob Dempsey. He and the other two officers formed a semicircle and moved toward Sarah and me.

"Dillard?" Dempsey said. "What are you doing in the middle of this?"

"Just lucky, I guess." Sarah was still fighting and cursing. I'd seen her go into alcoholic rages before, and I knew there wasn't much hope of calming her down anytime soon, at least not without the aid of some kind of sedative.

"So this is your sister," Dempsey said, "I've heard a lot about her."

"Yeah. Could you guys help me out here? My niece is in the backseat of the Mustang."

"You want me to cuff her?" Dempsey asked.

Before I could answer, Sarah managed to get herself into position to knee me in the groin, and she did so with all the force she could muster. I felt the sensation of pain and nausea rise into my stomach and staggered away as the officers closed in on her. My mind clouded with the pain, causing Sarah's screams to sound as though they were coming from inside a metal dumpster. I bent over and retched while the officers grabbed Sarah, lifted her off the ground, and carried her to one of the cruisers.

By the time the nausea passed, Sarah was in the backseat of a police car, beating against the windows and screaming. Had she been anyone else, she would most certainly have been pepper-sprayed, maybe even tasered. I walked over to her Mustang. The door was still open, and I looked into the backseat. Gracie was in the car seat, calmly looking out the window in the other direction.

"Hi sweetie," I said.

She recognized me immediately and grinned. "Unka Joe!"

I flipped the driver's seat forward, reached across her, picked up a blanket, and tucked it snugly around her.

"I'll be right back, sugar. You're going to come spend the night with me and Aunt Caroline."

"You gonna live?" a voice behind me asked. It was Dempsey.

I winked at Gracie and turned to face him. "I think so."

"We have ourselves quite the little situation here."

"Looks like it's under control now."

"I called the paramedics," he said. "They're on the way. What I'm worrying about is what I'm going to do with her after they get her to the hospital and she calms down."

"Just let her go," I said. "I'll take the baby home. I'll pick her car up, and I'll pick Sarah up at the hospital later. I'll make sure she doesn't cause any more problems."

"You sure about that? Because I don't think it's such a good idea. What I've got here is a DUI and endangerment of a child. And who knows what I'll find if I search this vehicle. We've got a crowd of people watching and two rookies who know who you are but don't know much about you. What I'm saying is that people are going to hear about this, you know what I mean? People like my boss, county commissioners, lawyers, judges, you name it. This is going to get out."

"So?"

"So giving a break to the district attorney's sister, especially one with a prior history like hers, isn't exactly great for my reputation in the law enforcement community."

I took a slow breath and tried to think. The pain in my groin was starting to subside, but I still felt thick and sluggish. What Sarah had done was stupid, no doubt. But she was in a lot of pain, and in my mind, I rationalized that she hadn't hurt anyone.

"Look, Dempsey," I said. "You can't make a DUI case because you didn't see her driving the car. She wasn't in legal control of the car when you got here because I had her keys. For all we know, her boyfriend drove her here, they got into an argument, and he walked away. The point is that unless you have a witness who saw her pull into the parking lot and get out of the car, you have no case."

"I'll bet you a month's salary that camera sitting up there on the roof will show her driving the car." He nodded his head at a security camera and I looked up. It was perched on the southwest corner of the building, an all-seeing eye of modern technology.

"You don't really want to go to all that trouble, do you?"

"I'm afraid I'm going to have to. I like you Dillard, always have. But there's a child involved here. I can't just let it slide."

I moved closer to him and lowered my voice.

"There are some things going on that you don't know about," I said. "I don't want to pull rank on you, but I'm the district attorney. She's my sister, and I'm not going to prosecute her. If you think you need to tell somebody about it, then do what you have to do. You can even arrest her if you want to, but the bottom line is that she isn't going to get prosecuted for this."

I looked at him steadily, waiting for him to make a decision. To my relief, he began to nod his head.

"All right," Dempsey said. "I'll fix it with these guys, but you owe me."

I reached into my wallet and pulled out one of my business cards, jotted my cell number on the back, and handed it to him. "Call me if you need anything. I mean *anything.*"

I heard the rumble of a diesel engine as the ambulance pulled in. The other two patrol officers were standing outside the cruiser watching and listening as Sarah made a complete jackass of herself. I reached into the back seat of the Mustang, unstrapped the car seat with Gracie still in it, and transferred it to my truck.

The last image I saw as I pulled out of the parking lot was Sarah. She'd stopped trying to kick the windows out just long enough to give me the finger.

CHAPTER SEVENTEEN

As soon as I left the grocery store, I drove home and picked up Caroline. We went back to the grocery store parking lot, and Caroline drove Sarah's car to the house that Sarah had inherited from my mother while I went to the hospital and gave them Sarah's personal information and health insurance card. One of the emergency room nurses came out and told me that Sarah had been sedated and would be admitted overnight. She gave me a phone number in case I wanted to call and check on her later.

After that, Caroline, Gracie, and I went out for pizza. We'd spent a great deal of time with Gracie, so she was comfortable and happy. She fell asleep in my lap a little after nine that evening, and I put her in our bed where she spent the night with Caroline, Chico, and me. Rio slept in his usual spot on the floor at the foot of the bed.

I wanted to get to the hospital early enough the next morning to catch whichever doctor would be caring for Sarah on rounds, so when I arrived at the Johnson City Medical Center hospital, it was still dark. I found Sarah's room, looked in, and saw that she was still asleep. Her chart was sitting on a work station just outside the door, so I picked it up and looked at it. I was particularly interested in the toxicology screen, and I was relieved to see that there was no trace of drugs in her blood. Her blood-alcohol level, however, was another matter. It was .029, more than three times the legal limit, definitely dangerous. I shook my head in disgust, set the chart back down, and walked back into the room. I sat down in the recliner next to the bed and closed my eyes, trying to decide exactly what I was going to say to her when she woke up.

About fifteen minutes later, a middle-aged nurse with a round face and stiff, brown hair flipped on the light. She began removing something from Sarah's wrist.

"Are you her husband?" she said brightly.

"Brother."

"She was so combative in the emergency room that they had to restrain her. We left them on in case she woke up in the middle of the night and decided to leave."

Sarah began to stir. She lifted her head and looked at the nurse, then at me.

"Where am I? Where's Gracie?"

"Gracie's fine. You're in the hospital. We'll talk about it after the doctor comes in."

The nurse took Sarah's vitals, and a couple minutes later a stodgy-looking redhead wearing a white lab coat walked through the door. A pair of reading glasses hung from a chain around her neck.

"Ms. Dillard," she said, "I'm Doctor Fritz. I see from your chart you had a busy night last night. The paramedics' report says you had a child in the car with you. What happened to the child?" Her tone was unfriendly and judgmental.

"My mouth tastes awful," Sarah said. "Do you have any toothpaste or gum or anything?"

"I'm sure the nurse will find you something. What do you remember about last night, Ms. Dillard?"

"Not much."

"I'm not surprised. You had enough alcohol in your bloodstream to float an aircraft carrier. Was this an isolated incident, or do you do this to yourself on a regular basis?"

"That's none of your business."

"Really? You seem to have made it my business. And who is this?" She pointed at me. "The lucky husband?"

"The lucky brother," I said.

"Since your sister doesn't seem to have any manners, I'll talk to you. She's obviously built up some tolerance to alcohol, or she would have been comatose last night. The blackout and the rage are symptoms of alcoholism, especially in a woman her age. She's been hydrated with intravenous fluids and given ibuprofen to combat the swelling in her brain. Since there don't seem to be any other medical problems, I'll discharge her immediately. I suggest you get her into an inpatient rehab program for a minimum of thirty days as quickly as possible. Have a nice day."

Doctor Fritz turned abruptly and walked out the door.

"Bitch," Sarah muttered as soon as the doctor was out of sight.

"We need to talk," I said. I stood and walked across the room to close the door.

"I don't feel like talking."

"Fine, then you can just listen." I stood at the foot of the bed and looked down at her, once again amazed at her remarkable physical appearance. She showed no signs of the abuse she'd heaped on herself the previous night. Her skin was smooth and taut, her eyes clear and bright. She'd folded her arms across her chest and was staring at the wall to her left.

"If I hadn't just happened to stop by the grocery store last night, you'd be in jail right now, and Gracie would probably be with Child Protective Services. You were already hammered and you were buying more beer. You'd driven to the store with Gracie in the car, and you were about to leave the store and drive some more. One of the checkout clerks called the police. I'm not going to go through the whole sad story, Sarah, but the police showed up and you made an absolute fool of yourself."

"Did I embarrass my little brother in front of his cop buddies?" she said sarcastically.

"What's wrong with you?" I snapped. "Didn't you hear what I said? You had *Gracie* in the car. That's a crime, Sarah. Thirty days in jail, minimum, and with your record, the judge will give you a lot more."

"I don't believe you," she said. "If that was true, the cops would be sitting here waiting for me to get out of the hospital so they could take me to jail."

"They're not here because I made a deal. I told them I'd make sure you go into a program and pull yourself together. If you don't go within a week, they get a warrant and arrest you."

The idea had come to me on the spur of the moment, when the doctor mentioned inpatient rehabilitation. Sarah had been through the twelve steps, she'd been to Narcotics Anonymous, but she'd never gone through an inpatient program. It sounded like a good plan to me, so I lied to her, hoping it would be for her own good.

"There's no way I'm going into a nuthouse for a month," Sarah said. "Where are my clothes?"

She threw the blanket back and started looking around the room. She spotted a plastic bag next to the wall beside the bed and picked it up.

"You're either going into a program or I'm calling the cop who wanted to arrest you," I said. "I'll call him right now. You'll be in jail by noon, and you'll stay there for at least six months. I guarantee it."

"No you won't," she said, pulling on her shorts. "You wouldn't do that to Gracie."

"I'd do it *for* Gracie! You're no good to her when you're like this. You're no good to anybody." I pulled my cell phone out of my pocket and wielded it like a weapon. "So what's it gonna be, Sarah? Rehab or jail?"

She sat back down on the bed and looked at me for the first time since she'd awakened. The stare was cold and contemptuous, a look I'd seen many times before.

"Why are you doing this to me?"

"Because I'm tired of cleaning up after you. Every time something bad happens in your life, you fall right back into the same old patterns. I've always felt sorry for you. I've always felt like your pain was somehow my fault because I didn't stop Raymond from raping you when we were kids, but that was almost forty years ago.

When Gracie was born, I thought you'd finally put all that behind you, but now look at you. You're selfish and pathetic, Sarah, and I'm not going to let you dump your baggage on Gracie the same way you've dumped it on everyone who's ever cared about you. You're going into rehab, and you're going to deal with this problem once and for all."

"Wow," she said. "That was quite a speech. I think maybe you missed your calling. You should have been a football coach."

"Shut up and put your clothes on. Let's get out of here."

"I'm not going anywhere with you."

"Yeah, you are. You're going home with me. You're going to stay with us until we find you a good program and you go into the hospital. We'll take care of Gracie while you're gone."

"I'm taking a cab home. I'll be out to pick up my daughter in a little while."

I started punching numbers into my cell phone.

"Enjoy jail," I said, and I walked out the door.

I'd dialed my own number, but I didn't send the call. I kept the phone to my ear as I walked down the hallway. A few seconds later, I heard footsteps behind me. I turned to see Sarah, pulling on her T-shirt and carrying her shoes.

"All right, I'll go," she said as she caught up to me. "But you're paying for it."

CHAPTER EIGHTEEN

When John Lipscomb and Andres Pinzon were eighteen, their lives—and their destinies—changed forever. It all started at a party. Andres was lifting a beer to his lips and looked around the room. Dozens of people were wandering through the house, drinking and laughing. A disc jockey was playing loud music on a large patio out back where dozens more were gyrating on a makeshift dance floor. Andres smiled. Life was good.

At eighteen years old, Andres no longer considered himself a stranger in a strange land. He'd been in America for five years now, and tomorrow he would graduate from prep school. In a few months, he'd be off to college at Harvard University, and from there, on to law school. He'd formed tight bonds with dozens of wealthy students from all over the country, bonds that would no doubt benefit him in the future.

Andres felt something hit him on top of the head, and an empty beer can fell into his lap. He looked around, knowing who it was.

"When are you going to grow up?" Andres said.

"When are you going to stop talking like a spic?"

John Lipscomb plopped himself down on the arm of the chair Andres was sitting in. The two boys, now young men, had become the closest of friends. After the initial fight, Andres found himself taken under the wing of one of the most unusual people he'd ever known. John was a walking paradox, a person who despised those with wealth and power but who also wanted desperately to become tremendously wealthy. He was capable of occasional acts of generosity, but he was more often inclined to ruthlessness. He was impulsive yet methodical, adventurous yet cautious. And he was always, always scheming.

Their fathers, both doctors, had also become close friends, and while the boys were in the eighth grade, it was decided that John and Andres would attend a prestigious private school together. Demeter Prep in Bethesda, Maryland, had an excellent pilot-training program, and since John's father wanted his son to become a licensed pilot like he was, Demeter was chosen. Both of the boys were bright—Lipscomb bordered on genius—and they were expected to make perfect grades. They did, although in different ways. Pinzon was scholarly and worked hard while Lipscomb perfected a long-standing tradition in the prep school world, that of cheating.

Halfway through Demeter, John began to suggest to Andres that they should attend the same college. Harvard was the natural choice since John wanted to study business and finance and Andres wanted to study commercial law. They'd been accepted a year earlier, and now both of them were well on their way to bright futures. They'd even discussed the idea of joining forces when they graduated, the corporate lawyer and the financier, and conquering the business world together.

"Come with me," John said. "I want to show you something."

He led Andres through the kitchen and downstairs, past the throng of dancers, and down a short hallway. John knocked softly on the door, and it quickly opened.

"Come on in, man," said Timothy Holden, a tall, slender party boy from Philadelphia that Andres knew only casually. "You guys have to try this stuff. It's amazing."

Andres entered a bedroom. Holden was pointing to a bathroom just to his left. John led the way.

"This is what I wanted to show you," he said.

Sitting on the vanity was a round mirror about the size of a dinner plate. On top of the mirror were four lines of yellowish-white powder, each about two inches long, a razor blade, and a short straw.

"Go ahead. I already cut it out for you," Holden said from beyond the door.

"Is that what I think it is?" Andres said.

Both young men had tried marijuana during their sophomore year at Demeter, but neither enjoyed the sensation and they hadn't used it again. They'd heard about this new street drug called cocaine, a drug that supposedly caused an intense, euphoric high and had the extra benefit of serving as a potent aphrodisiac, but this was the first time they'd actually seen it.

"Yeah, it's coke," John said. "Want to try it?"

Andres shook his head. "I don't think so."

"C'mon, man, this is the stuff everybody's going so crazy about."

"Nah, not interested," Andres said, and he turned and walked out the door.

Twenty minutes later, Andres was standing on a veranda overlooking a large swimming pool full of frolicking teenagers. The night air was cool against his skin, and in the distance, he could see the lights of Bethesda twinkling like fireflies. He heard the door open behind him and turned to see John stepping onto the veranda.

"So how is it?" Andres said.

"Intense, man, really intense. I see why people like it so much."

"So instead of going to Harvard, you're going to become a dope fiend?"

"No, man, I just wanted to try it. Listen, I've got this idea I've been running around in my head for a couple weeks, ever since I found out that Holden's been selling coke."

"He's selling it? Isn't that illegal or something?"

"I'm sure it is, but that's not the point. The point is that I talked to Holden, and he's too dumb to realize it, but there's a ton of money in it. I mean a ton. We could make a fortune."

"We? Are you talking about you and me?"

John took a long pull from his beer and leaned against the railing.

"You know where they're producing it, don't you? Colombia. Your native land. I'll bet you have relatives in the business."

Andres *did* have relatives in the business, several of them. He'd heard his father rant about them many times. Andres knew that five years ago, when the family moved from Colombia to the United States, at least four of his uncles and several of his cousins were in the marijuana-smuggling business. But now they, like many others, had moved into cocaine. A pound of marijuana would bring perhaps a thousand dollars in Miami, whereas a kilogram of cocaine would bring forty thousand.

"All you have to do is introduce me," John said. "My old man is getting me a used Cessna for graduation. We can fly down there, pick up the stuff, and fly it back. We buy directly from the source, cut out the middle men, and then we distribute to this ready-made market we have right here. Almost all of these people are going to big schools in big cities all over the country. We'll make a mint."

"We'll wind up dead," Andres said. "People in Colombia have been killing each other for years because of the drug trade. If we don't get killed, we'll probably go to jail."

"Stop being such a pussy. We're not going to wind up dead and we're not going to jail. This is the best chance we're ever going to have to make it big right out of the blocks. We make a few trips, get a stake together, and then use it to start up a business when we graduate from college."

"I don't know. It just seems like a line I don't want to cross."

John straightened up and stretched his arms over his head.

"I'm not taking no for an answer, *amigo*," he said. "Just do me a favor. You're good at math. Sit down with a pencil and a piece of paper and do the math.

Or better still, make one phone call to your family in Colombia. Find out how much a kilogram would cost us, then do the math. If you're still not interested, I'll find another way."

John turned and walked back toward the veranda door. He stopped just short and faced his friend.

"We've been together a long time," he said. "We make a good team. If you don't do this with me, you'll regret it for the rest of your life."

CHAPTER NINETEEN

Three days after the near disaster in the grocery store parking lot, we got a break. Jasper T. Yates, the Boone Lake busybody known as Turtle, called me on a Friday morning.

"I got somebody y'all need to talk to," he said.

"About what?"

"Them girls. He seen it."

An hour later, Bates and I were cruising slowly down a rough, muddy driveway that led to a small lot that bordered the lake. A cold front had moved into the area, and a thick, hard-gray sky hung low overhead. It was nearly dark, even though it was mid-afternoon, and silvery raindrops passed through the beams of Bates's headlights in a fine mist.

The man we were going to see was named Zachary Woods. I knew him as Zack. I'd defended him on an aggravated assault charge ten years earlier and remembered him as a tragic figure, tortured by memories of extreme childhood poverty and unspeakable cruelty at the hands of a perverted and violent grandfather. During the time I'd represented Zack, he'd come to trust me, and I hadn't forgotten the stories he'd told me of the beatings, the sexual assaults, and the constant hunger he endured while growing up in an isolated section of Grainger County. He'd spent much of his youth in the woods, left home when he was fourteen, and had eventually made his way to Washington County where he lived alone and had a reputation as the best stone mason in the area.

The incident that resulted in his arrest happened during a dispute over firewood. Zack, who was in his mid-thirties at the time and had never been in trouble with the law, lived in the same tiny trailer where he now lived. He had a neighbor named Tilman who kept stealing his firewood, which was Zack's only source of fuel in the trailer. Zack knew Tilman was the thief because he'd tracked him through the trees back to his home. After the third theft, Zack decided to put a stop to it. He set up a blind near his woodpile and waited in the cold darkness for Tilman to show up. Three nights later, close to midnight, Tilman came creeping through the woods. As soon as Tilman loaded his arms with firewood, Zack stepped out and confronted him. But rather than drop the wood and run, Tilman, who was much bigger than Zack, dropped the wood and pulled a knife. Zack had a knife of his own, and unfortunately for Tilman, he knew how to use it. Tilman wound up in the hospital with over two hundred stitches in his arms, chest, and back, and Zack wound up in jail. Tilman showed up for the preliminary hearing and lied through his teeth, but when we went to trial, he just couldn't explain why he was on Zack's property in the middle of the night, why the firewood was dropped exactly the way Zack explained it, why a knife with his fingerprints all over it was lying on the ground near the firewood, and why his blood-alcohol level was more than twice the legal limit. The jury acquitted Zack in less than an hour.

As soon as we parked, I saw the trailer door open and Zack stepped out. A massive, brindle pit bull was barking fiercely and straining against a logging chain that had been fastened to a steel pole in the ground. Zack didn't have a telephone and didn't know we were coming. People who wanted him to do stone work for them had to leave their name and number on a corkboard at the marina where Turtle worked, and Zack would call them from there. He was medium height and wiry—all muscle, sinew, and bone—wearing a camouflage cap. He had a prominent chin, eyes that always seemed to be moving, and he was wearing work pants, combat boots, and a sleeveless, white T-shirt. He was looking at the car suspiciously.

I got out of the car, and he recognized me immediately. His face seemed to relax as he walked past the dog. I felt something unusual under my feet and looked down. The driveway near the trailer was covered with flattened aluminum cans.

"Poor man's asphalt," Zack said, approaching the car. "I ain't seen you in a coon's age, Joe Dillard. What brings you out here?"

I introduced Bates. "We need to talk to you about something," I said. "It's important."

"That damned gravy eater," he said.

"Beg your pardon?"

"Turtle. I oughta know better than to open my mouth around him. Might as well write it on a billboard."

"Mind if we come in out of the rain?"

"There's barely enough room in there for me. How about I sit in the back of this fine automobile the sheriff's driving? As long as you promise not to arrest me."

"Promise," I said. "Hop in."

As soon as Zack was settled in the backseat, I turned around.

"No point in beating around the bush, Zack. Turtle says you saw something on the lake Saturday night."

"I didn't want no part of it," he said, "but it's been eating at me. In my sleep, you know? I keep seeing it in my sleep. That's probably the reason I told the gravy eater. I knew he wouldn't be able to keep it to himself, and I figured y'all would be coming around sooner or later."

"What did you see?"

"I saw a man dropping a body into the lake off the back of a big houseboat."

"Tell me about it."

"I dropped me a few catfish jugs near the bank in this little cove not far from my place around midnight. There were still some crazies out on the lake, but it had thinned out quite a bit. Right around five in the morning, I headed back out to check on them. The houseboat was anchored in the cove, but I didn't think nothing about it. I picked up the first jug, and then I heard some bumping and banging on the boat, so I looked over, and I saw a man dragging something. Couldn't much tell what it was at first, but then he hoisted it overboard and it splashed into the water. It was a body. A woman's body. She was naked."

"How close were you?"

"Maybe ten feet. I was in my canoe. I just sat there and stared. I didn't really know what to do. The man didn't notice me. He went back inside, and then somebody fired up the engine and the boat pulled out of the cove. I paddled over to where the girl went in, poked around a little with my paddle, and found her a foot or so below the surface. I pulled her up, but she was already dead. There wasn't nothing I could do for her, so I just let her slide back into the water. When I started to paddle out of there, something bumped my boat. It was another girl. She was dead too."

"Why didn't you report it?" Bates asked.

"I don't exactly have fond memories of dealing with the law," he said. "And if I'd reported finding those bodies in the lake at five in the morning, who would've been your first suspect?"

Bates nodded but didn't answer.

"Did you get a good look at the man?" I said.

"It was dark, but the moon was shining off the water and the running lights were on. I could see him."

"Would you recognize him again?"

"I reckon I would."

"What did he look like?"

"Gravy eater like Turtle, only this one eats his gravy by the bucket. Lard ass. Dark-haired."

I looked over at Bates. "Show them to him."

"Let me ask you a question," Bates said. "You ever heard of John Lipscomb?"

"Don't reckon I have."

"Nelson Lipscomb?"

"Not that I can say."

"Andres Pinzon?"

"Nope. Why?"

I'd called Bates as soon as I heard from Turtle, and he'd had his investigators put together three separate photo lineups: one that included John Lipscomb, one that included Nelson Lipscomb, and one that included Andres Pinzon. Bates pulled a manila envelope from the glove compartment and handed the lineup that included Nelson over the seat to Zack.

"Recognize anybody?" Bates said.

Zack pored over the photos for a couple of minutes.

"Never seen any of them," he said, handing the lineup back to Bates.

Bates repeated the process with the lineup that included Andres Pinzon. Nothing. Finally, he passed the lineup that included a photo of John Lipscomb to Zack. It took less than ten seconds.

"That's him," Zack said, tapping the sheet with a thick, calloused finger. "That's the gravy eater I saw."

I felt my heart accelerate. "Let me see, Zack."

His finger was resting on the photo of John Lipscomb. I looked at Bates, who appeared to be more worried than excited.

"Are you absolutely sure?" I asked. "No doubt in your mind?"

"Not a bit. That's him."

Bates handed him a pen. "Circle the photo and put your initials on it," he said.

"Would you be willing to get up on a witness stand and repeat this in front of a jury?" I said.

Zack hesitated. "You think it'll come to that?"

"It might."

He took a long breath. "Well, sir, that's the man I saw. If I have to, I'd swear an oath on it."

A few minutes later, after Zack had gotten out of the car, we were driving back down the muddy driveway. Bates broke the silence.

"What do we do now, Mr. District Attorney?"

The decision I was about to make was by far the most important of my brief career as district attorney general. While it was true that we now had an eyewitness who said he saw John Lipscomb dumping a body into the lake, it had been my experience that eyewitness testimony was often unreliable and easily assailable at trial on cross-examination. And even if Zack had seen Lipscomb dumping a body, we had no idea which body. Was it Lisa, who died of an overdose? If it was, then Lipscomb was guilty only of illegally disposing of a corpse, a misdemeanor, unless we could prove that he'd provided the drugs that killed her. It was certainly easy enough to assume that the act of dumping a body and the act of murder were connected, but we still had no way of proving it.

I asked myself what seemed to be a simple question: what was the *right* thing to do? When I was younger, I tended to view the world in terms of right and wrong, black and white. The distinction between the two came naturally to me then, or at least I thought it did. But as I grew older, witnessed more, experienced more, the line between right and wrong—at least in terms of morality—began to dissolve, and the two concepts began to bleed over into each other until a river of gray separated them, a seemingly unfathomable river with swirling tides that pulled me in different directions.

We could keep investigating, hope to find the boat, hope that another witness would come forward, and hope that Nelson Lipscomb would crack under the pressure of the drug charge and turn on his brother, but I believed there was little chance of any of those things happening. We could attempt to make a deal with Nelson, offer him a walk on the drug and weapons charges in exchange for information regarding the murders. But the truth was that we really didn't have much leverage with Nelson. He'd been arrested in the past, but he'd never been convicted. Given the standing of his family in the community and the very real possibility that powerful people would make influential calls and/or visits to the judge on Nelson's behalf, the worst punishment Nelson was likely to receive was probation. Finally, I could set up a meeting with Pinzon, John Lipscomb's lawyer, and tell him that we had a new witness, someone who actually saw Lipscomb dumping one of the bodies, and attempt to negotiate some kind of deal with him. But that would be like showing your hole cards before the flop in a game of Texas Hold'em. The defense would know what we had much too early, and they could adjust their strategy accordingly.

When I was practicing criminal defense, I'd been highly critical of prosecutors who indicted people prematurely, before their case was locked up, in an attempt to play one defendant against the other. The old "first one to the prosecutor's office gets the deal" strategy almost invariably resulted in a perversion of the truth, and I'd told myself that I would never use it.

I went back over the facts as I knew them: three dead young women; Erlene's identification of the bodies and her story about "Mr. Smith" hiring the girls every year; Erlene's identification of Nelson Lipscomb as Mr. Smith; the bouncer's testimony that he saw the girls get into a white limo; Turtle's testimony that he saw Nelson get out of a white limo with three blond girls at the marina, get onto the *Laura Mae*, and drive away; the limo driver's statement that he dropped Nelson and the girls off at the marina; the caretaker's testimony that he saw John Lipscomb and Andres Pinzon get onto the same boat a short time later and then leave unexpectedly early in the morning; the fact that the boat belonged to John Lipscomb's corporation and was nowhere to be found; and now Zack's testimony that he had seen John Lipscomb dump the body of a young woman over the side of the boat that morning.

There were no other suspects. The only reasonable conclusion I could draw based upon the evidence we'd gathered was that someone aboard the *Laura Mae* that night strangled two of the girls and dumped three bodies, and it seemed the only way to find out what really happened was to take a risk. If I was wrong, I knew I would be humiliated far beyond anything I'd ever experienced and that my legal career would most likely be over. Even if I was right, there were no guarantees we would ever convict anyone for the murders.

I rolled the window down as we crossed the DeVault Bridge near Winged Deer Park. The rain had stopped, but the wind had freshened and the clouds were becoming even darker. It had been five minutes or more since Bates asked me the question. Then I heard a voice inside my head: *"I was banging your wife. Didn't she mention it?"*

"We go to the grand jury," I said without looking at Bates. "We indict all three of them for second-degree murder, and we let the chips fall where they may."

CHAPTER TWENTY

I t didn't take long for the young Andres Pinzon to come around to John Lipscomb's way of thinking. I can't say I was surprised, especially after I heard how much money they made.

A week after Lipscomb made the suggestion that Pinzon "do the math," Pinzon got in contact with his uncle Eduardo back in Envigado, Colombia. The conversation was awkward at first—Eduardo and Andres's father had been estranged for years—but it quickly became cordial. Four days later, Pinzon and Lipscomb flew in the used Cessna 421 Lipscomb had been given as a graduation gift to a three-thousand-acre ranch twenty miles southeast of Miami, a ranch owned by a shell corporation controlled by Eduardo, who flew up from Colombia to meet the boys. He treated them like royalty, intrigued by his nephew's suggestion during the phone call and eager to expand his burgeoning cocaine business in the United States.

Lipscomb and Pinzon took their maiden drug-smuggling voyage to Colombia in June, a month after they graduated from Demeter Prep and nine days after they met with Eduardo Pinzon in Florida. They flew from Elizabethton, Tennessee, to the airstrip on Eduardo's Florida ranch, refueled, and set out for another small airstrip in the jungle near Santo Domingo in the Dominican Republic where they refueled again and rested for a couple hours. From there, they took off for yet another remote airstrip thirty miles southeast of Cartegena in northern Colombia. Eduardo met them again, but this time he had five kilograms of cocaine with him. The price was seventy-five hundred dollars a kilo. Eduardo had agreed to "front" the drugs to his nephew, but just before Andres boarded the plane to return to Tennessee, Eduardo put his arm around him and pulled him off to the side of the runway.

"If you don't come back here and pay me in a month," he said, "you'll get a visit from my *sicarios.* Business is business."

The *sicarios* were paid assassins, a different kind of debt collector. Ten years later, in the early nineties, Pablo Escobar's *sicarios* terrorized Colombia's government. They killed dozens of politicians, judges, lawyers, and police officers. They wiped out entire families, once even planting a bomb aboard an airplane that killed over a hundred innocent passengers. The target in the bombing, a politician who supported policies detrimental to Escobar's drug-smuggling interests, decided at the last minute not to board the plane, but it didn't matter. The *sicarios* shot him to death in his car two days later.

Pinzon knew that if his uncle sent *sicarios* to the United States, both he and Lipscomb would be dead, even if they handed over the money. They'd kill him just for the inconvenience of having to travel—and to send a message to anyone else who might think about paying his drug bill late.

But there were no late payments. Initially, Lipscomb and Pinzon's biggest problems were keeping up with their customers' insatiable demand and what to do with all the cash they were making. They sold their product, uncut, for two thousand dollars an ounce to their prep school friends from Demeter, who would dilute the cocaine with baby laxative by as much as a third and sell it by the gram. Lipscomb and Pinzon had customers at prestigious universities all over the country—Yale, Brown, Harvard, Stanford, Princeton, USC, UCLA, Duke—universities where the students had means. Their only shipping expense was the postage charged by the U.S. Postal Service, and they didn't ship the product until they'd received their money, cash only. After expenses, Lipscomb and Pinzon made just over three hundred thirty thousand dollars on the first five kilos. Three weeks after their first trip to Colombia, they flew back, paid Eduardo Pinzon in cash, and picked up ten more kilos.

When the cash started to pour in, the two of them traveled to Boston at Uncle Eduardo's suggestion and consulted with a lawyer. They presented themselves to the lawyer as two business students who wanted to start their own investment firm. The lawyer was dubious about their prospects for success, but he agreed—for a fee of seven hundred dollars—to assist them in setting up a corporation. As soon as the paperwork was approved by the state of Massachusetts, they set up corporate accounts at five different banks in Boston and began making large cash deposits. By the time the summer was over, Equicorp had over a million and a half dollars in cash.

There were a couple things that impressed me as I learned of Lipscomb and Pinzon's early ventures. They showed remarkable maturity, discipline, and ingenuity for nineteen-year-old boys. They didn't run out and buy fancy cars. They didn't hang out in bars. They didn't host big parties and chase women. Pinzon didn't use cocaine at all, and Lipscomb used it only occasionally, at least early in the venture. They kept to themselves and they kept their mouths shut.

The only money they spent was for business purposes. They rented stash houses in quiet neighborhoods where they stored, separated, and packaged their product, and they never used the house more than once. If a banker happened to question where all the cash was coming from, they made it worth his while to keep quiet. Lipscomb used pay phones near the apartment to conduct all their business. But probably the most impressive thing they did was resist the urge and the pressure to expand their operation. They kept it small and manageable, and it paid off in spades.

Lipscomb and Pinzon made another run to Colombia during the Thanksgiving break that first year. By then, their customers were literally begging them for more product, so they bought fifteen kilos. All of it was gone in less than two weeks. They went back the week before Christmas and picked up fifteen more. On January fifth, John Lipscomb deposited the cash that made each of the unlikely pair of nineteen-year-olds from Tennessee millionaires. He arrived back at their apartment with two bottles of Dom Pérignon and three and a half grams of pure Colombian cocaine that he'd been saving for the occasion.

"Let's party," Lipscomb said to Pinzon when he walked through the door, holding up the bottles in one hand and dangling the baggie of coke in the other.

"You know I don't use that stuff," Pinzon said, "and I thought we agreed that you'd stay out of it too."

"Ah, c'mon, *amigo*. We deserve this. We've been busting our butts. We've made over two million bucks. It's all good. Why don't you loosen up a little?"

"Because loosening up could get us caught."

"Look. I know this girl named Mallory. She's cool. She loves to party, and she won't say a word. I'll call her up, ask her over, and we'll take turns getting laid. How 'bout it, buddy?"

"No thanks."

"Okay, suit yourself," Lipscomb said. He put the bottles on the counter and picked up the phone. "But you seriously need to get laid, dude. I'm beginning to wonder if you're going gay on me."

Mallory arrived an hour later. Lipscomb introduced her as Mallory Vines. She was pretty, blonde-haired with a creamy complexion and huge breasts, just the kind of girl that attracted Lipscomb. Pinzon said hello and then disappeared into his bedroom where he spent the remainder of the evening listening to music and reading Pablo Coelho's *The Alchemist*. He turned off the music and light at eleven and heard the sound of Lipscomb's headboard banging against the other side of the wall.

At two thirty, Pinzon was awakened by a frantic Lipscomb.

"Get up," Lipscomb said. "I need your help."

Pinzon could tell by looking at Lipscomb that he'd been using. His eyes were wide, his pupils dilated, and beads of sweat had formed across his flushed forehead.

"I told you I'm not interested," Pinzon snapped.

Lipscomb grabbed him by the arm.

"Get up, man! I think she's dead."

"Dead? You're joking, right?"

"C'mon!"

Lipscomb walked out, and Pinzon got up and followed. Mallory was lying naked on her back on Lipscomb's bed, her blue eyes staring at the ceiling. Pinzon felt her wrist for a pulse, then her neck. He put the back of his hand near her lips to see if he could feel any sign of breathing. There was nothing.

"What did you do to her?"

"She did a lot of coke, man. She started talking crazy. Then she started jerking and spazzing and then her eyes rolled back in her head and she just went quiet. I tried mouth-to-mouth and CPR, but it didn't do any good."

"Did you call 9-1-1?"

"Are you crazy?"

"We can't just leave her here like this, John. We have to call someone."

Lipscomb approached to within a few inches of Pinzon's face. There was anger and desperation in his eyes. His upper lip was drawn back tightly like a snarling dog. He poked Pinzon in the chest with his finger.

"We're not calling anybody," he said. "If we call an ambulance, they'll bring the police with them. Even if I flush the coke down the toilet, they'll do tests on her and they'll find out what killed her. Then they'll start nosing around in our lives. Do you want that, huh? Do you want them nosing around in our lives?"

Pinzon's eyes dropped to the floor.

"What are we going to do with her?"

"Get dressed," Lipscomb said. "I know what to do."

CHAPTER TWENTY-ONE

The following Monday, a little after eleven, I was looking over the subpoenas for the grand jury witnesses when I sensed someone walking though the door. I looked up, and my heart lightened. It was my daughter, Lilly, auburn-haired like her mother, green-eyed like Sarah and me. She was wearing an orange University of Tennessee T-shirt covered by an open, black jacket and a pair of jeans. She was trim, athletic, ridiculously young and vibrant, and smiling the radiant smile that always turned me into a ball of pliable putty.

"Hi Daddy," she said brightly.

"Lilly! What are you doing here?" I stood and bashed my thigh against the corner of the desk as I hurried around to embrace her. Pain shot through my leg, but I ignored it and limped the last couple of steps.

"I came to take you to lunch," she said.

"Why aren't you in school? Have I missed something?"

She hugged me tightly around the neck and kissed me on the cheek. She'd done it thousands of times, but the touch of her lips against my skin and the warmth of the embrace always warmed me.

I cupped her face in my hands. "Has anyone told you lately what a drop-dead gorgeous young lady you are?"

"I don't think I've heard 'drop-dead gorgeous' lately."

"That's a crime. Give me the name of every boy you've seen in the past month, and I'll put them all in jail. So what are you doing here? This is your third year in college, and it's the first time you've ever showed up unannounced."

"I've been missing you. And there's something I need to talk to you about. Can you get away for an hour or so?"

"Absolutely. Where do you want to go?"

"Someplace private."

I ordered takeout from The Firehouse in Johnson City, and we drove to Rotary Park off Oakland Avenue. Something was bothering her because she was quiet and seemed distracted in the car. Lilly was rarely distracted, and she was never quiet. I'd been on hour-long walks with her in the past during which the only syllables I uttered were, "uh-huh." When we got to the park, we walked through the woods to one of the small pavilions and sat down at a picnic table. The day was overcast and a bit chilly, and the canopy of oak leaves rustled in the breeze above our heads.

"Is this private enough?" I asked, opening a Styrofoam container of salad and sliding it across to her. She smiled halfheartedly and started picking at the salad with a plastic fork.

"So what's on your mind, Lil? Is everything okay?"

"I guess it depends on your definition of okay."

"Spit it out. You know you can talk to me about anything."

"I'm afraid I've let you down."

Her bottom lip began to quiver slightly, and her eyes became translucent with tears. I couldn't imagine what she'd done, or what she thought she'd done, that would upset her so. Lilly had been entirely too easy to raise, a child that was as close to perfect as I could have hoped for. She was a tremendous student, she worked hard at dance and theater, and she loved to read. She'd never been moody or rebellious; she didn't drink, smoke, or use drugs; and she'd managed to stay away from boys until after her senior year in high school. She'd started dating a young man named Randy Lowe just before she went off to the University of Tennessee, and they were still together. She was almost a prude in some respects, so much so that one evening when she was fifteen years old, I offered her twenty dollars just to say "shit." She blurted out the syllable and stuck out her hand. The word sounded so strange, so out of character coming from her lips that it was hilarious, and I laughed so hard that my stomach cramped. I paid up though, and it was the only time I'd ever heard her curse.

I reached across the table for her hand as tears began to run down both of her cheeks.

"What is it, Lil? Tell me."

She looked down at the salad, took a deep breath, and let it out slowly. Her eyes rose up to meet mine.

"I'm pregnant," she said softly.

The words were so unexpected, so utterly shocking, that I stopped breathing for a second. I released her hand and straightened up, momentarily unable to think, to feel, or to understand. The phrase echoed in my subconsciousness like I was standing at the precipice of a deep canyon listening to an echo, but instead of fading, it grew louder.

"Excuse me," I said, and I stood and walked a few steps away from the table, trying to gather my thoughts. Pregnant? Lilly? Impossible. Caroline and I had had the pregnancy conversation with both Jack and Lilly dozens of times. Don't get pregnant. Don't get someone pregnant. If you're going to have sex, use some kind of contraception. You're not ready for a child. Get your education, find a career, get married, then have a baby if you want one. Set the parameters for the child's life; don't let a child set the parameters for yours. I stopped ten feet from the table, turned, and asked the dumbest question I possibly could have asked.

"How? How did this happen?"

"I made a mistake."

"A mistake? I don't think I'd call this a mistake, Lilly. This is more along the lines of monumental blunder. What are you going to do now? What are you going to do with a baby?"

"I'll love it, Daddy. The same way you love me."

I walked back over to the table and stood over her. Part of me wanted to hug her and part of me wanted to smack her.

"It's a little more complicated than that," I said. "Have you thought this through at all? What about school? What about dance? And theater? What about your career? How are you going to feed this baby and clothe it and shelter it? Dammit, Lilly! How could you be so stupid? What about your future?"

"Stop yelling at me!"

"I'm not yelling!"

"Yes you are!"

"No I'm not!"

"I'll have the baby and raise it. We'll work it out somehow."

"You don't have the first clue about how to raise a child. It's not like they come with instructions."

"You and Mom will help me."

"Your mom and I have lives of our own. We have plans of our own, and right now our plans don't include raising another child."

"Fine, then I'll raise it myself."

She got up from the table and started walking down the path toward the parking lot. I stared at her for a minute, still incredulous.

"Where are you going?"

"I'm going back to school."

"How are you going to get back to your car? Walk?"

She kept going.

"Lilly! I'm sorry, all right? Come back here and let's talk."

She stopped and turned.

"No more yelling," she said.

"Okay."

"If you yell again, I'm leaving."

"I promise."

She trudged back up to the table and sat down heavily. She refused to look at me, and I knew she was angry. I suppose she expected a sympathetic response from me, which is exactly what she should have gotten, but the utter shock of her revelation had rendered me temporarily unable to feel compassion.

"You have a choice, you know," I said, and I immediately regretted it.

"Is *that* what you want me to do?" Her eyes blazed with fury, and I found myself face-to-face with no less formidable a force than maternal instinct. "You want me to have an abortion? I should have known. Always the lawyer. Your precious law says I can kill it in the first trimester, so that's what you want. You'd rather me kill my own child than cause you any inconvenience."

She was standing again, glaring at me. My little girl had grown into a woman somewhere along the line, and I'd missed it. She was protecting her unborn child like a mother grizzly, and she regarded me as a threat rather than a father. I backed away a few steps and shoved my hands in my pockets, feeling a chill and a sense of shame.

"I apologize for even suggesting it," I said. "I don't want you to have an abortion. You'd never forgive yourself. I'd never forgive myself. I just don't understand how you could have done this."

She took a deep breath and let it out slowly.

"It was the third anniversary of our first date," she said. "I cooked dinner at my apartment. Spaghetti. We ate by candlelight. We had a glass of wine with dinner. It was the first time I ever drank alcohol. Then we had another. Before we knew it, the bottle was gone and we were ... we were .... I'm sorry. I really am. I know how much this disappoints you, but you have to forgive me. I need you. I need you more than ever."

"Have you told your mother?"

"Not yet. I wanted to tell you first. I figured if you killed me, it would save me the trouble of having to tell Mom too."

"Come here."

I opened my arms and she walked to me. I wrapped her up and kissed her on top of the head as she began to sob.

"It's all right, baby," I said. "We'll figure it out. We always have."

As Lilly cried, I squeezed her tighter. A vision entered my mind, and a smile gradually spread over my face. I pictured a tree covered in brightly colored lights on Christmas Eve. Beside the tree stood a wide-eyed toddler, eagerly tearing the paper away from a gift-wrapped package.

"You know something?" I said. "I'm too young to be a grandfather, and you're too young to be a mother. But I suppose there are worse things. Don't worry, baby. Like your mother says, everything will be all right."

CHAPTER TWENTY-TWO

John Lipscomb graduated from fledgling drug dealer to illegally disposing of a body to murderer in three years. His best friend and co-conspirator, Andres Pinzon, went along for the ride. Pinzon could have walked away early—maybe. But the allure of easy money and a nagging sense of fear kept him in.

Then, one day when he was twenty-one years old, Pinzon opened the passenger side door and slid into John Lipscomb's new Mercedes. It was precisely the type of vehicle they'd agreed to stay away from. It was flashy and expensive, the kind of car that attracted attention.

"I hate this car," Pinzon said as Lipscomb climbed in behind the steering wheel. "It screams, 'Look at me! I'm rich!'"

"You're probably the most uptight person I've ever known," Lipscomb said. "When are you going to learn to relax a little?"

"We've been under the radar so far. I'd like to stay there."

"Your friend is very wise," a heavily-accented voice said from the backseat. Pinzon spun around, frightened.

"Who are you?" Pinzon asked.

"I'm surprised you don't recognize him," Lipscomb said. "He's your second cousin on your father's side."

The man in the back nodded. He was young, only a few years older than Lipscomb and Pinzon. He was wearing a shiny, gray sport coat over a baby-blue button-down with an open collar. His black hair, which was the same color as his lifeless eyes, was combed straight back from his forehead. He looked like a South American wise guy. He had a deep, pink scar that ran from the corner of his mouth to his left temple in the shape of a scythe blade.

"What's he doing here?" Pinzon said.

"He's going to take care of something for me."

"Does he have a name?"

"Some people call him Santiago. Others call him *El Maligno*. Sit back and enjoy the ride."

El Maligno meant "the evil one." Pinzon had heard of him. The man in the backseat was a *sicario*.

"Where are we going?"

"To the airport."

Pinzon looked out the window as Lipscomb drove through the streets of the Back Bay toward Logan International Airport. The Charles River gleamed bright green in the sunlight, but as they passed through the long shadows cast by the buildings on Beacon Hill, Pinzon began to feel a strong sense of uneasiness.

"Why are we going to the airport?" he asked Lipscomb.

"To pick up a friend."

"Which friend?"

"A new friend. You've never met him."

"How can he be a friend if I've never met him?"

"He's a friend of mine. You can call him a business associate if you want."

The cryptic nature of Lipscomb's answers, coupled with the stranger in the backseat, deepened Pinzon's anxiety. Lipscomb's behavior had become increasingly erratic over the past three years. He'd gained more than forty pounds since their freshman year at Harvard, and he spent more time in clubs than in the classroom, having developed a seemingly insatiable appetite for female companionship, especially blonde-headed females.

After the Mallory Vines incident, Pinzon had been unable to sleep in their apartment and had moved into a studio flat on Newbury Street. The image of Mallory's lifeless face lying on Lipscomb's bed haunted Pinzon nearly as much as the cavalier manner in which Lipscomb had disposed of her body. Lipscomb had dressed her, and the two of them had draped her arms around their shoulders and taken her down to Lipscomb's car as though she were passed out from drinking. Pinzon's involvement ended there, but Lipscomb later told him that he'd taken Mallory to the stash house they were renting at the time. He enlisted some help, he said, to cut up her body and load it into a cooler, which was subsequently loaded onto Lipscomb's plane. Mallory's body was dropped—in pieces—out the windows of the plane into the Atlantic Ocean a hundred miles off the coast of Maine. They'd never heard another word about Mallory Vines. Pinzon wondered if the "help" Lipscomb had enlisted was sitting in the backseat now.

"That's got to be him," Lipscomb said as he pulled up to the curb outside the United Airlines terminal at Logan. A tall, slim young man wearing a fringed, buckskin jacket, blue jeans, and cowboy boots was leaning against the building smoking a cigarette. Lipscomb threw the Mercedes into park and got out. Pinzon watched as Lipscomb approached the cowboy. They talked for a minute, and the cowboy followed Lipscomb back to the car. He climbed in behind Pinzon.

"This is my man, Tex," Lipscomb said as he pulled out into traffic. "He flew all the way up here from Dallas just to meet us and take care of a little business. Tex, this is my friend and partner Andres, and the gentleman sitting next to you there is my buddy Santiago."

Pinzon turned and nodded at Tex, wondering what Lipscomb was up to. The only time Lipscomb did business face-to-face was in Colombia. Everything else was done strictly by phone and by mail. It had been that way for three years. They'd stashed almost twenty million dollars without drawing any attention to themselves, and with the exception of Mallory Vines, everything had gone smoothly. Pinzon glanced at Tex, who had curly, dark brown hair, a rugged-looking face with deep dimples in his cheeks, and grayish eyes that were darting around nervously. Pinzon wondered whether he held the key to some huge, untapped market in Texas that Lipscomb was interested in.

They drove in silence for forty minutes north along I-95 toward the Rhode Island state line. Lipscomb exited the interstate and turned east toward the ocean. A couple minutes later, he turned left onto a gravel road.

"This is my newest place," he said over his shoulder. "You're gonna love it."

A half mile down the gravel road, Lipscomb pulled up to a locked metal gate.

"Here," he said to Pinzon, holding out a key. "Lock it back up after I drive through."

Pinzon unlocked the padlock and removed the thick chain that secured the gate. As soon as Lipscomb pulled the Mercedes in, Pinzon replaced the chain and the lock and got back into the car.

"Can't be too careful," Lipscomb said, winking at Tex.

They drove a couple hundred yards along a dirt driveway through a stand of tall pines. In a clearing beyond the pines was an old, white farmhouse flanked by a dilapidated barn. Lipscomb pulled the Mercedes around to the back, got out, and said, "Come on, we can talk inside."

Pinzon opened his door and climbed out, but Tex, who had been silent since they left the city, didn't move.

"I think I'll just wait out here," Tex said.

"Look, you said you need more product so you can catch up," Lipscomb said. "This is where I'm keeping it. Come on inside. It'll just take a minute."

"You can just bring it out to me."

"Santiago, would you please convince Tex that it'd be in his best interest to come inside?" Lipscomb said.

Pinzon watched as *El Maligno*, who had stayed in the backseat next to Tex, reached beneath his left arm and pulled out a long-barreled revolver.

"Get out of the car," he demanded, and Tex opened the door.

Lipscomb led the way as the four of them walked in through the back of the house. The paint on the outside was cracked and peeling and most of the windows were broken out.

"It's a bit of a fixer-upper," Lipscomb said as he led the way through a run-down kitchen and into what was probably once a dining room. Pinzon could feel his knees shaking as he listened to the breeze whistle through the windows. He looked around and noticed that the floor of the room they were now standing in had been covered with a thick sheet of plastic. One rickety chair sat in the center.

"Have a seat," Lipscomb said to Tex.

"What are you doing, John?" Pinzon said.

"I'm about to teach this gentleman some manners."

"I don't want any part of it," Pinzon said. He turned and took a step back.

"Stop right there!" Lipscomb roared.

Pinzon froze. He'd never before heard that tone of voice from Lipscomb. He turned to face his friend.

"You know something, *amigo*?" Lipscomb said. "I'm beginning to question your commitment. The only thing you do with the business these days is ride down to Colombia with me. You don't sort, you don't package, you don't ship, you don't deal with the customers, you don't handle the money. And now you want to walk out on me in the middle of a meeting. If it wasn't for your connection with Eduardo, I wouldn't need you at all anymore."

"You're crazy—do you know that?" Pinzon said. "What is it, the money? Do you think you have power now? Do you think you can just do whatever you want with no consequences? We got into this business to make money, not to hurt people."

"Who said anything about hurting anyone?" Lipscomb said. "We're just going to have a discussion."

By this time, Tex was sitting in the chair with *El Maligno* standing a few feet away, the gun pointed at Tex's forehead. Pinzon looked down at Tex and felt pity. A dark spot had formed on Tex's jeans between his legs, and he'd started to cry.

As Lipscomb's girth had widened, he'd taken to wearing elastic suspenders. He hooked his thumbs in the front of the suspenders just above his waist and began to circle Tex slowly.

"Okay, Tex ol' buddy," he said, "how much money did you bring me today?"

Tex babbled something incomprehensible. Lipscomb kept circling.

"You remember Reid Kilgore?" Lipscomb said to Pinzon. "He went to SMU down in Dallas. He met Tex here at a party. Reid said Tex was good people but he'd fallen on some hard times. Tex told him his mother and father had both been killed in a car accident, but that he'd be flush as soon as the estate went through probate. He told Reid he could move ten ounces, easy. So for the first time in my career, I agreed to front product to somebody. I sent him ten ounces of pure powder. That was almost four months ago. He was supposed to send me my money within thirty days. Two months later, I called this lying piece of garbage. He said he'd get the money right to me. Didn't you, Tex? Another month went by, and I realized we had a serious problem. So I called Tex back and invited him to fly up here at my expense so we could work something out. I told him I'd be willing to front him some more product until he could get back on his feet. He was kind enough to agree to come up. In the meantime, I got a hold of Eduardo who got a hold of Santiago here. I paid Eduardo to fly Santiago up here on his private jet. Which means I've spent almost twenty thousand dollars to ask Tex this question. Where's my money?"

"I don't … I thought … I don't have it with me," Tex blubbered. "Please, give me another chance. I'll get the money."

"Wrong answer," Lipscomb said. "Santiago, shoot him in the kneecap for me so he doesn't try to get away."

The gun roared and Tex screamed. He dropped to the floor and rolled onto his side, clutching the wounded knee.

"John! What are you doing?" Pinzon yelled. He rushed over to Tex's side and knelt beside him. Blood was gushing through his fingertips.

"Get away from him," Lipscomb said ominously.

"I'm not going to let you kill him."

"You don't have a choice," Lipscomb said. "The only choice you have is whether you want to go with him."

"Eduardo would gut you," Pinzon said, looking uneasily at Santiago.

"Actually, Eduardo thinks you might be weak," Lipscomb said. "He and I have become close. He realizes who's making this business work. I've done a few things on the West Coast you don't even know about. Eduardo's making more money than he ever thought possible. I'll admit it would be problematic if you were to come up missing, but it's something I'm willing to deal with if you insist on acting like you're not a part of this. So what's it gonna be? Are you with me or against me?"

Pinzon stood and started to move away, but Tex grabbed his ankle.

"No," Tex said pitifully. "Don't leave me."

Pinzon jerked his foot away.

"I'm not going to be a part of murder," he said to Lipscomb. "I'm going outside."

He took a few steps, expecting to hear the gunshot any second.

"You're a part of it," Lipscomb said. "You're a part of *all* of it."

CHAPTER TWENTY-THREE

T wo nights after Lilly's unexpected visit, Caroline and I were bustling around the kitchen preparing dinner. We were expecting guests. They weren't supposed to arrive until eight, but I hadn't been able to get away from work until after six and was running behind. The grand jury had been notified of a special session and would meet the following Monday to consider the case against the Lipscomb brothers and Andres Pinzon. Bates and his people had served subpoenas on all the witnesses, and I believed we were as ready as we were ever going to be.

Sarah was scheduled to go into a rehab program called Daybreak in Asheville, North Carolina, the following morning. Caroline, with Sarah sitting next to her, had researched several places thoroughly on the Internet. They'd settled on Daybreak because of its excellent reputation and because it was close enough to allow us to bring Gracie over for visits on the weekends. Caroline and Sarah had made dozens of phone calls, checking out the facility, the doctors, and the program. I was encouraged that Sarah seemed so enthusiastic, that she recognized how important this phase of her life would be for both her and her child. She'd seemed to settle in nicely at the house with Caroline and me over the past several days and was attentive to Gracie. I found myself hoping that perhaps, finally, we'd hit on something that might work for her. If it didn't, I'd be spending thirty grand for nothing.

I was standing over the stove, stirring a reduction for chicken marsala, when Sarah walked in.

"Mind if I go by the house and pick up a few things?" she said. "I need to button the place up, too, since nobody's going to be there for a month."

I glanced over at Caroline, who was checking on a loaf of French bread in the oven.

"Can it wait until after dinner? One of us will give you a ride."

"I think it's probably best if I'm not here for dinner, and you don't need to give me a ride. I'm perfectly capable of driving over there and driving back."

Sarah's car was still parked in the driveway at her house, right where we'd left it after the incident at the grocery store. She hadn't driven since I brought her home from the hospital, and we'd made sure that she spent very little time alone.

"I don't know if that's such a good idea," I said.

"I promise I'll be good, big brother," she said. "I'll leave Gracie here as a hostage so you know I won't stray. It'll only take a while. I'll be back before ten."

I hesitated. Considering her track record, I wasn't inclined to give her the opportunity to do something stupid, especially since we'd be driving her to Asheville in the morning. The temptation to get high one last time might prove to be too much for her.

"C'mon, Joe, I made *one* mistake," she said.

"You've made lots of mistakes."

"I'm doing everything you asked. Except for that one night, I haven't had a drop to drink in almost two years. I'm going to the nuthouse tomorrow for a month, and in case you've forgotten, I'm a grown woman. Stop treating me like a teenager. If I'd wanted to, I could have snuck out any time during the past week. I know you leave your keys in the truck."

There wasn't much more I could say. If she'd wanted to go on a binge, she could have done it, and I knew if she was going to be successful with the treatment, she'd ultimately have to do it on her own.

"You'll go straight there and come straight back?"

"Yes, master. Straight there and straight back."

"Take the truck."

Ten minutes after Sarah left, Lilly and her boyfriend arrived. His name was Randy Lowe, and as much as I wanted to choke him for getting her pregnant, I liked him immensely. He was a bright, handsome kid, twenty-one years old, with a solid build, sandy-brown hair, and optimistic, energetic blue eyes. He was taking pre-med courses at the University of Tennessee and wanted to become a pediatrician. Caroline and I greeted them warmly, and a few minutes later, we sat down at the table to eat. Caroline was to my left, Lilly to my right, and Randy sat directly across from me. Gracie was in a high chair between Caroline and me, babbling happily.

"I assume you two have given this as much thought as your mother and I," I said after everyone was settled and the food had been passed around the table.

"We know exactly what we're going to do," Lilly announced confidently.

"Really? Enlighten me."

"We're going to finish the semester at UT and get married on December seventh," she said. "Then we're going to transfer up here to ETSU and move in with you guys. The baby isn't due until April, so I think I'll be able to finish out the spring semester. I'll take the summer off and finish up next year. Randy can go to med school at Quillen after he graduates, and in the meantime, you and mom and Randy's parents can help us take care of the baby."

I looked at Caroline, who was doing all she could to suppress a smile, and then at Randy. He was staring at his chicken. His arms were folded across his chest and his face had gone pale.

"Are you all right, Randy?" I asked.

He nodded.

"Are you sure? You look like you're going to throw up."

"I'm okay."

"Have you told your parents about this little situation?"

Randy's parents had divorced when he was young, but he'd come through it remarkably unscathed and remained close to both of them.

"Yes, sir."

"What do they think?"

"They probably think about the same thing you think, sir."

"So they think you're an idiot? A moron? An immature dipstick who allowed himself to think with his one-eyed monster instead of his brain?"

"Daddy!" Lilly said. "Stop it."

"You know something, Randy? I'm sitting here having a meal with you right now, but what I'd really like to be doing is cutting your pecker off with a dull knife."

"I said stop it!" Lilly yelled.

"It's all right," Randy said. "I deserve this."

I wasn't angry, but I couldn't resist taking a few potshots at him.

"Let me ask you something," I said. "Have you ever heard of this little invention called a condom? I guess maybe it's a bit of a primitive device by modern standards, but it works. It comes in this little foil package. All you have to do is take it out of the package and slide it over your joystick before you hop in the sack, and *voila!* No baby. They sell them in pharmacies and convenience store bathrooms all over the country."

"I didn't mean to, sir," he mumbled.

"You didn't mean to what? You didn't mean to have sex with my daughter or you didn't mean to get her pregnant?"

"Get her pregnant."

"So you meant to have sex with her."

"Well ... I ...."

"You're a pre-med major, right? You know that having sex sometimes leads to reproduction? In fact, if I'm not mistaken, I believe that having sex is the primary means of reproduction for the human species, isn't it?"

His face was going from pale to pink. He sat there motionless, looking forlorn and deflated.

"So if you meant to have sex with her and you understand that having sex leads to reproduction, yet you did nothing to prevent it, how can you sit here and tell me that you didn't mean to get her pregnant?"

"I was drunk."

"Ah, yes, of course. The universal excuse. I'm sorry, Your Honor, I didn't mean to cut her head off with an axe. I was drunk. Have mercy, Judge, I didn't mean to run over that child. I was drunk. I'm sorry, Mr. Dillard. I didn't mean to knock up your daughter. I was drunk. And now, since you decided to get drunk, and since you didn't mean to get Lilly pregnant but you did, my wife and I get the opportunity to help you and my daughter raise a brand spankin' new child. Thank you, Randy. From the bottom of my heart, thank you."

I shoved a fork full of chicken into my mouth and smiled.

"Wow," I said. "This is good stuff. Dig in."

CHAPTER TWENTY-FOUR

We sat at the table for more than an hour following my rant. Caroline had waited several minutes before she spoke, but she finally managed to ease the tension, and we ended up talking seriously about what we needed to do to prepare for the birth. Gracie became fussy about thirty minutes into the conversation, so Caroline took a brief break and put her to bed. Randy even ate a couple bites of his supper, and eventually his face returned to its natural color.

I didn't really mind that Randy and Lilly would be living with us. The house had seemed too empty and too quiet since the kids went off to college. I didn't mind the fact that they were getting married either because, from everything I'd observed over the past three years, they genuinely loved each other. And the more I'd thought about it, the more the idea of having a grandchild appealed to me.

I glanced at the clock around 9:45 and suddenly realized that I'd forgotten about Sarah. I got up from the table, picked my cell up off the counter, and punched in her number. She didn't answer. I hit redial. Same result.

"She's not answering," I said to Caroline, who had started to clear the table.

"She said she'd be back by ten. Give her the benefit of the doubt."

"Why won't she answer her phone?"

"Maybe she turned it off or left it in the car. Maybe the battery's dead. Relax. She'll be here soon."

I put the phone down and helped Caroline, Lilly, and Randy clear the table, load the dishwasher, and clean up the kitchen. By the time we were finished, it was a little after ten. I dialed Sarah's number again. No answer.

"I guess I'd better go over there and see what's going on," I said.

Lilly and Randy were driving back to Knoxville, so I kissed Lilly goodbye and punched Randy in the shoulder. Caroline stayed home with Gracie, and I drove her car through Johnson City to the house on Barton Street where I was raised. Sarah's Mustang was in the driveway, along with my truck. I walked up to the front door and opened it, fully expecting to find her sitting at the kitchen table or in the den, drunk and belligerent, but as soon as I stepped inside, I knew something was wrong. The house was filled with the powerful odor of gasoline.

"Sarah?"

I walked down the hallway off the kitchen toward the bathroom and bedrooms, the smell getting stronger with each step.

"Sarah!"

I wondered whether she might have gone over the edge, whether she had decided to kill herself rather than go through rehab and burn Ma's house down in the process. The bathroom door was closed, but there was light shining beneath it. I opened the door and looked inside, but there was no sign of her. I heard a moan. It was coming from Ma's old bedroom, just down the hall. I walked quickly to the room and flipped on the light.

Sarah was lying faceup on the bed, wearing only a bra and panties. Her eyes and her mouth had been covered in silver duct tape, and her arms and legs were both spread. Her wrists and ankles had been fastened to the bedposts with barbed wire. The bedding beneath her was soaked in gasoline.

I hurried to the side of the bed. "It's me," I said. "It's Joe." I reached down and removed the tape from her mouth as gently as I could.

"Get it off my eyes," she said. "Get it off my eyes."

She yelped as I pulled the sticky tape from her eyelids.

"What happened?" I said. "Who did this?"

"Get me out of here."

I went to work on the barbed wire next. It had been cut into lengths of about eighteen inches and wrapped like bread ties around her wrists and ankles. I got the wire off her right wrist and right ankle first. She had a few puncture wounds, but they didn't look too serious. As I moved around the bed to free her left wrist and ankle, I saw a gas can sitting on the floor. There was a cigarette lighter on top of it.

"Hurry up," she said.

I freed her and took my phone out. I was punching in 9-1-1 when she grabbed my wrist.

"Don't," she said. "Let's just go."

"You need to go to the hospital," I said, "and I need to call the police."

"Please, not now. Hand me a blanket from the closet. You can call the police after you get me out of here."

She stood while I got her a blanket. I wrapped it around her and started leading her to the front door.

"Who was it?" I said.

"I don't know. Two of them, I think."

"They were waiting for you when you got here?"

"No. They must have followed me. They came in just a few seconds after I got here. It happened so fast. One second I was walking down the hall and the next I was on my back in the bedroom with tape over my mouth and eyes. They cut my clothes off. The knife was so cold, Joe."

"Did they … did they—"

"They didn't rape me. They didn't say a word until after they poured gas all over me. I thought they were going to burn me alive. Then one of them—he had a Spanish accent—put his lips next to my ear and said, 'Tell your brother to back off. Next time we won't be so gentle.'"

CHAPTER TWENTY-FIVE

S arah's physical wounds required only first aid. The psychological damage was impossible to assess.

Tell your brother to back off.

The message had to have come from Lipscomb or Pinzon or both. The more I thought about it, the more I seethed. The murder case was getting out of control. At first, the suspects had done what normal suspects do— they'd gotten rid of as much evidence as possible and run off to Nashville. But then, unlike normal suspects, they started applying heavy political pressure. Since that hadn't worked, it appeared they were willing to resort to terrorism.

After I got Sarah home and settled in, I called the police and went back to her house. I also called Bates and filled him in, but the attack had occurred inside Johnson City, so the city police would handle the investigation. The crime-scene unit didn't find anything, which didn't surprise me. When they were finished and everyone had left, I locked the place up and drove back home. It was four in the morning.

The next morning, we decided against taking Sarah to Asheville to rehab. After what she'd been through, we decided that being around family would be best for her. She said she wanted to stay with us for a while, and that was fine with me.

On Monday morning, I was back in the office early. The grand jury was scheduled to meet at nine. Proceedings conducted by grand juries, at both the federal and state level, are supposed to be secret. Grand jurors, clerks, police officers, judges, and prosecutors are forbidden by law from disclosing anything that occurs while the grand jury is meeting. Each county in Tennessee has its own grand jury—twelve people, plus a foreman, randomly selected by drawing names of registered voters from a box. The grand jury's purpose is to issue indictments, official pieces of paper that formally charge a person with a criminal offense. They serve for one year—the foreman serves two years in Tennessee—and they meet at the beginning of each term of criminal court. They can also be called into session under special circumstances, and that's what I'd done.

Typically, only the police officer who is handling the case appears before the grand jury. He or she lays out the case, and the grand jurors have the opportunity to ask questions. If the grand jurors wish, the district attorney can provide them with legal advice or even question the witness. The officer then leaves, and the grand jury votes on whether to return an indictment.

In this case, however, with so much at stake, I decided to call all our witnesses in. The father of the boy who originally spotted Lisa testified, as did the other two people who reported finding the other two girls. Hobie Stanton, the medical examiner, Erlene Barlowe and her bouncer, Turtle Yates, Hector Mejia, Zack Woods, the limo driver, and the fisherman who saw the *Laura Mae* being removed from the lake all testified. Bates brought his laptop and showed the grand jurors the phone calls Nelson Lipscomb made from the back of the cruiser, and by that time, we had his phone records and knew the calls were to his mother and his brother, John. It took the grand jurors less than half an hour to vote yes to indicting all three men, and the court clerk issued warrants for their arrest. I handed the warrants to Bates.

"Don't pick Nelson up until the other two are arrested and brought back here," I said. "Put them in the same holding cell, and make sure you have it wired."

"Done," Bates said. "How long you reckon it'll take to get them out of Nashville?"

"Depends. To be honest, I'd just as soon have you and a couple of your guys drive down there and pick them up, but we better go through the normal channels. Call the Davidson County sheriff and see how he wants to handle it."

"I'll call him from the office," Bates said. "I reckon I'll record it, too."

"Why? You think there's going to be a problem?"

"It's Nashville, Brother Dillard."

Bates left. He called me forty minutes later.

"The Davidson County sheriff says he isn't going to arrest John Lipscomb and Andres Pinzon unless he's instructed to do so by either the district attorney or the governor," Bates said. "These boys must have a bunch of clout."

"Try the Nashville Police Department."

"Already did. Same problem."

"I'll call the Davidson County DA."

The Davidson County district attorney's name was Clayton Williams. It took the rest of the afternoon to get him on the phone, and when I did, his attitude was one of detached ambivalence.

"The possibility that you might be seeking our assistance has been previously brought to my attention," he said after I introduced myself and told him why I was calling.

"I beg your pardon?"

"The governor and the attorney general have already contacted me. They both say that an obscure prosecutor in a far corner of the state is seeking to further his own career by undertaking a dangerous miscarriage of justice at the expense of two prominent businessmen from Nashville. It has been strongly suggested that if you call, we should refuse to cooperate with you in any respect and notify them immediately. So that's what I'm going to do, Mr. Dillard. I have no intention of intervening on your behalf, and as soon as I hang up, I intend to call both of them back."

I held the phone away from my ear, stupefied by the arrogance of the political elite.

"Are you telling me you're refusing to honor a lawful warrant? You're refusing to arrest two men who have been indicted for murder?"

"We'll arrest them at the direction of either the governor or the state attorney general."

"So that's it? That's all you have to say to me?"

"No, I'd also like to tell you to have a wonderful day," he said, and he hung up on me. I called Bates back immediately.

"Meet me out at my house," I said. "We need to take a little walk through the woods."

CHAPTER TWENTY-SIX

The next morning, Bates and I went public. I had Rita Jones call every print, television, and radio reporter within a fifty-mile radius. I called the Associated Press reporter in Knoxville personally and invited her to come up for a press conference. I worried, briefly, about my obligation to keep the results of grand jury proceedings secret, but the warrants had been faxed to another law enforcement agency, and politicians all over Tennessee knew about them. As far as I was concerned, they were no longer secret, and even if there was a legal argument that they were, the secrecy was serving only to impede the judicial process.

At the press conference, which I held in one of the courtrooms because of the number of reporters present, I told them that the grand jury had indicted two wealthy men from Nashville for the murders of the three young women, and that the Nashville authorities were refusing to cooperate. I also told them that the highest levels of government in the state of Tennessee were also attempting to interfere in the process, and I said, flat out, that the governor himself was involved. I mentioned the state attorney general, and I made sure I took a well-deserved swipe at the Tennessee Bureau of Investigation for refusing my request to help with the investigation. I respectfully declined to give them the names of the men who had been indicted, but Bates may have given the names to them. Or maybe one or two of his investigators leaked the names. I preferred not to know.

The result was exactly what I'd hoped. The reporters attacked the story like sharks after a dead marlin. The headlines the next morning were along the lines of: "Multi-millionaires Enjoy Protection of Pols." The stories named Lipscomb, his brother, and Pinzon. They outlined the evidence we had, and because of the uproar, the governor's office, the state attorney general's office, and the TBI director's office were all deluged with calls.

On Wednesday morning, as soon as I walked into the office, Rita handed me a stack of messages. Lawyers representing all three men had called. The governor, the state attorney general, the director of the TBI, four congressmen, two senators, the Davidson County sheriff, and two dozen reporters all wanted me to call them back. I tossed all the messages into the trash except the one from the Davidson County sheriff.

"You've put a lot of people in an extremely difficult position," Sheriff Lane Masters said when he picked up the phone.

"It isn't difficult," I said. "Just do your job."

"Have you talked to Mr. Lipscomb's lawyer?"

"Pinzon?"

"No, his criminal defense lawyer."

"Sure haven't."

"Do you intend to?"

"Sure don't."

"It might be in your best interest to allow them to turn themselves in. Let them fly up there on their own plane, go through the booking process, and post their bond."

The bond had been set at a million dollars apiece. I had no doubt they would be able to come up with the money. They'd be out of jail a couple hours after they arrived in Washington County.

"I might have agreed to that a couple days ago," I said, "but now I think it'd be best to treat them like everyone else. Take them to jail, and Sheriff Bates will send a couple of his deputies to pick them up."

"You don't care much about your political future, do you Mr. Dillard?"

"Can't say that I do."

"Must be nice. So you really think you can convict them of murder?"

"I wouldn't have indicted them if I didn't."

"You have a lot of experience with this kind of thing, do you?"

"I've tried plenty of murder cases."

"Okay, partner. Leon Bates vouches for you, so you can have it your way. We'll pick them up in a couple hours and I'll notify your sheriff. I expect you'll be hearing from some mighty angry people in the near future. Good luck to you."

Less than thirty seconds after I hung up, Rita buzzed me.

"It's the governor. Do you want me to tell him you're out?"

"I'll talk to him," I said, and I punched the flashing button.

"I just want you to know that if John Lipscomb isn't convicted of murder, I'm going to the legislature, and I'm going to have you removed from office," Governor Donner said. "There better not be any plea bargains, no reduced charges, nothing. He pleads guilty to second-degree murder or a jury convicts him. Otherwise, you're gone, my friend."

"I'm not your friend."

Donner laughed. "That's the first intelligent thing I've heard you say, Dillard. I'm going to take great pleasure in watching you go down in flames."

The line went dead.

I knew I was in dangerous territory. Unfamiliar, dangerous territory. I'd never gone up against the kind of power—or the kind of people—I was facing. Lipscomb had plenty of money, he had high-dollar lawyers, and he had political clout. That, in itself, wasn't so dangerous, but I knew he was also willing to cross lines. The attack on Sarah proved it.

The entire investigation had turned into a runaway train, and I was the engineer. I wasn't about to jump off though. I had to keep going. Whether it was for Erlene and her girls, for Sarah, or to serve my own foolish pride, I didn't know, but I couldn't back down. If I did, how could I ever look my wife, my children, my sister, or even myself in the eye again? As I sat there with the governor's threat echoing in my head, I felt a burgeoning sense of dread unlike anything I'd ever experienced.

These people weren't just hoping to beat me in court.

They wanted to destroy me.

The Davidson County sheriff did what he said he'd do. Lipscomb and Pinzon were arrested in their posh Nashville office a couple hours after the sheriff and I spoke on the phone. We let Nelson Lipscomb dangle, hoping he might come running to my office, beg to make a deal, and tell us what happened on the boat. I suspected that Bates was illegally tapping Nelson's cell phone, but I didn't mention it, and if he was, nothing came of it.

As soon as we heard Lipscomb and Pinzon had been arrested, Bates sent Rudy Lane and a patrol deputy to Nashville in a van to pick them up. They left late in the afternoon, were going to spend the night at a hotel near the jail, pick up the prisoners bright and early, and have them back in time for a one o'clock arraignment. There was a provision in the Rules of Criminal Procedure that allowed their lawyers to appear on their behalf, so I knew as soon as they'd been booked at the jail and their bonds had been posted, Lipscomb and Pinzon would be traveling straight to the airport to their private jet and would fly back to Nashville.

I awoke early, as usual, the morning of the arraignment, fixed myself a cup of coffee, and drank it in the cool darkness on the deck. The crisp morning air felt good against my skin. The stars were beginning to fade, and I could hear the whine of a small outboard motor, no doubt a fisherman, rounding the bend in the channel below. There was a slight breeze blowing in off the water, carrying with it an earthy, musty odor. I finished the coffee, went back inside, dressed in my running gear, grabbed a small flashlight, and Rio and I took off down the trail that bordered the bluff above the lake. Chico remained in the house, curled up between Caroline and Gracie on the bed.

Forty minutes later, I was back at the house, drenched in sweat. I walked around to the front and started up the driveway to get the morning paper. I glanced toward the woods, which looked like an out-of-focus, black-and-white photograph in the faint, gray light of predawn. Rio, who'd been investigating the base of a maple tree behind me, came loping up the driveway. I could hear his claws scraping against the asphalt as well as his breath, which always reminded me of a locomotive. Just as he passed me, he stopped and let out a low growl.

"What's wrong, big boy?"

I looked ahead and could make out two dark shapes at the top of the driveway, side by side, ten or fifteen feet from the road. They weren't moving. Rio continued to growl—a deep, throaty, threatening sound. I reached down to calm him and noticed that his teeth were bared, something he did rarely. I'd stuck the flashlight into the pocket of the hooded sweatshirt I was wearing, so I reached in and retrieved it. I pushed the button and cast the beam at the shapes. They were still about fifty feet away, eerily still and silent. I couldn't tell what they were.

"Hello? Who's there?"

No answer.

I reached down with my right hand and grabbed Rio's harness. He resisted, apparently not wanting to go any closer to the objects. I let go of the harness and started walking, very slowly, to the road. The shapes in the driveway gradually came into focus. My first thought was to turn and run back to the house, but I couldn't. I had to see if they were real. I moved closer still.

Ten feet away, I stopped.

"Oh, no," I murmured. "Please, please, no."

The breeze shifted slightly and the smell of blood filled my nostrils. I turned my back to the bodies and began to vomit.

CHAPTER TWENTY-SEVEN

As the last bit of bile erupted from my stomach, a frightening realization gripped me. I was up against something I'd never encountered—a terrorist. The bodies in my driveway were placed there for one reason, to strike terror into my heart.

Rio had moved over to my side but was still growling. I stood unsteadily, my thighs like molded gel, and turned back toward them. Both had been duct-taped into chairs and were sitting side by side, their torsos covered in dark blood, their faces luminescent in the pale light. Their chins weren't resting on their chests as they should have been. Instead they were sitting up straight, eyes open, their death stares seemingly tracking me like the eyes in a portrait. I pulled Rio back down the driveway and walked through the kitchen into the bedroom.

"Caroline," I whispered. Her eyes opened and she smiled.

"What time is it?"

"A little after six. You need to get up, baby. Things are about to get a little crazy around here."

"Crazy? What do you mean?"

"Just get up and get dressed. I'll explain in a few minutes."

I kissed her on the forehead and went back into the kitchen. Rio paced nervously back and forth between the front door and the kitchen door. I dialed Bates's cell number.

"There are two bodies in my driveway," I said when he answered. My voice was quivering involuntarily. "You need to get over here with your crime-scene people and a couple ambulances, but I don't want you to do it through the normal channels. Use your cell phone. I don't want the media crawling all over my place, and I don't want them crawling all over this crime scene."

"Do you know them?" he asked.

"Yeah. So do you. Come as quick as you can. I'm going back outside."

Caroline walked into the kitchen wearing a robe. I watched her fix herself a cup of coffee and sit down at the table.

"What's going on, Joe?"

"Something bad has happened. Two people have been murdered. They're in our driveway."

She set her coffee cup down and looked at me like I had suddenly started speaking a foreign language.

"In our *driveway*? What are you … what?"

"I'm not sure what's going on yet."

"Are you sure they're … how could this … are you sure they're dead?"

"They're dead."

"How? I mean … who? Who are they?"

"Witnesses. Against John Lipscomb."

"Have you called the police?"

"Bates is on his way. Stay inside, and try to keep Rio from going nuts when they show up."

I turned away from her and walked to the door. I wasn't looking forward to going back outside, but I felt like I needed to. I didn't think they should be alone, and at some level, I felt responsible for their deaths.

I closed the door behind me and walked back up the driveway. It was lighter now, but the sun still hadn't cleared the eastern horizon. All the stars except Venus had faded into the grayness. I walked slowly, consciously taking deep breaths in an attempt to quell the fear and anxiety coursing through me. I briefly entertained the thought that perhaps I'd experienced some kind of mental spasm, that a group of neurons in my brain had misfired and created an illusion, complete with the smell of blood. I actually *hoped* I'd gone temporarily insane and that when I went back outside, the bodies wouldn't be there.

But they were. Frozen, like bloody mannequins, continuing to stare silently at me in death. I still had the flashlight, and as I got to within five feet, I shined it onto the body to my right. It was Zack Woods. I circled him, careful not to get too close. Duct tape—a lot of it—had been wrapped around his forehead, shoulders, thighs, and calves. A piece of two-by-four had been shoved between his back and the back of the chair, obviously before the tape was applied. His head had been fastened to the board with the tape. That's why he was sitting up straight.

The other body was Hector Mejia, Lipscomb's care-taker, whom I'd met only briefly at the Washington

County Jail. He'd also been duct-taped to a chair and braced with a two-by-four.

I looked around at the surrounding hills. I wondered whether the killer was hiding in the woods, watching me survey the scene he'd so carefully crafted, enjoying my shock and horror. Maybe he was looking at me through a rifle scope. I shook off the thought and turned my attention back to Zack and Hector.

The first sight of them had been so shocking that I was unable to concentrate, unable to look closely, to examine the scene with any kind of analytical thought. But I'd managed to calm myself, and I looked closely at Zack's face. It was a horrible sight. His mouth was open, his lips were black, and blood had poured down his chest. His throat had been cut, a gaping wound three inches wide surrounded by a black crust of dried blood. I looked at the wound and noticed something unusual, something protruding from his throat a couple inches beneath his chin. I moved a step closer then recoiled, nearly vomiting again.

It was Zack's tongue. Whoever did this wasn't just a killer. He was a psychopath.

Bates came rolling down the road in his BMW about five minutes later, followed by two marked cruisers, two unmarked cruisers, a crime-scene van, and two ambulances. None of them were flashing their emergency lights. I walked to the top of the driveway and watched while they parked along the curb, got out, and followed along behind Bates to where I was standing. Bates stopped next to me and peered down the driveway at the backs of Zack and Hector. The others—eight men and two women, all in uniform—stood silent and stone-faced, each one preparing in his or her own way to deal, once again, with man's inhumanity to man.

I was grateful we didn't have neighbors close by. When I bought the property, one of the things that appealed to me the most was the isolation. The land that abutted to the east was TVA land and would probably not be developed, at least not in my lifetime. The land to the west was owned by a young farmer named Graves. He was the closest neighbor, and his house was almost a mile away.

"Who are they?" Bates said quietly.

"Zack Woods and Hector Mejia."

"Shit." Bates rarely used profanity.

"Look at their throats," I said. "I've never seen anything like it."

Bates glanced over his shoulder. "Let's go," he said, and the group moved forward.

I walked alongside Bates until we were standing where I had stood earlier, just a few feet in front of Zack and Hector. He looked at them for several seconds, then bent forward and rested his hands just above his knees. I thought for a moment that his reaction was going to be the same as mine, that he was going to vomit, but his eyes were fixed intently on Zack's throat.

"This ain't good, Brother Dillard. This ain't good at all. Do you know what this is?"

I didn't understand the question. Of course I knew what it was. Two dead people with their throats cut in a manner I'd never seen placed in my driveway. I waited for him to continue.

"It's called a Colombian necktie. It's usually something that happens in the drug trade. I've been to seminars and I've seen photos, but this is the first time I've seen it around here. Look at this."

Bates pulled on a pair of latex gloves and moved close to Zack. He squatted.

"See here?"

He pointed with his pinky finger and moved it diagonally a couple inches from the center of the wound to beneath Zack's jawline on both sides.

"After they cut the throat, they make a deeper incision here and here. They cut the cartilage away from the larynx, reach through with their fingers, and pull the tongue down through the wound. Looks like a little tie, see?"

"It's sick," I said.

"It's a message, delivered directly to you. A pretty simple message."

He came out of the squat and took a step back, removing the gloves and stuffing them into his back pocket. Then he took his cowboy hat off with his left hand, turned it over, and started running the index finger of his right hand around the inside of the brim.

"Same message as with Sarah," I said. "Back off."

"This one's a little louder. It means stop doing what you're doing or we'll do the same thing to you."

"Joe?"

I heard a familiar voice behind me. I turned to see Caroline, who had dressed in jeans and a gray hoodie, walking cautiously toward me. I didn't like the look on her face.

"I wish you hadn't come out here," I said.

"Who are they?"

Caroline moved next to me, and I put my arm around her shoulders. She stared at Zack and Hector.

"One of them takes care of John Lipscomb's property at the lake. He told us he saw Lipscomb and a man named Andres Pinzon get on the boat with the girls the night they were killed. The other is Zack Woods. He said he saw Lipscomb dumping one of the girls off the back of the boat that morning."

"But why? Why are they *here*?"

"We're not sure yet. Please go back inside."

"I don't want to go back inside. I want you to tell me why these people are here. This is my home too, you know."

The tone of her voice was agitated, bordering on frantic.

"We think the men we've arrested for the murders are responsible for this, Mrs. Dillard," Bates said. "But don't let it worry you. We'll take care of it."

"Don't worry? You'll take care of it?" I could see the veins in Caroline's neck pulsing. "They kill two people and bring them to our house for the whole world to see and you're telling me not to worry? Are you serious?"

"They're trying to scare us," I said.

"Well, *it's working*! If they can do something like this, what's to keep them from killing us too?"

"I'm the district attorney, Caroline. They're not going to kill a district attorney."

"Really? They'll kill his witnesses and dump them at his doorstep but they won't kill him? Why? Because they're so *terrified* of him?"

"We have work to do here, Caroline. We have to take care of these people—"

"They're not people anymore! Look at them!"

I'd never seen her so hysterical, but I certainly couldn't blame her. Telling her about it inside the house was one thing, but this was something else, something she could see and smell. I took her by the arm and began leading her to the house. She jerked away from me but kept walking. When we got to the door that led into the kitchen, I opened it for her and she walked through. I closed it and went back outside. One of the crime-scene techs was beginning to pull the tape from Hector.

"Thanks a lot," I said to Bates.

"What?" he said.

"For setting her off like that."

"I ain't too good with women."

"That's obvious. How could they have known about Zack and Hector? The witnesses weren't listed on the warrants."

"Your guess is as good as mine, brother. Maybe a leak in the grand jury."

"How much longer before you're done here?"

"Couple hours. You in some kind of hurry?"

"Lipscomb and Pinzon should be at the jail by noon, right? I plan to be waiting for them."

CHAPTER TWENTY-EIGHT

I gave my statement to Rudy Lane about finding the bodies in the driveway, after which I hung around for another half hour or so and watched as Bates and his people finished their forensic examination of the crime scene. I went back inside before the EMTs loaded Zack and Hector into the ambulances and took them off to the medical examiner's office.

Caroline was waiting for me in the kitchen. She was leaning back with the heels of her hands resting on the corner of the counter. She didn't look as though she'd cooled off.

"I want to know exactly what's going on," she said as soon as I closed the door. "I want to know why those two people were killed. I want to know who killed them. I want to know why they were put in our driveway. And the most important thing I want to know is *what you're planning to do about it.*"

"I'm not going to talk to you if you can't keep your voice down."

"I'm upset! What do you expect?"

"Where are Sarah and Gracie?"

"Upstairs. Why?"

"I don't want them to hear this."

"Never mind about them. Explain it to me!"

"We told you—they were both witnesses against John Lipscomb. That's why they're dead. As far as who killed them, I don't know. Lipscomb or Pinzon or both probably hired someone to do it, but there's no way of proving it, at least not yet. They put them in the driveway as a message to me. They want me to back off, to let them go. As far as what I'm going to do about it? I just don't know yet."

I walked over to her and put my hands on her shoulders.

"I'm sorry, Caroline. I guess I should have done things differently."

"Stop it. Don't patronize me. You said one of those men saw Lipscomb get on the boat and the other one saw him drop a body into the lake, which means they were extremely important, if not indispensable, to your case, right?"

"Right."

"So now they're dead. Do you even have a case?"

"Not much of one. But we—"

"Then why don't you back off? You can put a stop to this right now. Just back off."

"Not a chance," I said. "What kind of message would that send? Kill a couple witnesses and the state will give up?"

She started pacing around the kitchen.

"I don't care about messages," she said. "I've had all the messages I can handle. What I care about is you not winding up like those men in the driveway."

"You're overreacting."

"And you've got your head in the sand. What will it take, Joe? Don't you see these people are different? They're not going to let you win."

"This isn't about winning and losing. It's about right and wrong."

"Spare me the sanctimony. This is about your ego. This is about you showing the bad guys they can't mess with Joe Dillard."

"Maybe it is," I said, "but if you think I'm going to let some scumbag drop a couple dead bodies on my doorstep and then tuck my tail between my legs and run, you don't know me like I thought you did."

I turned my back on her and walked off toward the bathroom to take a shower. She gave me a parting shot as I cleared the door.

"You're going to wind up dead in a gutter somewhere. And where will that leave us?"

I was seething when the transport van that contained John Lipscomb and Andres Pinzon showed up at the jail at ten minutes before noon. Caroline's words rang in my ears, and the look of terror on her face as she stood gazing at Zack Woods and Hector Mejia sitting in my driveway with their throats cut was branded into my brain.

Bates and I were standing in the booking area waiting for Lipscomb and Pinzon to walk in. A large gathering of media was in the parking lot. Bates was talking about Nelson Lipscomb, who had apparently left town.

"With his brother's money and contacts, he could be anywhere," Bates said. I barely heard him. "I reckon not picking him up right off the bat wasn't such a good idea."

I didn't respond.

"You okay, Brother Dillard?"

I nodded.

"They'll make bond," Bates said. "If any one of them is determined to run, there isn't much we can do about it. But we'll find Nelson. Don't you worry. We'll find him."

The steel door buzzed, and Lipscomb and Pinzon walked through. Both of them were wearing uniforms issued by the Davidson County jail, and both were handcuffed and shackled. Pinzon looked like a mannequin, but Lipscomb had a narrow-eyed look of defiance on his fat face.

"I want to talk to Lipscomb alone," I said to Bates.

"Bad idea. You seem a little upset."

"I want to talk to Lipscomb. Alone. Now. Put him someplace where there aren't any cameras and where nobody can see or hear us."

"You're about to do something you'll regret," Bates said.

"Take his cuffs and shackles off."

Bates walked over and whispered something to Rudy Lane, who took Lipscomb by the elbow and led him to a cell in the far corner of the booking area. I followed closely behind. I'd dressed in a pair of dark-gray dress slacks and a white, button-down shirt for the arraignment, which was scheduled to start at one o'clock. I'd left my tie and my jacket in Bates's office.

Lipscomb hesitated at the cell door, but Rudy shoved him inside. The door was steel, painted gray like everything else around me, with a small window at eye level. I stood outside the cell while Rudy removed Lipscomb's cuffs and shackles. My peripheral vision began to close in, and within seconds, I could see only what was directly in front of me. As soon as Rudy was finished, I walked in.

"Close the door behind you," I said to Rudy without taking my eyes off Lipscomb, who was standing in the middle of the cell three or four feet in front of me.

"You sure about this?" Rudy asked.

I didn't answer. Rudy eased by me, the door clanged shut, and I stepped to within a foot of Lipscomb.

"Is this where I get the rubber hose treatment?" he said.

I backhanded him across the mouth with my right hand. A loud *thwap* echoed off of the concrete block walls as Lipscomb stumbled backward.

"That's for what you said about my wife."

I moved close to him again. The backs of his legs were against the concrete bunk. A small stream of blood was already trickling from the corner of his lip to his chin.

"Your wife is a slut," he mumbled, and I slapped him so hard with my open right hand that my palm and fingers immediately went numb. He fell back onto the slab and his head thumped into the wall.

"That's for what you had your hired thugs do to my sister. Who told you about Zack Woods and Hector Mejia?" He didn't respond, so I leaned down close to him. "I know what you are, and one way or another, I'm going to prove it and put you away for good. If you think killing a couple witnesses and planting them in my driveway is going to keep me from making you pay, you've underestimated me. If you or any of your murdering friends come anywhere near me or my family again, I'll hunt you down and do the same thing to you that they did to Zack and Hector."

Lipscomb folded his hands in his lap and rested the back of his head against the wall. The laughter started slowly and quietly, like a train pulling out of a station, but it soon gained momentum and volume, a frightening, high-pitched cackle that sounded like it was emanating from the labyrinths of hell. I stood over him, panting like a wild animal. I wanted to beat him to a bloody pulp, a feeling that intensified as the laughter assaulted my eardrums. I reached down and grabbed the front of his jumpsuit and was pulling him to his feet when he spit a stream of mucous and blood directly into my face. I drew my fist back, ready to break his jaw.

"Dillard!" The voice was Rudy Lane. I froze.

The warm, sticky fluid on my face began to sicken me, and I let Lipscomb go and backed away. I hurried out the door past Rudy and turned left down the hallway that led from the booking area. Behind me, I heard Lipscomb's voice.

"You're a dead man, Dillard! Do you hear me? A dead man!"

CHAPTER TWENTY-NINE

I walked straight out the front door of the jail and to my truck, forgetting completely about the tie and jacket I'd left in Bates's office. I felt disoriented, disconnected from the world around me, and I started to drive aimlessly. A short while later, about ten miles west of Jonesborough, I drifted off the road on US 11-E and sideswiped the railing of a bridge that crossed a creek near the Telford community. The noise of metal grinding jolted me back to awareness, and I slowed the truck down and pulled to the side of the highway. I shut the engine off, gripped the top of the steering wheel with both hands, and rested my forehead on them. I didn't want to move or think. I just wanted to melt away.

I don't know how long I sat there, but eventually I became aware of a tap, tap, tapping. When I realized someone was knocking on the window, I pulled myself together at least enough to look to my left. A bearded face came into focus.

"You all right in there, partner?" I didn't recognize him. He was wearing denim bib overalls and a green-and-yellow John Deere cap. I sat back and nodded my head, unwilling to roll the window down.

He stood there, looking at me intently for a few seconds.

"The world ain't such a bad place, you know. All you gotta do is look for the good. It's all around you."

He turned and walked away to his vehicle, and I looked at the clock on the dashboard. I was due in court in half an hour for Lipscomb and Pinzon's arraignment. I turned the rearview mirror toward me and looked at my face. There was dried blood around my mouth and smeared on my cheeks where Lipscomb had spit on me. I looked down at my shirt and it, too, was speckled with small blood stains.

I pulled back onto the highway, made a U-turn, and headed back to Jonesborough. It was lunchtime, so with any luck the office would be empty. I parked in the back lot at the justice center and used my key card to go in through a door that led directly to our offices. I made it to the closet in my office where I kept an extra set of clothes without seeing anyone. I grabbed the suit and was about ten steps from the bathroom when Rita Jones walked around the corner. She stopped in midstride and gasped.

"What happened to you?"

"Nothing."

I kept walking and ducked into the bathroom, leaving her standing in the hallway. I went straight to the sink, took off my shirt, and started washing the blood from my face. I should have locked the door behind me because a few seconds later, Rita walked in.

"You're bleeding," she said.

"It isn't mine. This is the men's room, in case you didn't notice."

"There's a lot of talk going on about you around here."

"What are they saying?"

"They're saying you've gone off the deep end. They're saying the governor is going to have you removed from office."

"Doesn't really matter, does it? You're the one who runs this place."

"I'm serious, Joe. I know you've been through a lot lately with Sarah and Caroline and everything that's going on here at work. Are you okay? I mean really okay?"

I'd known Rita for nearly twenty years. She was an excellent secretary and paralegal. She was also a beautiful redhead with a body and demeanor that reduced most men to driveling idiots. She'd wrecked more than her share of marriages, and in years past, had taken more than one shot at wrecking mine. I'd always managed to fend her off, and I liked her, but at that moment, I didn't feel like talking. I was queasy and had to put both hands on the sink for a minute as a wave of dizziness swept over me.

"I'll be fine," I said. "I had a rough morning, that's all."

"Maybe you should see someone. A professional."

"A shrink?"

"Someone who can help you work through some of the things that have happened to you."

"I appreciate your concern, Rita, but I'll be fine. Now if you don't mind, I need to change my pants."

"You look terrible," she said.

"Thanks."

"I mean it. You look like you haven't slept in a month and you're pale. You should see a doctor."

"Will you please get out of here so I can finish getting ready to go to court?"

"Fine, but if you need to talk, you know where to find me. And Tanner is in his office. I'm going to tell him to go to court with you. You look like you could use some help."

I stayed in the bathroom splashing cold water on my face until a few minutes before one. The nausea wouldn't go away, so just before I walked out the door to the courtroom, I went into one of the stalls and stuck my finger down my throat. I gagged several times, but nothing would come up. I hadn't eaten that day.

I took the back steps up to the main courtroom, which still smelled of new carpet and fresh paint. Court wasn't yet in session, but Tanner Jarrett was already sitting at the prosecution table, six lawyers were sitting at the defense table, and the gallery was packed with reporters and camera crews. As soon as I walked through the door, a group of reporters surged toward me.

"Mr. Dillard! Can you confirm there have been two more murders? Mr. Dillard! Is it true that the victims were left in your driveway? Mr. Dillard! Mr. Dillard!" I looked past them and saw Erlene Barlowe leaning against the wall at the back of the courtroom.

A bailiff stepped to the front and warned the crowd to turn off their cell phones and stay quiet. When he was finished, he walked over and knocked lightly on the door to the judge's chambers. The door opened, and Judge Adams walked through with a flourish, chin held high, black robe flowing behind him.

"All rise," the bailiff called, "the Criminal Court of Washington County is now in session, the Honorable John Adams presiding."

Adams, the newest judge in the district, was a blue-blood alcoholic. Judge Leonard Green, who'd been on the criminal court bench for decades, had been murdered a year earlier. The state supreme court promptly appointed a former medical malpractice attorney named Terry Breck to replace Green. Breck was bright and personable, and it appeared that at last, we finally had a decent judge. But Breck succumbed to a heart attack a couple months later, and John Adams, a former ambulance chaser who just happened to be a member of the lucky sperm club—his father made a fortune in the textile business before the industry packed up its sweatshops and moved abroad—entered the picture.

Adams was a young, bombastic buffoon. He claimed to be a direct descendent of President John Adams and even had a brother named Quincy. He also claimed to have ancestors that traveled to America on the *Mayflower* and loved to regale anyone who would listen with stories of the hardships endured aboard the ship, as though he'd experienced them firsthand. He wore lots of tweed and cardigan sweaters beneath his black robe and smoked a curved pipe. But he knew nothing about the law. He didn't know the rules of criminal procedure, didn't know the rules of evidence, and interpreted written opinions and case law with the logic of a third grader. He'd had more rulings reversed on appeal during his first year in office than most judges accumulated in a decade, yet he seemed unfazed, blissfully unaware of his own incompetence, bathed in the power of the mystical black robe.

"You okay?" Tanner whispered.

"I'm fine."

"Rita was right. You look awful."

Judge Adams took his seat and surveyed the crowd. He had judge-length, strawberry-blond hair that he parted in the middle, a small nose between small, hazel eyes, a narrow face, and cheeks flushed by the legendary amounts of Scotch he consumed each evening.

The bailiff called the case and I looked over at the six lawyers. Collins Brubaker, the president of the Tennessee Bar Association whom I'd insulted when we arrested Nelson Lipscomb, was the only one I recognized.

"Feeling a little outnumbered, Mr. Dillard?" the judge said. Tanner and I were the only people at the prosecution table.

"Outnumbered, maybe, but not outgunned," I said.

Brubaker stood.

"Collins Brubaker, appearing on behalf of Nelson Lipscomb, Your Honor. The defendants are waiving their right to appear at arraignment. They also waive their right to a formal reading of the indictment. We have an agreement on bail, which the court has already signed."

"The state moves to revoke bail," I said without standing. "We'd like them held in jail pending trial."

"But Mr. Dillard signed the bail agreements," Brubaker said. "Unless there has been some material change in circumstance—"

"I signed the agreement before Nelson Lipscomb disappeared and two of our witnesses were murdered," I said. "I've changed my mind."

I heard scrambling behind me as the reporters jockeyed for position.

"Order!" Judge Adams said, banging his gavel dramatically. "What are you talking about, Mr. Dillard?"

"Two people who testified before the grand jury and who would have testified against these defendants were murdered last night. Their throats were cut and they were placed in the driveway outside of my home. We tried to serve an arrest warrant on Nelson Lipscomb this morning, but the sheriff's department can't find him."

The scrambling turned to silence. I looked over at the group of lawyers at the defense table. Only Brubaker was standing. He'd apparently been elected to serve as the mouthpieces' mouthpiece.

"Your Honor," he said, "even if, in fact, two people have been murdered, as Mr. Dillard claims, it has no bearing on this proceeding unless he has proof that these defendants were somehow involved."

The nausea still lingered, and I found his voice irritating. I thought about walking over and smacking him across the face the same way I'd smacked Lipscomb.

"Even if, in fact, two people have been murdered?" I said to him. "Are you calling me a liar? Do you think I'd walk in here and lie about something like this?"

"You'll direct your comments to the court, Mr. Dillard," Adams said, "and you'll stand up when you do so."

"Forgive me if this sounds insensitive, Your Honor," Brubaker said, "but if Mr. Dillard's witnesses are deceased, perhaps the question we should be asking him is whether the state still has enough evidence to sustain this outrageous prosecution."

Judge Adams looked down on me.

"Well?" he said.

I stood. "Well, what?"

"Do you have enough evidence to sustain the indictment?"

"I have no intention of revealing the evidence we've developed to you or anyone else this early in the proceeding," I said. The law required me to provide discovery to the defense after arraignment, but I didn't have to do it immediately. I had some time. Not much, but I had some time. "If you're asking me whether I intend to ask you to dismiss the indictment, the answer is absolutely not."

As I spoke, I began to feel lightheaded and felt an irresistible urge to leave the courtroom.

"Excuse me," I said, and I started around the table toward the door. I took a couple steps, and the lights seemed to go out. I felt myself falling forward, and then I felt nothing at all.

CHAPTER THIRTY

When I woke up, I heard a siren and realized I was in the back of an ambulance. An oxygen mask covered my face, and there was an intravenous tube running from my arm to a bag on a stand. A middle-aged man in a paramedic uniform was sitting next to me. Rita Jones was on the other side, holding my hand. Her eyes were red and her makeup smeared.

"What happened?" I asked.

"Thank God you're awake," she said, squeezing my hand. "Do you know who I am?"

"You're my promiscuous paralegal."

She smiled broadly. "Don't talk," she said, "just rest."

"Caroline?"

"She's meeting us at the hospital. We're almost there. And don't worry about court. Tanner is taking care of it."

I followed her advice and closed my eyes, feeling groggy and exhausted. I remembered the arraignment, remembered becoming angry at Brubaker, but beyond that, nothing. A couple minutes later, the back door of the ambulance opened, and the paramedic, along with another paramedic and either a nurse or an orderly from the hospital, unloaded me and wheeled me into one of the trauma rooms inside.

I spent the afternoon with doctors and nurses prodding and poking and asking me questions. I managed to get at least enough information out of them to learn that they believed I'd had some kind of "cardiac episode," which, in laymen's terms, meant I'd had a stroke. I couldn't believe it. Caroline showed up about fifteen minutes after I arrived at the emergency room. She didn't cry, didn't really give any outward sign of her concern, but the look in her eyes was that of a deer just before it's hit by a car.

I was angry at myself for worrying her. Her day had started off with the bodies in the driveway, Lilly was pregnant, she still hadn't healed from her latest surgery, and now this. I asked her not to call the children until we knew exactly what was going on, and she agreed.

They moved me to a private room in the cardiac wing late in the day. Around four o'clock, a short, young black man entered the room. He was wearing the signature white lab coat and carrying a file. He walked up to my bedside and smiled.

"Mr. Dillard, I'm Dr. McKinney. I'm a cardiologist, and I'm going to be taking care of you."

His voice was nasal, his diction perfect. He had no accent, very much like a radio announcer. He was slightly overweight with a double chin, and was wearing brown, corduroy pants, a yellow turtleneck shirt that was too tight for his build, and ugly, comfortable shoes. He was geek through and through, not a smidgen of cool in him. He looked like the type who had spent a great deal more time studying than partying, and that gave me some comfort.

"Nice to meet you," I said. "This is my wife, Caroline." She was sitting in a recliner to my left. "What's the verdict?"

"We think you had a transient ischemic attack, what most people refer to as mini-stroke, most likely caused by a buildup of plaque that's blocking the carotid artery in your heart. We can't be certain, though, unless we go into the artery and take a look around. The stress test didn't show any abnormalities. I know you've been asked these questions before, but do you mind answering again for me?"

"Go ahead."

"You don't smoke?"

"Nope. Never have."

"How much do you drink? Please be honest."

"I get a little drunk on Christmas Eve and New Year's. Well, maybe more than a little drunk. And sometimes on the Fourth of July. Maybe a little tipsy on Valentine's Day. Other than that, I drink a few beers now and then, but I don't really drink much at all."

"Do you exercise regularly?"

"Almost every day. I ran four miles this morning. I still lift weights some, but not as much as I used to."

"Were you unusually winded after your run this morning? Unusually tired?"

"Felt the same as always."

"How would you describe your diet?"

"Normal, I guess."

"And it says here there's no history of heart disease in your family."

"Not that I know of. I'm not much of a genealogist, but none of my grandparents died from heart disease. My mother had Alzheimer's, and my father was killed in Vietnam."

"Yes, I see that here," he said, tapping on the chart. "I'm very sorry."

There was an awkward moment while I waited for him to continue.

"What about stress?"

"I hate that word," I said. "Things happen. Things happen to everybody. I deal with it the best I can."

He nodded methodically. If his skull had been transparent, I could have seen the gears turning inside his brain.

"Are you going through a particularly difficult time right now?"

"How should I put this? Let's just say that some unusual things have happened lately."

"Well, Mr. Dillard, it appears that you're one of those we can't really explain. You're young, you're fit, and your lifestyle is relatively healthy. There doesn't seem to be any family history that we can document, at least not in the past two generations. It's possible that some plaque has built up on the inside of your carotid artery and is restricting the flow of blood to your brain. A tiny piece of plaque may even have broken off and blocked an even tinier artery in your brain, which caused you to pass out. I'm going to schedule you for a heart catheter first thing in the morning. We'll go in and take a look around."

"Fine, but can I leave as soon as you're finished? I need to get back to work."

A frown came over his face. "It'll depend on what we find."

"You won't find anything," I said. "This was just a … a … an anomaly. A freak occurrence."

"I'll see you at six in the morning," the doctor said, and he walked out the door.

Caroline walked up next to the bed and reached down for my hand.

"It would be ironic, wouldn't it?" she said.

"What's that?"

"If such a good man wound up with a bad heart."

CHAPTER THIRTY-ONE

T here was a steady stream of visitors during the evening. Bates came by, as did Sarah, several people from the office, a few lawyers, Rudy Lane, and Caroline's mother. I was grateful for the visits, but I was embarrassed to be in a hospital bed. The last visitor finally left around 9:00 p.m.

"Go home," I said to Caroline, who was sitting in the chair next to the bed. "Get some rest."

"I'm not going home without you. There were two dead men in the driveway this morning, remember? Sarah has taken Gracie and the dogs and gone to my mother's. I'm staying right here."

In the aftermath of what happened to me in the courtroom, I'd been occupied with doctors and nurses and tests and needles and questions all afternoon. After that, the visitor parade started. But none of the visitors had said a word about John Lipscomb or the murder case, not even Bates.

"You're right," I said. "You're absolutely right. I must be losing my mind. Have you talked to Jack and Lilly?"

"I called them earlier. I didn't want them to hear about it from somebody else. It's been all over the news.

Mother said they showed footage of you lying on the floor in the courtroom."

"How considerate of them. The kids aren't coming home, are they? It isn't serious. I'm fine."

"They're worried. They've heard about the bodies in the driveway. That story is going national."

"It's funny how some things just seem to take on a life of their own, isn't it? When this case first started, when they pulled that poor girl out of the water, I thought it was going to be a drowning, or maybe a simple little who-dunit. You know, man and woman get drunk on their boat and get into an argument, man gets too aggressive, accidentally kills the woman, panics and drops her into the lake. But this is nuts."

"Can you convict them?" Caroline said. "Now that those two men are dead?"

"I don't know. I guess Bates and I will just have to keep working. Maybe something else will pop up."

We watched television for a little while. Around ten thirty, Caroline said she was hungry and was going to the cafeteria. I turned the television off and had just started to doze when I felt a hand pushing up and down on my chest. A dark figure was leaning over the bed, illuminated only by the lights from the parking lot outside the window.

"Mr. Dillard. Mr. Dillard, wake up."

The voice was whispering and accented, vaguely familiar, but I couldn't quite place it. I stared up, trying to focus. And then I realized who it was. Andres Pinzon. The first thought that entered my mind was that he'd probably injected me with some kind of poison and wanted to let me know who was responsible for my death.

"I suppose you're here to kill me," I said.

"We need to talk."

"The security in this place stinks."

Pinzon walked around the bed and sat down in the same chair Caroline had occupied a short time earlier. The place was eerily quiet.

"I need to tell you a story," he said, and he started talking. He talked briefly about his childhood in Colombia, and then he went into a long story about his relationship with John Lipscomb and how it had evolved. He told me about their venture into the cocaine business, about a young girl who died in Lipscomb's room, and about another young man who was murdered at Lipscomb's command. He talked about the fortune they'd made together and the moral compromises he'd made along the way. At one point, he said he'd sold his soul to the devil.

"Why are you telling me all of this?" I said when he finally hesitated. He'd been talking for half an hour.

"You charged me with murder. I want you to know that I've never hurt anyone."

"Who killed the girls?"

"I'm not going to tell you anything else unless you give me your word that you'll dismiss the murder charges against me."

"Not a chance."

"Let me ask you a question, Mr. Dillard. Are you familiar with how Colombian drug smugglers exact revenge? How they deal with people who betray them or who they think might be a threat to their operation?"

The images of Zack Woods and Hector Mejia with their throats cut came into my mind, along with what Bates had told me about the Colombian necktie.

"Why?" I said. "What do Colombian drug dealers have to do with three murders in my district?"

"The Colombians are famous, perhaps 'infamous' is a better word, for their creativity when it comes to revenge and domestic terrorism. If a smuggler is betrayed by someone in his organization or feels that he needs to send a message to someone who might be a threat—a prosecutor or a politician, let's say—he'll order his *sicarios* to murder the person in some sadistic way, but it doesn't stop there. Before the *sicarios* murder this person, they will capture or kidnap as many of his family as they can find. They'll take all of them to some obscure location, and the traitor or the prosecutor or politician will be tied up and forced to watch while his wife and daughters, maybe even his mother, are raped. If he has sons, they, too, will be sexually humiliated in the most shameful ways. Then the *sicarios* will murder the entire family. The traitor or the politician will be the last one to die."

"A *sicario* is what? A hired killer?"

"A paid assassin, loyal to one organization."

"And the reason you're giving me this civics lesson?"

"My lawyer told me about your witnesses on the plane back to Nashville. He said their throats were cut and they were placed outside your home. I'm guessing that their tongues were pulled out of the wounds in their throats."

"How do you know that?"

"It's the Colombian way. Your witnesses were killed by a Colombian *sicario,* probably more than one. They were probably led by a man named Santiago—they call him *El Maligno.* It means 'the evil one.' I've only seen him once in my life, when John hired him to murder the man I was telling you about earlier, the man who owed him money."

"We're not in Columbia, in case you haven't noticed."

"You don't understand, Mr. Dillard. John Lipscomb is a powerful man, a sociopath who has more resources than you can imagine and who has loyal contacts in the Colombian drug culture. They have different rules. They don't respect the law. John gave you your warning, and you responded by assaulting him in a jail cell. He was livid on the flight back from Nashville. I heard him yelling at his lawyer. He's going to have you killed, but before you die, you'll watch while your family is murdered."

I was silent for a full minute. Could he be serious? Was John Lipscomb really capable of having my entire family murdered? I thought again about the bodies in my driveway, the way it was staged, and I felt my pulse quicken.

"Turn the light on," I said. "I want to see your face."

Pinzon got up, walked around the bed, and turned on the light. He was wearing a long, black coat and had a black cap in his hand. He looked tired, and he looked scared.

"Tell me what happened to the girls on the boat," I said.

"I'll tell you everything, but I want your word about dismissing the charges."

"What difference does it make? From what you're saying, there isn't going to be a trial."

"I want to continue my life with my wife and child when this is over, just like you," he said. "I can't do it with a murder charge hanging over my head."

I swung my legs over the side of the bed.

"What happened to them, Mr. Pinzon?"

"I didn't see it."

"But you were there."

"I was on the boat, but I was asleep when it happened. John insists we come up here every year for a party. It's the anniversary of our takeover of an insurance company that took us from rich to ultra-rich. It's supposed to be a private celebration, but John bores easily. A few years ago he added girls and drugs to the mix. I stay away from both. I'm happily married and I don't do drugs. But John is … well, he's different."

"I asked you what happened to them."

"I drank too much. I passed out around two in the morning, but John was still going strong. He woke me up at around five fifteen and told me we had to leave. I asked him why and he said, 'Déjà vu, Boston.' I knew what he meant. The cocaine he gets is pure, straight from Columbia. He still has contacts there. The girl must have done too much of it. I knew she must have died. I asked him what we were going to do, and he said, 'Don't worry. I took care of it.' Nelson dropped us at the house, we went in and picked up our things, got on the helicopter, and flew back to Nashville. I read about the other two girls on the Internet after they were found, and I knew he'd killed them."

"But you didn't see it. Maybe Nelson killed them."

"John killed them. Nelson wouldn't have the stomach for it."

"Did you confront John about it after you read the news?"

"Of course I confronted him. He said they were strippers and hookers. He said it was like taking out the trash. Nobody would miss them. But then you arrested Nelson and you showed up in Nashville, and I knew things were about to get much worse. That's why I told you to let it go. You'll never convict him of anything."

"I'll make a deal with Nelson as soon as we find him. With both of you testifying, John will go to prison for the rest of his life."

"You won't find Nelson."

"Do you know where he is?"

"Nelson is dead. I suspected it when he didn't show up at the jail, but when my lawyer told me about the dead witnesses, I knew Nelson was dead, too."

"John Lipscomb would have his own brother killed?"

"John is capable of anything. I'm convinced the only reason I'm still alive is that the *sicarios* haven't had time to get to me. As soon as I got back to Nashville this afternoon, I gathered my family and got back on a plane. They're at the airport waiting for me right now. We're going into hiding until this is over, and I suggest you do the same."

The door pushed open and Caroline walked in.

"What's going on?" she said. "Is everything all right?"

"Everything's fine. This gentleman and I are just having a discussion. Give us a few minutes, would you?"

She walked back out, closing the door behind her. A hundred questions were whirling through my mind. I tried to slow my brain down, to concentrate on what was most important at the moment.

"What happened to the boat?" I said to Pinzon.

"It's been dismantled and is on a scrap heap somewhere. He didn't tell me who he hired to get it out of the water, and he didn't tell me where they took it. You'll never find it."

"Tell me again about this *sicario*. What did you say his name was? Santiago?"

"I've only seen him once, and that was twenty years ago. I know his reputation is that of a coldblooded killer. He has a scar on his face. It runs from the corner of his mouth on the left side all the way to his temple in a sort of half circle. Of course, by the time you recognize him, it will probably be too late."

"How do I find him before he finds me?"

"I don't know how to find him. Do you have any idea how John found out about your two witnesses or how he was able to direct the *sicarios* to them and to your house?"

"None whatsoever."

"You've been under surveillance since shortly after you arrested Nelson Lipscomb. So has your sheriff. John knows everything you do, everything you say. He knows where you are and what you're doing every day, all the time. He's become obsessed with you."

"Does he know I'm here?"

"Of course, the lawyers told him. I'm sure someone is calling the hospital every hour to check on your condition. There may even be someone in the building or in the parking lot."

"Who spies on a district attorney and a sheriff?"

"John Lipscomb does. When he needs information, he gets it. It would be wise for you to have your house, your vehicles, even your clothing, checked for listening devices and GPS transmitters. I'm certain your phones are tapped. There may even be video cameras."

Pinzon stood and started for the door.

"Wait, wait a minute. How can I stop him?"

He paused and turned to face me.

"Get your family to safety, Mr. Dillard. Do it quickly, and then wait for the *sicarios* to come. I'm sure it's already been set in motion. When they come, kill them."

"Kill them? Are you crazy? I'm not like Lipscomb. I'll have them arrested and throw them all in jail."

"Again, you don't understand. If you arrest them, someone else will come to finish the job. It's a matter of honor with the *sicarios*."

"So where does it end?"

"You must cut off the head. The only way you and your family will ever be safe is if John Lipscomb is dead."

CHAPTER THIRTY-TWO

As soon as Pinzon left and Caroline walked back in, I pulled the IV tube out of my arm and removed the monitors that were stuck to my chest. I stood up and was relieved that there was no dizziness or nausea. I stepped over to the small closet where my clothes were hanging and started getting dressed.

"Joe, what are you doing?" Caroline said.

"We have to go."

"What? Why?"

"Don't ask questions right now. Just follow my lead. I'll explain as soon as I can."

I picked up the phone on the table by the bed, dialed information, and got the name of a cab company. I told the woman who answered to have a cab waiting for us at a McDonald's that was about a half mile from the hospital.

"We're taking a cab?" Caroline said. "I have a perfectly good car in the parking lot."

"Shhhh, don't talk until we're outside."

As we walked down the hallway, I heard a voice behind me.

"Mr. Dillard! Mr. Dillard! Where are you going?" It was the nurse.

"I'm leaving."

"You can't leave. You're scheduled to go to the heart catheter lab first thing in the morning."

"I'll have to reschedule."

Caroline and I walked toward the elevators with the nurse hurrying along behind me, chastising, threatening, cajoling, pleading, trying everything she could to get me to stay. Instead of pushing one of the elevator buttons, I pulled Caroline through the door that led to the stairs. We hurried down five flights, went through a maze of hallways, and walked out of the hospital through the emergency room door. I avoided the parking lot, skirted the building, and started walking up a residential street that would eventually lead us to the McDonald's parking lot.

"Can I talk now?" Caroline said.

"Pinzon said our phones are tapped, there are GPS transmitters on our vehicles, and our house is wired for sound and video."

"Pinzon? You mean …?"

"Yeah. John Lipscomb's codefendant in the murders. That was him in the room back there."

"What did he want?"

"To warn me." I wasn't sure how much I should say. I didn't want to frighten Caroline, but I didn't want to lie to her either.

"Warn you about what?"

"The attack on Sarah, the bodies in the driveway, they were warnings. I just didn't have enough sense to realize what they meant. And then today, over at the jail, I made it even worse."

"What do you mean? What did you do at the jail?"

"I sort of smacked Lipscomb around a little. He said something about you when I first met him at his office in Nashville, something vulgar. He just did it to bait me, but I didn't forget. Then Sarah was terrorized. I knew it was him, and then the bodies this morning. I lost my temper."

"I don't understand. What does you losing your temper have to do with that man coming to your room?"

"It's a long story."

"Then I guess you better get started."

As we walked the last couple blocks to meet the cab, I told her everything Pinzon said in the hospital room. She listened without saying a word. When I was finished, she stopped on the sidewalk.

"So they're coming to kill us," she said. "Men are coming to kill all of us, including the children."

"There's no way to be certain, but I'm inclined to believe what Pinzon said."

"And this is happening because you lost your temper. How many times have I talked to you about your temper, Joe?"

"That isn't fair."

"We can't use our phones?"

"I don't want to risk it."

"Jack and Lilly need to be picked up and taken someplace safe. Immediately. Can you make that happen?"

"Jack's in Arizona. Lilly's in Knoxville."

"I know where they are! Can you make it happen? You're the one who put them in danger. Can you get our children to safety?"

I didn't respond to the comment about me putting the kids in danger. On one hand, I knew she was angry and frightened and didn't mean it. On the other, however, I knew she was right. Allowing my anger to overcome my sense of reason had always been a problem for me. I'd tried to control it, but like with Sarah and alcohol, there were times when I just couldn't. And now, as Caroline had just pointed out, I'd allowed my lack of self-control to put my children—not to mention my wife and sister and niece—directly in the crosshairs. If Andres Pinzon was right, we were already the targets of a group of foreign killers, something I would never have dreamed possible.

As soon as we got in the cab, I told the driver to take us to the corner of Highway 36 and Boring Chapel Road.

"Why are we going there?" Caroline said.

"You remember I told you about seeing Leah Turner? She's Leah McCoy now. She and her husband are both FBI agents. If anybody can get to Jack and Lilly quickly, it's the FBI."

It was midnight when we walked onto the McCoy's front porch, but there were a couple lights on. I rang the bell and waited. A few seconds later, Leah was standing in the doorway in a pair of purple pajamas.

"What the heck are you doing here?" she said. "I saw you pass out cold on the news. They said you're in the hospital."

"Listen, Leah, I have a serious problem. Can we come in?"

As we were walking in, an extremely large man came walking down a set of steps that led to the second floor.

"What's going on?" he said in a deep baritone.

"Meet my husband," Leah said. "Mack McCoy, Joe and Caroline Dillard."

We all said hello and Leah led us into the kitchen. She made coffee while I listened to a quick bio from her husband. He was one of those guys that ooze testosterone, a true man's man. He was at least six feet five, broad-shouldered, barrel-chested, and his neck looked as thick as a Brahma bull's. He said he'd been a Navy SEAL for six years, an FBI sniper, and a SWAT team member who was involved in the tragic and infamous David Koresh incident at Waco. He had worked in both Bolivia and Colombia on anti-cartel task forces; was an expert in weapons, explosives, surveillance, and counter-surveillance; and had played an integral part in the largest cocaine bust in the history of the United States. His closely clipped, dark brown hair was sparse atop a chiseled face, and his blue eyes gleamed like they'd just been coated with polyurethane.

Mack said he'd been following the news about the murders of the girls and the witnesses, and I filled him in on all the details, including Pinzon's revelation that Lipscomb wanted my entire family dead. I told him about Jack and Lilly, and he was on the phone immediately. When he hung up, he said, "Done. They'll both be at a hotel with an FBI escort in less than an hour."

"Thank you," Caroline said. "Thank you."

"Anybody else?" Mack said.

"My sister and her daughter are at Caroline's mother's place."

"We'll grab them up too, just to be safe."

"What do you know about *sicarios*?" I asked.

"Vicious, efficient killers. A lot of them are trained by mercenaries, former British SAS guys. They're completely loyal to their employers, and they don't give a tinker's damn about collateral damage."

"How would they get into the country?"

"From what you've told me, this Lipscomb is rich, right?"

"Filthy rich."

"He can smuggle them in through Mexico pretty easily if the money's right, or he may just have them flown in on a private jet."

"Just fly them in? Nobody will stop them?"

"It's a big sky, my friend. There's no way to police every private aircraft and airstrip in the world. Smugglers get billions of dollars worth of dope into the country every year. They're not going to have a problem getting a few guys in. Did this Pinzon give you any names? We might be able to track them through Interpol or NAGDIS."

"He said one of them is called *El Maligno*. He thinks his real name might be Santiago, but he isn't sure."

"Needle in a haystack. Lots of Colombians named Santiago. We'll run the nickname, though. Maybe we'll get a hit."

"So what should I do? Do you have any suggestions?"

"The first thing we need to do is sweep your house, find out if you're really being bugged, and if so, how sophisticated these guys are."

"The sooner the better," I said.

"Would now be soon enough? Hang on just a minute."

He picked up his phone again, and I listened while he convinced someone to come out in the middle of the night. He hung up and said, "We're all set. One of the TTA's is a buddy of mine. He'll be here in half an hour and follow us to your place."

"TTA?" I asked.

"Technically trained agent. Electronics geek. His name is Bernie Cole."

It was nearly one in the morning when we arrived at my house, just a couple hours since Pinzon's visit to the hospital. Leah, Caroline, and I rode with Mack while Bernie Cole, a light-skinned black man who looked to be around thirty-five or so, followed in a green van. Just before we pulled into the driveway, Mack got a call on his cell.

"Everybody's safe, at least for now," he said. "None of them are too happy about it, but they're out of harm's way." I reached over and hugged Caroline, but the phrase "at least for now" echoed inside my head. When would we be safe again? When would this end? *How* would it end?

"Where are the cable and phone boxes?" Mack said as he climbed out of the car.

I pointed to the corner of the garage. "Right behind that bush."

"Is there an attic with outside access?" he said.

I shook my head.

"Crawl space? Anyplace they could hide transmitters?"

"Yeah, I'll show you."

Mack, Bernie, and I walked through the dark to the side of the house, and I pointed out a crawl space beneath the garage.

"Wait here," he said, and he and Bernie, flashlights blazing, disappeared.

I stayed by Mack's car with Caroline and Leah until Mack returned ten minutes later with Bernie right beside him.

"Bad news," Mack said. "He was telling the truth, and it's sophisticated equipment. Top of the line. Some of it may even be original design. Bernie thinks the guys who are watching you are probably ex-bureau or CIA guys, maybe even black baggers."

"Black baggers?"

"Black baggers are agents who specialize in breaking into places and installing surveillance equipment. Nobody ever sees them. Not many people even know they exist."

"They must be good if they got past my German shepherd," I said. "What about the phones?"

"The land line is tapped. If I were you, I'd operate under the assumption that they're good enough at what they do to listen to your cell phone calls. How do you want to play this?"

"What do you mean?"

"There are cameras and video transmitters, so if we go in, they'll know it. We can either dismantle everything, or we can go back under the house and figure out exactly what's there without them seeing or hearing us and without disturbing anything. It just depends on whether you want them to know you're onto them. If they don't know you're onto them, maybe you can figure out a way to use the equipment against them."

"Leave it for now," I said, not really knowing why. I stood there for a minute while the four of them looked at me, waiting for me to say something else. Finally, I said, "What do we do next?"

"You need to figure something out," Mack said.

"What's that?"

"Where you're going to hide your family until this thing is over."

CHAPTER THIRTY-THREE

Caroline and I took turns driving the van we rented, and I managed to sleep for a couple hours. We'd picked up Sarah and Gracie and Melinda—Caroline's mother—and driven the rest of the night and the following morning. It took us just under eleven hours to get to O'Hare airport in Chicago. There we met Jack and Lilly, both of whom had been put on planes by FBI agents at the airports in Knoxville and Phoenix, and got back into the van. I explained what was going on while I drove east around the southern tip of Lake Michigan. Their reactions were what I expected—shock followed by anger followed by frustration. The bizarre circumstances had caused them to drop their lives. The FBI agents who picked them up had asked them to throw their cell phones away and not communicate with anyone until we picked them up in Chicago. Nobody knew where they were; it was as if they'd dropped off the face of the earth.

At Mack's instruction, we'd left town without talking to anyone. I bought two prepaid cell phones at a convenience store just before we left, called Mack, and gave him the numbers in case he needed to get a hold of Caroline or me. He said the kids could use the phones to notify whomever they needed to notify that they would be gone for a while. I handed mine to Lilly, knowing she would want to call Randy.

"Tell him you're safe, and that's it. Don't tell him where you are, where you're going, or why you left. The less he knows the better. Just tell him you'll be back as soon as you can."

"I can't believe we're going to hide like a bunch of cowards," Jack said.

"You didn't see what was sitting in front of the house yesterday morning," I said, "and you don't know what we're up against. These people have their own set of rules. It's something I can barely comprehend."

"So we're just going to sit in the woods and wait for the FBI to call?"

"No. You're going to sit in the woods and wait for *me* to call. Once I get you settled, I'm going back."

The amount of equipment the FBI tech agents found was mind-boggling. I got periodic reports from Mack via the cell phone. Tiny, high-resolution cameras that were capable of transmitting to a laptop computer in real time had been installed in every room in our house, along with a dozen miniature microphones that were so sensitive that Mack said whoever was listening could hear the dog scratching himself. GPS trackers and microphones had been installed in my truck and Caroline's car. Mack called in more TTAs who swept my office and then went to Bates's home and office. Everything was bugged. They'd been listening to every conversation and watching every move Bates and I had made since Nelson Lipscomb was arrested.

The more the agents discovered, the more naked and exposed I felt, and the angrier I became. Whoever they were, ex-CIA, ex-FBI, ex-military, they had invaded Caroline and me completely. I could imagine them watching me change the dressing on her wound, listening to our most intimate words, amusing themselves at our expense, and reporting everything to John Lipscomb, the master puppeteer. Lipscomb was probably plugged in himself, taking perverted pleasure in his god-like power. He'd used his money to kill three people—including his own brother—and effectively destroy the legal case against him. I had to do something to stop him.

I hadn't seen Bo Hallgren in five years, but I considered him to be my closest friend. Bo and I met at Fort Benning, Georgia, when we were just kids. Both of us had volunteered for the U.S. Army Rangers. We went through Ranger school and jump school together, were both assigned to the First Battalion of the Seventy-Fifth Ranger Regiment, and roomed together at Fort Stewart for two years. We wore each other's clothes, ate each other's food, and drank each other's beer. When I jumped onto the airfield at Point Salines in Grenada in 1983 with gunfire blazing from the ground below, Bo Hallgren went out the door right behind me. We'd experienced the same hardships and witnessed the same horrors, and I didn't think there was anybody better suited to watch out for my family.

After I was discharged from the Army, Bo stayed on. He spent twenty years in the Rangers. By the time he retired, he'd fought all over the globe, and he never received a scratch. He'd written to me occasionally and had stopped by to see me when he passed through Tennessee a decade earlier. He'd moved to a two-hundred-acre farm about fifty miles from Detroit, Michigan, when he left the army, and Caroline, the kids, and I had spent a night there five years earlier when we drove to the Upper Peninsula and stayed at Mackinac Island.

Bo was standing on the front porch of his white farmhouse when we pulled up. He was lean and sturdy, about my height, with short, reddish hair, a craggy face, and brown eyes. A golden retriever was running around the yard.

"Howdy, hillbilly," he said when I stepped out of the van.

We embraced while the band of weary travelers climbed out. Rio and Chico headed straight for the golden retriever, and while they spent a few minutes checking each other out, I looked around the farm.

"Still have the livestock?" I said.

"A hundred and twelve beef cattle, twenty-two pigs, and one horse," he said.

"I thought so. No mistaking that smell."

The morning was crisp and clear, the sky a spotless blue. The house was surrounded by soybean and cornfields that had already been harvested. There was a pond that covered the better part of an acre a hundred yards to my left, and a large patch of woods that stretched over the horizon to the north and south about three hundred yards to my right. The dirt driveway that led to the house was a half-mile long. The place was quiet and isolated, perfect for an old soldier, and a perfect place to hide.

"These troops of yours have grown like garden weeds," Bo said. He was the perfect host, shaking Jack's hand, hugging Caroline, Lilly, Melinda, and Sarah, and commenting on how cute Gracie was. "Come on in," he said. "Lucy can give your dogs the tour out here. I've got food ready. Hope you don't mind breakfast in the middle of the afternoon."

Bo lived alone—he'd never married—and the house was a monument to maleness and military order. It was spotless. There were weapons everywhere: shotguns, rifles, pistols, some of them obviously valuable antiques. There were also heads mounted in every room—deer, elk, bear, and even a wild boar. The smell of bacon filled the place, and I realized I hadn't eaten in a couple days. We walked into a dining room that had a table big enough for all of us to sit, and Bo started serving fried eggs, hash browns, bacon, ham, sausage, biscuits, gravy, even pancakes with maple syrup. It was a feast of fat and cholesterol, and tasted better than anything I'd ever eaten.

When we were finished, Bo offered coffee. I refused politely, went into the den, and sat down on an overstuffed couch. The next thing I knew, I opened my eyes and realized it was six o'clock in the evening. I'd slept for four hours.

I got up and looked around the house. Caroline, Lilly, and Gracie were asleep in a bed upstairs. Sarah and Melinda were watching television in the den. I couldn't find Jack or Bo, and the dogs were gone, so I went outside. I heard banging coming from the barn and walked down a small hill. Bo was beneath a huge combine beating on an axle with a ball-peen hammer. The smell from the pigpen was strong and acidic.

Jack, who was wearing jeans and a Peoria Javelinas T-shirt, was stroking the neck of a beautiful, black horse that was standing inside a large stall. He lifted his chin when he saw me but didn't smile, which was unusual for him. Jack was a good-looking, good-natured kid, dark-haired and dark-eyed, tall and thickly muscled. He'd always been the kind of kid who was willing to stand up for both himself and what he believed in, and I knew hiding out at Bo's wouldn't sit well with him. But I wanted him there not only for his own protection, but to be there in case something happened and Bo needed some help. Jack was good with weapons—he and I had shot a lot of skeet and done a lot of target practicing over the years—and he'd always been fearless, sometimes even a little crazy. There wasn't much I could ever say about it though. The proverbial apple fell right next to the tree.

Bo crawled out from beneath the combine. He was wearing a pair of camouflage coveralls and a military utility cap. He started wiping down the hammer with a rag—the barn was almost as clean as the house—and he put it in a toolbox by the stall.

"Feel better?" he asked.

"I think so, but I need to get on the road."

"So far all you've told me is that your family is in danger and you need a place to hide them," he said. "Give me some details."

I sat down on a bench next to the stall and told Bo everything, from the day the girls' bodies were discovered to our arrival at his place. Jack had heard it all, but I noticed he was listening intently.

"Do you have some kind of plan for dealing with these guys?"

"Not exactly, but I'll figure something out on the way back to Tennessee. We'll probably have to bait them somehow and then arrest them."

Jack, who hadn't said a word, came out of the stall and closed the half-door.

"I thought the man who came to the hospital, Pinzon, said the only way to stop them was to kill them," Jack said.

"I'm not a murderer."

"Let me ask you something," Bo said. "If you have good information that men are coming to kill you and your family and you decide to kill them first, are you really guilty of murder?"

"Preemptive self-defense isn't something the law recognizes as a defense to murder."

"So if you wanted to kill them legally, you'd have to wait for them to come to you."

"Yeah, I guess so. The law says a person can use deadly force, but the language is tricky. I'd have to be in 'reasonable fear' of serious bodily harm or death, and the legal definition of reasonable is indecipherable. Nobody knows what it really means, and I don't have any intention of getting myself into a situation where I might wind up at the mercy of a jury."

"But you're the district attorney, Dad," Jack said. "You're not going to prosecute yourself."

"If I hunt these guys down and kill them, there will be an investigation. I'm not exactly the fair-haired child with the political crowd right now. If the investigation shows that I was on the offensive, they'll get a special prosecutor and charge me with murder. I'm not up for that."

"If you arrest them, how do you know more won't come?" Bo said.

"I don't. As a matter of fact, that's exactly what Pinzon said will happen."

"So you're going to have to kill them," Jack said. "Them and this Lipscomb guy too. What other choice do you have?"

I looked at him for several seconds. "I honestly don't know," I said.

"What a mess," Bo said.

"Let's go back to the house. I need to say goodbye and get back on the road."

"You boys go on ahead. I'll be along in a little while."

Jack and I started walking slowly up the hill. He kept glancing at me, and I knew he had more to say.

"Spit it out," I said.

"I know you," he said. "You're worried about how you'll feel if you have to kill somebody."

"I can't kill anybody, Jack. It's like you said a few minutes ago. I'm the district attorney. I'm supposed to keep order by enforcing the rule of law through the courts, not by violence. And you're right. I *am* worried about how I'd feel if I killed someone. I don't see how I could live with myself."

He was quiet for a little while, but as we were drawing close to the house, he said, "We can't stay here forever. Eventually, we all have to go back. Lipscomb knows that. All he has to do is be patient. If he wants to kill us and he has all this money and power, he can do it. So let me ask you one more question. How would you live with yourself if Lipscomb or these men he's supposedly hired managed to find us and kill us?"

I looked into his eyes, and at that moment, that miniscule tick in time, I knew what I had to do. He didn't have to say another word.

CHAPTER THIRTY-FOUR

illy had made use of Bo's library and was reading in the den when Jack and I walked back into the house. "C'mon," I said to her, and she closed the book and followed us.

Caroline was in the kitchen with Melinda watching Sarah feed Gracie. I stood looking at them for a couple minutes, then I looked at Jack and Lilly, both of whom were standing beside me. This group of six was my family. All of it. I had no grandparents, no cousins, no aunts or uncles, no in-laws. Melinda and I weren't particularly close, but she was my wife's mother, and I felt the same obligation to her that I felt to the rest.

Would I die for them?

The answer was yes.

Would I kill for them?

If I had to.

"I need to get going," I said to Caroline.

"I know," she said without looking up.

Sarah wiped Gracie's face with a napkin, got up from her seat at the table, and walked around to me. She wrapped her arms around my neck in a rare show of affection.

"I want my little girl to be just like my brother," she whispered. "I want her to be brave and strong."

"I'm sorry, Sarah," I said. "I'm sorry you got dragged into this."

"It'll be over soon." She pecked me on the cheek and stepped back.

Caroline was next. She cupped my face in her hands and smiled.

"Come back to me," she said.

I fought to hold back tears and squeezed her tightly.

"I will."

Jack and Lilly gathered close to us and draped their arms over our shoulders. I could hear Lilly sniffling. We stayed locked in an embrace for a long time, none of us wanting to let go, none of us wanting to say goodbye.

"I love you," I said. "I love all of you with all my heart."

"Please let me go with you," Jack said quietly.

"You have to take care of my girls."

I took the deepest breath I'd ever taken in my life and broke away. I hugged Melinda, leaned over and kissed Gracie on the forehead, and walked out the door.

Bo was lingering next to the van. The back doors were open.

"I gathered a few toys for you," he said as I approached.

"Toys?"

"I was active duty for twenty years, hillbilly. You don't think I'd walk away empty-handed, do you? Here, let me show you."

A wooden crate about half the size of a casket was in the back of the van. Bo lifted the lid.

"You remember how to use these, don't you?"

I stared into the crate, wide-eyed. "Are those what I think they are?"

"Yeah, but they're a little different these days."

Bo gave me a brief tutorial on the equipment. I knew all the basics, but there were a couple modern refinements that took only a few minutes to learn. He'd packed the crate with clothing too, and I pulled out a pair of camo utility pants.

"Think they'll fit?" I said.

"Doesn't look like you've gone pork chop on me yet."

"I hope I don't have to use any of this stuff," I said as I started to climb in the van.

"Me, too, but better to have it than not, right?"

"I guess so. Thanks."

I looked toward the house. They were standing on the front porch. I could see that Caroline and Lilly were crying while Jack and Sarah were doing their best to remain stoic. Melinda had stayed inside with Gracie.

"They'll be fine," Bo said. "Don't worry about a thing."

"If something happens to me—"

"Nothing's going to happen to you. You're a Ranger."

"It was a long time ago, Bo."

"Doesn't matter. I remember what you were like when bullets started to fly, and I doubt you've changed. Are you going to have any help when you get back down there?"

"I hope so."

"Sure you don't want me to tag along?"

"It's not your fight, buddy."

"You ought to at least take that shepherd with you."

"Nah, he's my buddy too. I don't want to put him in harm's way."

I started the van and put it in reverse, taking a long, last look at the people on the porch. My eyes started to water again.

"I'll see you soon, hillbilly," Bo said. "Go give 'em hell."

As soon as I got on the road, I dialed Bates's number.

"It's Dillard," I said when he picked up.

"Where are you?"

"Driving. I'm on my way back. We need to get together as soon as I get there and figure out a plan."

"What kind of plan?"

"A plan to deal with this case. To deal with Lipscomb."

"There is no case. Zack Woods and Hector Mejia, your best witnesses, are dead. Nelson Lipscomb is missing in action. It's over."

I noticed he said "your best witnesses" instead of "our best witnesses" and wondered whether he was trying to distance himself. Leon Bates was not only a good sheriff, he was a master politician. He had excellent instincts when it came to figuring out which way the political winds were blowing, and they certainly weren't blowing in my direction.

"You got any idea what's been going on around here while you been off doing whatever it is you're doing?" he said. "The press is going nuts. The politicians are all over me. My office was bugged, my house was bugged, my car was even bugged."

"I know all that, Leon. Pinzon came to see me at the hospital last night. He told me about the surveillance. That's why the FBI came and checked everything out. We have to find a way to make a case on Lipscomb. Otherwise, he's going to—"

"Pinzon told you?"

"Yeah. He told me a lot. He's gone too. He's hiding."

"Then Lipscomb is the last man standing. He's the only one who hasn't run."

"Pinzon didn't run from us. He ran from Lipscomb. And Nelson didn't run either. Pinzon says he's dead."

"You know something, Dillard? I think maybe Pinzon is playing you for a fool."

"Don't be ridiculous. Have you forgotten about the phone call Nelson made from the cruiser? And what about Zack Woods? He identified Lipscomb. Hector saw him get on the boat. He killed those girls, Leon. I know it and you know it. We still have Turtle, and if we can get Lipscomb to trial, I think I can convince Pinzon to testify against him."

"You got no case, counselor. My advice is you get your butt back here and forget any of this ever happened. And you better start shoring up your end on the political side. There are a lot of people calling for your scalp. They—"

"Leon! Listen to me! Pinzon says Lipscomb has hired people to kill me, to kill my entire family."

"Is that a fact? Has it occurred to you that Pinzon might be pulling your chain? He's the Colombian. He's the one that would know how to hire men from Colombia for a hit."

"No, you don't understand. When he came to the hospital, Pinzon told me what happened on the boat. He told me all about his history with John Lipscomb. They dealt drugs together for years. They made millions. Lipscomb knows all about the Colombians. He's closer to them than Pinzon ever was."

"And you believe everything he told you?"

"Yeah, Leon. I do."

"He and Nelson are probably sitting on a beach somewhere drinking fruity rum with little umbrellas in the glass. They're probably laughing at all of us."

"They've gotten to you, haven't they? Who was it? The governor?"

"A lot of people—a lot of powerful people—think you're using Lipscomb as a career builder."

"But you know better, don't you?"

"Doesn't matter. The bottom line here is that this turns out bad for Joe Dillard no matter what. And if I stay with you, it turns out bad for Leon Bates too. You can't prove your case against John Lipscomb. You're going to have to dismiss it, and when you do, the hammer is going to fall. I'm thinking seriously about putting out a press release tomorrow that says I've done my best to be loyal to the district attorney through this entire affair, but that circumstances now lead me to believe that he is engaging in a personal vendetta against John Lipscomb and consequently the sheriff's department will offer no further assistance."

"You're kidding me, right? This is a joke."

"Afraid not. All the signs have been there, but I've been too close. I haven't been able to see the forest for the trees."

"What are you talking about?"

"You start off by treating the governor of the state like a bastard stepchild, then you barge into Lipscomb's office and damned near attack him. You make a decision to indict three men on thin evidence, you insist that they be hauled up here in a prison van, and then you assault Lipscomb at the jail. You top it all off by passing out flat on your face in the courtroom in front of God and everybody, and then you disappear. I may have been blind before, but I see the light now. You're unstable, Dillard. You might even be crazy."

"You know something, Leon?"

"What's that?"

"You're about to find out just how crazy I can be."

CHAPTER THIRTY-FIVE

My next call was to Erlene Barlowe's cell. I asked her to wait for me after her club closed. If I pushed it, I could be there by three in the morning.

I crossed the Tennessee border a little after midnight and rolled into the back parking lot at the Mouse's Tail around 3:00 a.m. I'd called Erlene again ten minutes earlier, and she said she'd be waiting. I'd never been inside the Mouse's Tail, but I had fond memories of that back parking lot. It was there that Erlene had handed me a quarter of a million dollars in a gym bag several years ago—my fee for defending a young friend of hers who had been accused of murder back before I became a prosecutor. I pulled up to the back door and waited less than a minute before I saw her walking out, dressed in a tight, sequined red top with a red boa around her neck, black spandex pants, and spiked heels. She walked up to the driver's side window.

"Are you okay, sugar?" Erlene said. "Last time I saw you, you were face down in the courtroom."

"I'm fine. Can you go for a ride?"

"I thought you'd never ask."

She walked around, climbed in, and I pulled back onto the road.

"Are you sure you're okay?" Erlene said. "What are you doing out at this time of the night?"

"Sit back. It's a long story."

I recounted the story of Pinzon's visit to the hospital, the surveillance at my house, the threats, the Colombian killers who were supposed to be on their way to kill my family, and the trip to Michigan. I also told her everything Pinzon had said about Lipscomb.

"So he killed them," she said. "You're sure of it."

"Afraid so, and it looks like he's going to get away with it. I'll never get him to trial, Erlene, and even if I do, I'll never convict him. He's already killed three girls, two witnesses, and his brother. He's going to try to kill me, and there's a chance he might come after you. I know you didn't see him that night, but you and your bouncer can link Nelson to the girls, and if John thinks it might still get back to him somehow …. I'm not trying to scare you, but it's something you should think about."

"Don't worry about scaring me, sugar. The man I'm afraid of hasn't been born yet."

"Pinzon said the only way to stop Lipscomb is to get rid of him. I don't think I can do it. At least I don't think I could do it and get away with it."

"I don't reckon you could."

"How do you feel about revenge, Erlene?"

She contemplated the question for a few seconds.

"You know, my granddaddy, God rest his soul, used to have these sayings about revenge. He'd say, 'Child, the best revenge is to live well,' or, 'Revenge is a dish best served cold.' But you know something? My granddaddy always reminded me of a cow standing in a field chewing her cud. My granny walked all over him and so did anybody else that took a notion. I never put much stock in the things he said."

"I know what you mean. I've never been one to let people trample on me."

"Me either."

"There's one more thing. It looks like Sheriff Bates has bailed on me. He said he thinks I'm crazy."

She let out a little whistle. "I swan," she said. "I knew that man was more politician than lawman. I reckon I'll have a little surprise for him next time he comes sniffing around here. Maybe a hidden camera."

"Bates? Bates comes out here?"

"You didn't hear that from me, sugar."

"I guess everybody has their secrets."

"What are you planning to do, sweetie?" Erlene said. "I mean, you said your family's all tucked away safe and sound, but you're back here. You're up to something."

Erlene put on the air of a Southern belle—even if the belle was a little on the sleazy side—but I knew what was underneath the façade. She was a tough, intelligent woman who existed on the fringe of lawlessness. During the time leading up to the trial of the friend of hers I defended, a key prosecution witness wound up dead of an apparent drug overdose, but I always suspected Erlene was behind it.

"I'm going to take care of the Colombians myself, but that still leaves Lipscomb. What are the chances of you helping me out with him?"

"You know something? I think somebody John Lipscomb has wronged may just decide to take matters into her own hands. Somebody who knows how to get things done."

"I hope whoever it is acts fast."

She reached across, put her hand on my arm, and squeezed.

"Have faith, baby doll," she said. "It's a powerful thing."

PART III

CHAPTER THIRTY-SIX

A half-hour later, I parked the van in a stand of trees a half mile from the house, got out, and walked around to the back. I opened the crate Bo had given me and pulled out a set of camouflage fatigues, a pair of jungle boots, a black stocking cap, a pair of gloves, a flashlight, and some web gear. I reached back into the crate and grabbed an M16 assault rifle that was equipped with a thermal-imaging sight, four thirty-round clips of ammo, and a sheathed, Yarborough knife. I used electrical tape from the crate to tape the Yarborough to the web gear and clipped the flashlight on. I stuck three of the clips into an ammo pouch, slapped the other one into the receiver, pulled back the charging handle to load a round into the chamber, made sure the safety was engaged, and started walking cross-country through the woods.

It was chilly and there was a stiff breeze. My earlobes began to tingle, so I pulled the stocking cap down farther on my head. It was terrain I'd walked many times, a large tract owned by the Tennessee Valley Authority that was adjacent to my property. I made my way slowly through the darkness, fallen leaves dry and crackling beneath my feet, until I came to the trail that I ran on several times a week. I followed the trail along the bluff above the lake and knelt at the edge of the woods about a hundred yards from the house. I stayed there without moving, listening to every sound, until around 5:00 a.m. The house, with the exception of a couple lights Caroline and I had left on, was dark and still. Nothing stirred—no insects, no animals, no birds, nothing. It was as though I was the only living creature on earth.

I took the prepaid cell out of my pocket and dialed Mack McCoy's phone number.

"I figured you for an early riser," I said when he answered.

"Where are you?"

"In the woods outside my house. Any chance you and Bernie Cole can come out?"

"Be there in an hour."

As the gray light of dawn began to emerge, I started scouring the area around the house, looking for signs that someone had been there: cigarette butts, wrappers, cans, bottles, any type of trash that might indicate surveillance. I looked for depressions in the grass and weeds, especially on the higher ground, but found nothing that alarmed me. It appeared that the *sicarios* hadn't arrived yet. I wondered about what Bates had said to me on the phone. Maybe I *was* crazy. Maybe Pinzon was the killer and had hatched an extravagant plot to extricate himself from the murders. Maybe there weren't any *sicarios*. Maybe no one was coming. Maybe Pinzon had tried to force me into hiding to buy himself some time.

I heard vehicles approaching on the road and looked down the hill. Mack McCoy's car was in the lead, followed by the van Bernie Cole had driven the other day. I took the web gear off, set it down next to a tree stump, and laid the M16 beside it. I came out of the woods just as Mack and Leah were getting out of the car at the top of the driveway. Both of them reached for their weapons. I held my hands up.

"It's me! It's Dillard!"

"Damn, son, have you looked at yourself in a mirror lately?" Mack said as I approached. "You look rough."

I hadn't bathed or shaved in two days.

"Did you get everybody squared away?" Mack said.

"Yeah, they're safe. They're with an old friend on a farm in the middle of nowhere in Michigan."

"What are you doing dressed up like GI Joe?" he said.

"I spent the last few hours out here watching the house. I was afraid someone might be in there, but nothing's moved so far. I've been walking the property since dawn looking to see if anybody's been around, but I didn't find a thing." I looked at Bernie Cole, who had gotten out of the van and walked up next to Mack. "I need to know exactly what's in the house, and I need to know if there's a way to disable it."

"Disable it?" Bernie said.

"Shut it off completely."

"That's easy. They're using your power supply. All you have to do is flip the main circuit breaker and cut the power to the house. Everything but the phone tap goes dead."

"You've missed quite a circus around here the past couple days," Mack said. "The media's on a feeding frenzy. You should see the story in the paper this morning, what the sheriff is saying. He's telling everybody you've come unhinged."

"I know. I talked to him yesterday. What do you think? You think I'm a nut case?"

"I might if it wasn't for Leah. She's said a lot of good things about you. If I wasn't so secure in my masculinity, I might be jealous."

I looked at Leah, who was still standing on the passenger side of the car. She winked at me and shrugged her shoulders.

"I was with Pinzon for more than an hour at the hospital," I said to Mack. "I saw how he acted. I've misread people before, but I don't think he was lying. Lipscomb is responsible for the murders of the girls, and he's behind the murders of Zack Woods and Hector Mejia. I think he had his brother killed too."

"You're probably right," Mack said. "I've checked into some of the things you told me before you left. The girl in Boston, Mallory Vines, checks out. She was reported missing and was never seen again. And the other guy, Tex. His name was probably William Rogan, reported missing from Grand Prairie, Texas. His parents had been killed in an automobile accident, he was a student at SMU, and he went by the nickname of Tex. Never a sign of him after he got on a flight to Boston."

I breathed a sigh of relief. "Good. I guess that's good."

"There's more," he said. "You want the good news or the bad news first?"

"Guess I could use a little good news about now."

"We got a hit on the *El Maligno* nickname you gave me. He's worked for Eduardo Pinzon for twenty years.

Eduardo Pinzon just happens to be Andres Pinzon's uncle."

"Right. That's what he said. 'Uncle Eduardo.'"

"First name is Santiago. Last name is Guzman. Has a nasty scar on his left cheek just like you said."

"So you can track him?"

"That's the bad news. I called an old buddy in Colombia and asked him if they could get eyes on this guy. They know him well. They know where he lives, where he hangs out. They should have been able to find him, but they couldn't."

"Which means?"

"It could mean he took a vacation to Guadalajara or Rio de Janeiro or someplace."

"Or it could mean—"

"Right. He's on his way up here, but that isn't the worst of it. My Colombian buddy told me that *El Maligno* is responsible, directly or indirectly, for at least a hundred and fifty murders. He and his boys blew up a plane in Colombia with over a hundred people on it back in ninety-eight. They were trying to kill a Colombian presidential candidate, but the guy got cold feet and didn't take the flight. This *El Maligno* tracked him down and shot him in his car two days later. Killed his wife and daughter, too. He's a bad, bad hombre."

We stood outside the house for more than an hour. Bernie showed me a rough diagram he'd drawn of the devices that were in the house and explained what areas they covered while Leah and Mack milled around impatiently. The video cameras were everywhere, even in the garage, and the microphones, at least theoretically, would pick up every word uttered—even whispers— from anywhere inside.

"There's nothing outside?" I asked Bernie. "Did you check the workshop out back?"

"I checked everywhere," he said. "Didn't find a thing."

"Just what are you planning?" Mack said. He'd walked up behind Bernie and was hovering over his shoulder. Leah stayed a good distance away. She was looking out over the lake, acting like she was interested in what she was seeing. I remembered Leah as a strong, independent, sometimes domineering woman, but she'd obviously met her match in Mack.

"I have something in mind," I said.

"What can we do to help?"

"I don't think you should be here."

"Why not?"

"Because I don't have a lot of choices."

"Meaning?"

"Look, I've only known you for a few days. You weren't in on the beginning of this, and I don't think you want to be around for the end. If this *El Maligno* comes, someone is going to die here. If the media and the government and Bates and everybody else think I'm crazy now, what's it going to look like if there's a gun battle on my property? Even if I make it out alive, there are going to be some serious repercussions."

"Yeah, well, chances are you won't make it out alive if you try to do this alone," Mack said.

"This case—this *situation*—has been like a hurricane. It started small and now it's grown into something uncontrollable, something deadly. You and Leah just transferred here. You need to think about your own careers, about your reputations. If they come, I'll be lucky to live, and if I do live, I'll be lucky to stay out of jail. There are people on both sides of this that would like to see me dangling from the end of a rope. So you guys need to distance yourself from me. What do the politicians call it? Plausible deniability?"

Mack put his hands on his hips and took a couple steps in my direction. I'm not a small man, but he dwarfed me. Being in his presence was like standing in front of Zeus.

"I think maybe I like you, Dillard," he said. "You know why? Because I'm not some run-of-the-mill, dipstick FBI agent, and you're not some run-of-the-mill, dipstick prosecutor. I wish you were in the U.S. attorney's office. You and I could get some things done."

I smiled for the first time in days.

"Tell you what," I said, "I'll make a deal with you. You have other work to do, right? Go do it. My plan, if you can call it that, is to go inside and let them see me on the video equipment so they know I'm here. After that, I'm planning to sit out in the woods, watching, until they come, *if* they come. So here's the deal. If you'll agree not to tell anyone I'm here, if you'll just let me handle this my way, I'll agree to call you the second I see something that looks like it might be bad. And if I call you, I'll expect you to come running."

He regarded me intently with those brilliant blue eyes for a few seconds. He was trying to read my mind, to decide whether or not I was lying.

"Deal," he said, "but I want to know what kind of weapons you have."

"A shotgun and a pistol. They're both in the house. I think I have three double-ought buckshot shells for the shotgun and some bird shot. I have maybe fifteen rounds for the pistol. I'm not prepared to fight a war with anyone."

"Is that it? A shotgun and a pistol? I don't know exactly what kind of firepower these guys will bring if they come, but it'll damn sure be more than a shotgun and a pistol."

"Maybe. Probably."

"You're going to get yourself killed, Dillard."

"You were a SEAL," I said, "a professional soldier. Which enemy is the most dangerous, the enemy you least wanted to fight?"

He thought for a minute before he started nodding his head.

"The man who's defending his own home."

"And that's what you're looking at. This ground we're standing on, that house, those buildings, this is my home. My wife and I built a life here, we raised our children here, and now John Lipscomb has taken it from us. He's taken our lives, and I don't intend to let it stay that way. If he sends soldiers, *sicarios*, hit men, assassins—whatever you want to call them—if he sends them here, I'm going to kill them."

"And when Lipscomb hires more? You going to kill them too?"

I thought of the conversation I'd had with Erlene. She'd gotten the message. I had no doubt she had her own people working on doing the same thing to Lipscomb that he'd been doing to others.

"I don't think Lipscomb will hire any more," I said.

"Why would you think that?"

"Just call it a hunch. I think Lipscomb's train is about to run off the tracks."

CHAPTER THIRTY-SEVEN

After Mack and Leah left, I walked back through the woods to the van and curled up underneath a poncho. I slept restlessly for a few hours, terrified by a nightmare, one in which Caroline, Lilly, and Sarah were being gang-raped by men wearing black hoods. I'd been gagged and tied to a chair, my eyelids taped open, and I was being forced to watch helplessly. Jack was in another chair across the room, his throat cut and his tongue pulled out through the wound. The sound of John Lipscomb's laughter boomed through the scene while the men sweated and grunted and brutalized the women in my life. I woke up just as the man who was raping Caroline raised a knife to her throat.

I changed back into the clothes I'd been wearing the day before, started the van, drove it around to my workshop, and unloaded the crate Bo had given me. I cut several two-by-fours that were lying in a pile into four-foot lengths and used a cordless drill to bore two holes into each end. As soon as I was finished, I drove the van back to the hiding place and for the third time walked through the woods to the house. I opened the front door with my key and stepped inside.

I don't think it had ever been so quiet inside the house. I walked through each room, looking around, trying to act like I didn't know I was being watched. I went into the kitchen and fixed myself a sandwich, sat down at the kitchen table, and ate it slowly.

I spent the better part of the next two hours convincing myself that setting an ambush with the intention of killing men wasn't wrong. I thought about Osama bin Laden and the terror he'd inflicted on an entire nation, a nation in which I'd been raised, a nation of laws. How did we react? We went hunting for blood, just as we should have. It took ten years, but we finally killed that miserable coward.

John Lipscomb was no different in my mind. He was a criminal and a terrorist, a murderer of defenseless young women as well as a coward who hired others to do his killing. The difference was that I knew his men were coming, and I knew where they were most likely to strike.

A thought popped into my head as I recalled the conversation I'd had with Bo Hallgren in his barn. I walked over to a drawer in the kitchen and took out a pen and a small notebook. I set the notebook on the table in front of me, opened it, and wrote down the words "reasonable fear."

Was I in reasonable fear of seriously bodily harm?

Damned right I was.

Would the law allow me to use deadly force?

If they came to my house, the answer was yes. A man's home is still his castle in the eyes of the law.

I finished nibbling on the sandwich and started gathering things: photographs, an old wedding album, a cedar chest full of memories, and I carried it all to the outbuilding. I didn't know what was going to happen, but I knew with what I was planning there was a possibility that a fire might start. If it did and I couldn't put it out, I didn't want some of the things Caroline and I cherished to burn.

On my last trip to the workshop, it started sprinkling. A clap of thunder startled me, and I looked to the southwest, the direction from which most of our weather came. A huge, black thunderhead was rolling across the mountains, moving steadily in my direction. I picked up Bo's crate and carried it to the corner of the house, just outside the garage, as the sky grew steadily darker. I went back to the workshop one last time, gathered up the two-by-fours, the drill, and some four-inch wood screws, and carried it all to the crate.

I walked inside the house again. Bernie Cole had made me a diagram, so I knew where the cameras were. I was so geared for a fight that I wanted to walk up directly in front of a camera and say, "Here I am. Come and get me," but I resisted the impulse. I could hear the wind whistling outside. I walked down the steps to the basement and flipped the main circuit breaker.

The house went black.

I hurried back upstairs and out through the garage. I made two trips carrying the crate, the lumber, the screws, and the drill into the house. I changed quickly back into the fatigues, boots, and web gear, smeared some camo paint on my face, and went to work.

There were five doors into the house: one in the kitchen that led to the deck, one in the den that led to the deck, one in Jack's old room downstairs that led to the patio, one in the kitchen that led to the garage, and the front door. I barricaded the two doors that came off the deck and the door to Jack's room by screwing three two-by-fours into the door frames on the inside. I left the other two doors—the front door and the door from the garage to the kitchen—unlocked.

I opened the crate and started pulling out the real toys Bo had given me: claymore mines. Claymores are roughly the size of a thick, hardback book, and they weigh only about three and a half pounds. The outer shell is green and made of plastic. They're convex in shape, about eight inches long, five inches high, and a little less than two inches wide with the words "Front Toward Enemy" stamped into the front panel. They're filled with seven hundred steel balls, each about an eighth of an inch in diameter. The balls are held together by an epoxy resin and propelled by a C-4 explosive charge.

I'd used claymores when I was a Ranger. They're deadly, but the best thing about them is that they can be aimed in a particular direction. They don't send shrapnel flying three hundred sixty degrees like other conventional land mines. They have a sight on the top so that a soldier can aim them. They'll spread the steel balls about sixty degrees at fifty yards away. I didn't need a sixty-degree spread though. My prey was going to be in a much more confined area.

I placed one claymore about fifteen feet from the front door and another about fifteen feet from the door that went from the garage to the kitchen. I camouflaged both of them by covering them with dark towels. There are several ways to detonate claymores, but Bo had given me four laser triggers, the latest improvement in the technology, and I set the beams so that anyone who walked four feet inside the doors would be met by a hail of ball bearings traveling at four thousand feet per second. I set one in the den and one at the top of the stairs that led to Lilly's room—places where an intruder who entered through a window was most likely to walk. As soon as I was finished, I pulled the M16, the ammo, the knife, the flashlight, and a poncho out of the crate, pushed it into the garage, and went outside into the storm.

When I got to the place where I planned to spend the night watching, I took the cell phone out of my pocket and texted a message to Caroline: "All is well. Talk in morning. I love you." I turned the phone off and sat back to wait.

I certainly didn't plan it when the house was being built, but building on the bluff above the lake gave me at least a bit of a tactical advantage. If someone wanted to sneak up and try to get inside, they couldn't do it from the lake side because of the sheer rock cliffs. That meant they would have to come through the woods or walk across an open field on the opposite side of the house. They could come directly down from the road, but I didn't think they'd be that lazy.

I'd been over it dozens of times in my mind in the past twenty-four hours. From which direction were they most likely to come? I didn't know how sophisticated their weapons or their equipment would be. Would they have night-vision devices like the scope I had? Would they have grenades or rockets? Were they planning on destroying the house and anyone in it? From what Pinzon had told me, I thought they most likely wanted to take me alive, if at all possible, so they could torture me or force me to watch my family die. They might even want to take me to Lipscomb so he could derive some pleasure at my expense.

The weather was both a blessing and a curse. It would help me move silently, but it would do the same for them. I'd walked up to the same rise where I was standing when Leah and Mack arrived that morning. It gave me a clear view of three sides of the house. I couldn't see what was going on in back, but I didn't believe they'd come from there. I spent the next four hours lying on my belly, peering through the thermal sight and listening. Five vehicles passed on the road below me at different times during my wait, and each one set my heart racing.

The rain slacked off to a drizzle a little after midnight. I could hear the low rumblings of thunder as the storm glided off to the east. I lay there for another hour as doubt began to eat at me, and I began to tell myself I was a fool. Around one, I heard the sound of another vehicle coming down the road, but this was different, louder.

I rose up and looked in that direction. There were three vehicles driving toward me. As they passed the driveway, they slowed ever so slightly, and something told me it was about to begin.

Three vehicles? I wondered how many people were in them. I thought briefly about the promise I'd made to Mack McCoy to call him. I turned the phone on and noticed my hands were trembling. I told myself to calm down and changed my mind. It was me against them. There would be no cavalry.

The vehicles had driven off into the darkness to the west, and I waited for them to return, telling myself to breathe deeply, to rely on the training I'd received so long ago, to remain steady in the confusion, the noise, the chaotic terror of men trying to kill each other. I thought about Caroline and Jack and Lilly and what I was willing to sacrifice for them and their safety. The answer, as it had always been, was everything. I listened for the sound of a vehicle, thinking they might turn off their lights, approach slowly, and park close by so they could get in and out fast. Nothing. Maybe the vehicles had been a group returning from a party or a bar, maybe a bunch of kids.

And then I saw the first *sicario.*

In the thermal sight, he was glowing like he was beneath a black light, approaching slowly from the northwest. They'd apparently driven a ways past my place and then walked back. He was carrying a rifle. I not only felt my heart pounding, I could hear it.

Th-thump. Th-thump.

A couple seconds later, I saw another image, then another, then another, and then another.

Th-thump. Th-thump. Th-thump. Th-thump.

I waited several seconds, panning them as they walked across the field that abutted my property and into the yard on the west side of the house.

Five of them.

I started crawling.

CHAPTER THIRTY-EIGHT

Two of the men moved around the front of the house and stepped up onto the porch. One of them knelt at the door while the other hung back a few feet. By this time, I'd crawled to within a hundred feet of them, beneath a holly bush Caroline had planted a couple days after my mother died. I couldn't make out what they were doing. I couldn't even see them without looking through the infrared scope.

I expected them to try the unlocked door and walk through, but a few seconds later, they ran off the porch and there was a loud explosion. They'd blown the door open, probably with a small C-4 charge. A half second later, I heard another explosion that came from around back. They'd coordinated their attack. I'd barricaded the door in back, but there was no way a few pine two-by-fours would stand up to plastic explosive. I cursed myself for underestimating them.

I could have shot the two in the front, but I waited, hoping they'd go inside. They crept back onto the porch, and through the scope, I saw one of them toss something through the opening where the door had been. There was another explosion, a flash-bang grenade, and they rushed in. Less than a second after they cleared the doorway, the first claymore exploded and I knew they were dead. Two down.

I panned the thermal scope to a man who'd been squatting next to a spruce tree near the driveway. He moved backward several yards to a pin oak for better cover. I put the crosshairs on the side of his head and squeezed the trigger. He crumpled and lay motionless.

Three down. Two left.

They were most likely inside, coming up the steps from Jack's room toward the kitchen. The claymores I'd set didn't cover that part of the house. I could wait to see if they stumbled into one and blew themselves up, or I could go in and try to kill them myself. I flipped the selector switch on the M16 to full-automatic and ran for the front door.

As I cleared the doorway, the smell of C-4, blood, and intestinal fluid filled my nostrils. I stepped on one of the men who'd been hit by the mine and nearly fell. I flipped the flashlight on for just a couple of seconds and pointed it at the men who'd rushed the front of the house. They were bloody corpses. The front entrance had been decimated, but there were no fires. I squatted next to the stairs that led up to Lilly's room—less than five feet from the stairs that led down to Jack's—and shouldered the M16, listening for a creak, anything. A few seconds later, I heard a faint sound. They were coming up the stairs. I peered through the scope. One of them appeared in a half crouch.

I opened up on him and tracked the weapon to my right and down, firing a dozen shots through the sheetrock wall in less than a second. I heard several thumps, but I didn't move. I stayed there for almost a minute, listening, the barrel of the M16 still pointed at the doorway. The rain outside had stopped. The wind had died down. The house was completely still. The last two men were dead on the staircase. They had to be.

I stood and eased my way to the opening, keeping the weapon trained in front of me. I flipped on the flashlight. The two men were lying on top of each other on the landing below. One of them groaned, and I started cautiously down the steps. I pressed on the carotid of the man who was on top but felt nothing. I grabbed his collar and rolled him to the side. The man beneath was breathing laboriously. I knelt next to him. His eyes were open, and he looked at me.

"*Ayudame,*" he whispered. "*Ayduame.*"

"I don't know what you're saying."

"Mother of God, help me." The English was so heavily accented I could barely understand.

I took the knife out of its sheath and cut the black fatigue shirt he was wearing down the front. There were three small entry wounds from the M16 rounds: one just above his collar bone on the left side at the base of his neck, another a couple inches from his left nipple near his armpit, and a third in his abdomen, about three inches beneath his sternum. All three wounds were bleeding, but the wound above his collar bone was lethal. Dark blood was spurting from it with every beat of his heart.

I set the M16 down next to me, sliced a piece of fabric from his shirt, balled it up in my hand, and started applying pressure to the wound in his neck. His eyes hadn't left my face.

"Are you the lawyer?" he said.

"You're dying," I said as his eyelids fluttered. "Make your peace."

The corners of his lips turned up slightly.

"So are you," he said.

I saw a flash of white light as something crashed into the back of my head, and then there was nothing.

CHAPTER THIRTY-NINE

Five men had walked through the field to the house. Four had gone on the attack while one stayed back. The claymores took two of them, and I'd killed two more on the stairwell. I'd put a bullet in the head of the man outside, and when I killed him, I thought he was probably *El Maligno*, the boss, supervising his little raid from afar.

I was wrong.

I looked around, straining to see in the darkness. There was a sharp pain at the base of my skull where I'd been struck by something, probably a rifle or pistol butt, and my head felt like it was being squeezed in a vice. I was sitting up, but I couldn't move. A beam of a light came on and shined directly into my face.

"Ah, so you're finally awake," a voice said from behind the beam. It was a deep baritone, accented, although not as thickly as the man on the stairs. "I was afraid I might have hit you too hard, maybe put you into a coma. That would have been too bad."

It was then that I realized why I couldn't move. I'd been taped to a chair, just like Zack and Hector, with a board running up the middle of my back.

"This is a nice place," the voice said. "Look at all the damage you've done. You should be ashamed."

My first instinct was to ask him who he was, but I knew. Footsteps approached and the light came closer. He stopped less than a foot in front of me and knelt. He held the flashlight beneath his chin, pointing upward. It was a macabre image: a long, thin jaw, flat nose, and black eyes. His lips curled into a smile.

"This is the last face you'll ever see."

I saw the scar. It was him. It was *El Maligno*.

"Where is your wife? Your son and daughter? You can't save them. I've been given my instructions. I've been paid. They can't hide forever, you know. As a matter of fact, I feel certain they'll come to your funeral, and when they do, I'll be waiting. Señor Lipscomb wanted you to watch them die, but that doesn't seem possible now."

He stood up and backed away. A few seconds later, he said, "Smile," and there was a flash.

"He wants photos," *El Maligno* said.

I struggled against the tape, but it was useless. It was like I'd been laced into a full-body straightjacket.

"I'm wondering about you," he said. "I've killed so many. It's interesting to see how people react when they know they're going to die, that all hope is lost. Some beg, some pray. Most of them soil themselves. Some try to be brave, but in the end, they cry. How about you? Will you cry?"

"I'll hunt you down in hell."

"Ah, defiance! Excellent! Would you like to know what I'm going to do to you? I'm going to cut your throat, but I'm going to do it slowly. Shallow incisions.

I'll probably have to make three, maybe four of them before I get to the jugular. I'll be taking photographs along the way for Mr. Lipscomb's enjoyment. When I cut the jugular, I'm going to stand here and watch you bleed out. And then I'm going to cut your tongue out and take it to Señor Lipscomb as a souvenir."

I heard the click of a folding knife and suddenly, my mind began to take me to another place. I was barely conscious of the maniac approaching me. I felt at peace, almost serene. I saw Caroline in a white dress, standing on a beach next to a calm, clear ocean inlet. Her back was to me, and a soft, warm breeze was lifting her hair ever so slightly. She turned to me, smiling, and waved.

"I'm coming," I said.

Something cold and sharp pressed against my neck.

There was a flash of bright light and the room seemed to explode. Caroline dissolved as the flashlight *El Maligno* was carrying dropped to the floor.

I became aware of someone to my right. Another flashlight beam illuminated a body on the floor at my feet. Then someone was kneeling. A hand reached out and pressed fingers into the flesh of *El Maligno's* neck. I recognized the shape of a cowboy hat.

"He's dead," a voice said.

It was the most welcome voice I'd ever heard, and it belonged to Leon Bates.

CHAPTER FORTY

I wanted to leave, to get straight back to Caroline and the kids, but I stuck around while Leon and his people did what they had to do. Before long, the place was crawling with sheriff's department investigators, deputies, and emergency medical people. I gave a written statement to Rudy Lane while deputies and investigators tagged and bagged evidence and the medical folks carted away the bodies. Bates gave Rudy a written statement too, which reassured me. He also showed Rudy a digital camera that El Maligno had been carrying.

"There's a photo of brother Dillard on this camera," Bates said. "I'm not gonna show it to you because I don't think he'd want anybody to see it. If anybody questions how we handle this investigation, it'll be my hole card."

It was good to know that Leon was back on my side. If anyone could keep the politicians at bay, it was him.

After I talked to Rudy, I went into the bathroom and took the longest shower of my life. I dressed and walked around the inside of the house surveying the damage. The front entrance was destroyed and so was the entrance in back where they'd blown the door. The claymore had torn up a couple walls and shattered three windows. I'd put a dozen holes in the sheetrock by the stairwell leading to the basement. The bodies were gone, but there was still blood all over the place. It was pretty bad, but it was fixable. I figured it would take in the neighborhood of ten thousand dollars to get it back to where it was. I was so punchy that I actually wondered for a second whether my homeowner's policy might cover the damage. I looked out the front window and saw news vans parked about a hundred yards up the road. Somebody had already leaked the story. By daybreak, dozens of gawkers were standing in the road like a herd of cattle.

Mack and Leah McCoy showed up about the same time the reporters began arriving. I was sitting in the kitchen drinking a cup of coffee when Mack strode into the room and stopped five feet away from me. I'd taken a half dozen aspirin by that time and my head was still pounding. He folded his arms across his massive chest and glowered at me.

"You lied to me," he said.

"Not exactly. It happened fast, Mack."

"That's not what I'm talking about. It's obvious you didn't need my help, but from the looks of this place and from what I've already heard, you had more than a shotgun and a pistol."

It was the second time he'd made me smile.

"You're right. I lied."

"You know something? I always thought the Rangers were overrated. I guess maybe I was wrong."

"Wow, Mack, I'll bet you don't say that often."

"So what about your wife and kids? You said they're in Michigan. When are they coming back?"

I'd called Caroline and told her, without giving her many details, that I was okay and that I thought it might be over. She wanted to get Bo to take everyone straight to Detroit so they could fly home, but I told her to sit tight. There was one more thing I needed to confirm.

"Not yet," I said to Mack. "I have to talk to someone first."

I texted Erlene Barlowe a couple hours later. I was surprised she responded immediately since her club didn't close until three in the morning. She was up, though, and agreed to meet me at the edge of a Walmart parking lot in Colonial Heights. She pulled up in her red Mercedes and motioned for me to get into her car, so I climbed in the passenger side. She was wearing a black-and-white, cheetah-print blouse with a plunging neckline and her usual black, spandex pants. She smelled like incense and cinnamon. She drove out of the parking lot and pulled onto Highway 36.

"They're talking about you on the radio, sugar," she said.

"What are they saying?"

"Must have been some gunfight. They're making it sound like the OK Corral."

"Yeah, it was pretty intense."

"They're saying the sheriff was involved."

"He showed up out of nowhere," I said. "I don't know when and I don't know why, but if he hadn't, I'd be dead."

She looked over and gave me a coy smile.

"Leon's a good boy," she said, "but like any man, he needs a little guidance now and then."

"What do you mean, a little guidance?"

"He just needed a little talking to is all. Leon forgets sometimes what's really important in life. He gets too involved in all that political mess, worries too much about what people think. I just reminded him what a good friend you've been. I reminded him how you stood up for him in front of that judge a few years back and how you let him take the credit when that awful Satan worshipper got killed and—"

"Wait just a second," I said. "How could you possibly know about that?"

She winked at me, the smile still on her lips.

"You and Leon?" I said. "How long? How serious is it?"

"A Southern girl doesn't kiss and tell, sweetie."

I shook my head in disbelief. Leon Bates and Erlene Barlowe. Damn. Truth really was stranger than fiction.

"So you're the reason he showed up?"

"I wouldn't put it exactly like that," she said, "but then again, maybe I would. I suppose my influence had something to do with him keeping a close eye on you last night. You know what he told me? He said you're the bravest man he's ever known. One of the smartest too. He said those boys that came gunning for you didn't have a chance. He also said he didn't feel the slightest bit of remorse over shooting that last man—what did he call him? El Malarkey or something like that. He said he didn't feel a bit bad about shooting that man in the head. Said he'd do it again in a skinny minute."

I chuckled at the thought of Bates using the phrase "skinny minute."

"You've already talked to him then," I said. "You guys must be pretty close."

"Stop it, sugar. I'm not going to reveal any intimate details. All I'll say is that the sheriff and I have formed a mutual respect for each other."

Mutual respect. She was priceless.

"What about John Lipscomb?" I said.

Her eyes tightened just a tick and her voice took on a more serious tone.

"I'm not going to say much about him either, but I'll tell you just a couple things. First, you don't have to worry about him anymore. And second, I'm told he peed his pants and cried like a baby."

"So it's over?"

She nodded.

"My girls can rest in peace now, and you can go ahead and tell your family it's safe to come back home. John Lipscomb is in hell where he belongs."

By that time, Erlene had pulled onto I-81 and was now taking the ramp to I-26, headed south toward Johnson City and Erwin.

"Where are we going?" I said.

"John Lipscomb isn't the only person in the world who has money," she said. "I've got a beautiful place in the mountains over by Asheville. It's less than an hour away. I have a private chef who is fixing us a lunch fit for a king. There'll be wine and champagne and fancy fixin's all over the place. We're going to have us a little victory celebration."

"Just me and you?"

"Leon's meeting us there, sugar. It'll be fun."

CHAPTER FORTY-ONE

The clock on the courtroom wall read 9:02 a.m.
It was a Tuesday morning and Judge Adams had just
entered. He was holding what he called a "miscellaneous day," a session of court that involved the judge
taking a few pleas, hearing a couple motions, and asking
about the status of upcoming trials. It was a slow day by
criminal court standards. There were only thirty cases
on the docket. The gallery was less than half-full. There
were no reporters or cameras. I wouldn't normally have
been in the courtroom. Tanner Jarrett usually handled
miscellaneous days in Judge Adams's court. But I had an
announcement, one that I had shared with exactly two
people: my wife and Leon Bates.

It had been less than two weeks since the battle with the
Colombians. None of the men I killed had any identification on them, nor did *El Maligno*, the murderer whose
brains were blown out by Leon Bates. Mack McCoy leaked
information about him to the media though, which helped
solidify the notion that what I'd done was at least under-
standable. There was a huge blitz that lasted about a week.
There were newspaper stories, television stories, Internet

stories. Reporters tried to get in contact with me, but I refused to indulge them. They lingered outside my home until I finally turned Rio loose on them. Talking heads pontificated on television, discussing the morality and the legality of what I'd done. I didn't pay much attention.

And then, like all big stories, it fizzled out.

My family arrived at the Tri-Cities airport a few hours after the lunch I shared with Erlene Barlowe and Bates. It was obvious that the two of them had developed far more than the "mutual respect" Erlene had mentioned. They acted like a couple of love-struck teenagers. The kids hung around for a couple days, but then Jack went back to Arizona to continue his baseball career, and Lilly went back to Knoxville to finish out the semester. Sarah swore the experience had sobered her enough that she didn't need to go to rehab. I was skeptical, but given the circumstances, I let it slide.

Caroline and I made love as soon as we managed some privacy. And then we made love again, and again. I couldn't get enough of her. It was intense, and it was beautiful.

Andres Pinzon came out of hiding a week after the gunfight and was running Equicorp. John Lipscomb had disappeared without a trace. Most people thought he'd run away to escape prosecution for the murders of the three girls, and Leon Bates reinforced that notion at every opportunity.

I stood after Judge Adams got settled in.

"I have an announcement for the court," I said. "The state is moving to dismiss all charges against John Lipscomb, Andres Pinzon, and Nelson Lipscomb."

Judge Adams raised his nose like he was sniffing and looked around the courtroom. An announcement of such magnitude would normally have been accompanied by fanfare. Bates was standing about fifteen feet to my right, near a door that was used by attorneys, clerks, and probation and police officers.

"Dismissing the charges?" Judge Adams said. "Just like that?"

"Yes, judge. Just like that. Our most important witnesses are dead. We can't prove our case."

"Are you moving to dismiss with prejudice or do you want to be able to reinstate the charges later if you develop more evidence?"

"With prejudice."

Judge Adams was stunned, but there was nothing he could do, nothing he could say. The decision of whether or not to prosecute a case fell directly to the district attorney general. The judge hesitated for about thirty seconds, but then he said in his most formal tone, "Very well. Case dismissed with prejudice."

I walked to where Bates was standing and put my arm around his shoulders.

"Step into the jury room with me for a minute, would you?" I said.

We walked into the empty room where jurors deliberate during trials. I pulled an envelope out of the inside pocket of my jacket and handed it to him. It was addressed to Lincoln Donner III, the governor of Tennessee.

Bates looked at it and said, "Is this what I think it is?"

"Caroline and I have talked about it a lot, Leon. I'm not a politician."

"You're right about that, Brother Dillard."

"Deliver it in person, will you?"

"With pleasure. You want me to give him that old Johnny Paycheck line?"

I smiled and nodded.

"Yeah, Leon, that'd be perfect. Tell him he can take this job and shove it."

Thank you for reading, and I sincerely hope you enjoyed *Reasonable Fear*. As an independently published author, I rely on you, the reader, to spread the word. So if you enjoyed the book, please tell your friends and family, and if it isn't too much trouble, I would appreciate a brief review on Amazon. Thanks again. My best to you and yours.

Scott

ABOUT THE AUTHOR

Scott Pratt was born in South Haven, Michigan, and moved to Tennessee when he was thirteen years old. He is a veteran of the United States Air Force and holds a Bachelor of Arts degree in English from East Tennessee State University and a Doctor of Jurisprudence from the University of Tennessee College of Law. He lives in Northeast Tennessee with his wife, their dogs, and a parrot named JoJo.

www.scottprattfiction.com

ALSO BY SCOTT PRATT

CONFLICT OF INTEREST

By

SCOTT PRATT

This book, along with every book I've written and every book I'll write, is dedicated to my darling Kristy, to her unconquerable spirit and her inspirational courage. I loved her before I was born and I'll love her after I'm long gone.

CHAPTER ONE

lifted my arms and allowed the guard to run his hands all over me. He was a young man, maybe twenty, just starting his career at the sheriff's department. They start all of the new deputies at the jail. It familiarizes them with the "local talent," so to speak, and teaches them how to deal with the same kind of incorrigible conduct they'll encounter later on patrol. I looked at the name stitched into his black pullover shirt as he finished frisking me. It was Freeman. I mused at the irony while he grunted something unintelligible and waved me through the metal detector.

I walked down the gunmetal gray halls and heard the shouts of inmates, the echoes of clanking iron doors, and the buzzing of electric locks. I'd been practicing criminal law in one form or another for almost twenty years, and the sounds I was hearing had become familiar. They were still disconcerting to a degree—I disliked everything about confinement and mistrusted almost everything about governmental authority—but over the years I'd come to accept them as a part of my life, much the way one who lives in a polluted city comes to accept the foul odor in the air.

My name is Joe Dillard, and I was at the Washington County Detention Center on a Sunday night at ten o'clock to see a man who, from what his family and a couple of his friends said on the phone, wanted to hire me. They said he would be willing to pay me a substantial amount of money to act as his defense lawyer in a criminal case. They said he was being railroaded.

I'd never met the man, but from what the people I spoke to during a flurry of telephone calls said, he was a hardworking businessman. An entrepreneur. A success story. He wasn't world-class rich, but he was far from poor. He could pay a good fee, they kept saying. He could pay a really good fee. One person suggested that he could afford as much as a hundred thousand dollars.

I didn't know whether I wanted to get involved, but the lure of a hundred grand elicited a promise from me that I would at least go down to the jail and talk to him. Before I did, however, I spoke to the police officer who was in charge of the investigation and to a couple witnesses. I didn't like what I heard.

His name was Howard French. He was forty. He had a wife and two teenage girls. He owned and operated a company he'd inherited from his father. The company manufactured cabinets and countertops and employed fifty people. I looked him over as he walked into the interview room in his bright orange jail jumpsuit. He was a shade under six feet tall and more than a little overweight. His hair was brown and cut like a banker's and his eyes were brown. He had lots of deep acne scars in his cheeks. He looked extremely uncomfortable in the handcuffs and shackles. You'd think most anyone would look uncomfortable in handcuffs and shackles, but it isn't so. I'd met guys that wore them like old socks.

Howard French had been charged with second-degree murder. He'd been in jail for less than twenty-four hours and would certainly make bond as soon as he was arraigned by a judge the following morning. He sat down stiffly in the steel chair as the guard walked out and closed the door.

"Thank you for coming, Mr. Dillard," he said. "Thank you for coming." He was nodding like a bobble-head. I reached out and shook his cuffed right hand.

"I'm sorry about what happened," I said.

He cocked his head to the left and said, "What do you mean?" Somehow I knew he'd say that.

"I'm sorry about the girls."

"Oh, me too. I can't tell you how sorry I am about those two young ladies. But I didn't have anything to do with it."

"You didn't?"

"No, I swear it. Not a thing."

I resisted the urge to get up and walk out the door. I'd been there for less than a minute, and he'd already lied to me.

"Why don't you give me your version of what happened, Mr. French?"

"Call me Howie," he said. "Everybody calls me Howie. Okay, well, I went to the Bay House to eat supper, you know? I finished eating and walked outside and there was all this commotion up at the top of the parking lot by the street. Tires squealing and a big crash and a fireball and all, so I ran up there to see what was going on. When I got to the street there was this car that was upside down on its roof. It was on fire and there was this police officer and a woman dragging someone away from the fire and then the police officer went back to the car but the fire was getting hotter and he couldn't get close to it."

"So you walked out of the restaurant just as it happened?"

"Yeah. Just as it happened."

"What time was it?"

"I'm not real sure. Around ten o'clock I guess."

"Doesn't the Bay House close at nine?"

"Maybe. I'm not sure."

"You were eating alone on a Saturday night? Where were your wife and kids?"

"They were busy. They went to a movie or something."

"Did you go anyplace else before you went to the restaurant?"

"I rode around some."

"You were driving your red Viper?"

He nodded his head enthusiastically.

"I love driving that car," he said. "It's a cool car, you know? Really fast. Five hundred horsepower. It'll fly."

His eyes lit up when he talked about the Viper, the fool. He was forty years old and running around town in a hopped-up muscle car like a kid half his age.

"Do you race it?" I said.

"No, no. I don't race it. I just drive it around."

"Do you ever race it on the street? You know what I mean. Pull up next to somebody at a red light and rev the engine, see if they want to go a few blocks?"

"Nah, I've had plenty of people try to get me to race, but I don't pay attention."

I sat back and folded my arms. I wasn't all that pleased about being there so late on a Sunday, and his nasal tone—plus the fact that he was lying through his teeth—was quickly getting on my nerves.

"How about we cut the crap, Mr. French?" I said. "I came down here because some members of your family and a couple of your friends called me and asked me to consider defending you. You've been charged with second-degree murder because the police and several witnesses say you were drag racing on a busy street when there was a lot of traffic around. A young girl was killed and another was burned so badly she'll never be the same. The one who was killed, do you even know her name?"

"Yeah, I know her name. Of course I know her name. It's been all over the news."

"What was it?"

"I think it was maybe Britney?"

"That's right. Britney James. And the girl who was with her in the passenger seat? The one who is in a coma right now? Do you know her name?"

"I think maybe it's Jane."

"Jane Clouse. Do you know what they were doing when David Burke slammed his Mustang into the back of their car?"

"People are saying they were maybe looking at some pictures."

"Right. Britney James had been crowned home-coming queen at her high school on Friday night, about twenty-four hours before this happened. Her best friend Jane Clouse had taken a bunch of pictures. They had them developed at Walgreen's. They'd just picked up the pictures and were sitting at a red light when the Mustang you were racing hit them going a hundred and thirty miles an hour."

"I wasn't racing—"

"Stop," I said, holding up my hand. "Just stop. The impact ruptured the gas tank in the little Honda Britney was driving. It also snapped the driveshaft in two, lifted the car off the ground, turned it over, and sent it more than two hundred feet down the street. Do you know that at least four different witnesses have told the police that you were sitting at a red light next to the Mustang revving your engine less than a half mile away a few seconds before the crash?"

"They saw me? They saw my face?"

"I don't think anyone saw your face, but they saw a red Viper."

"So?"

"Is this really the way you want to play it? Is your defense going to be that you weren't even on the road when the crash happened? That the red Viper everybody saw must have belonged to someone else and that you just happened to be dining a couple hundred feet from the wreck? I don't know this for a fact, but I'd be willing to bet that you're the only guy within a hundred-mile radius of Johnson City, Tennessee, who owns a red Dodge Viper."

His shoulders slumped and his chin dropped. He hesitated a few seconds before taking a deep breath.

"I can't go to jail," he said. "I might have been at the red light next to the Mustang. The Mustang might have been revving its engine. The guy who was driving it might have been trying to get me to race him. I might have started to race him, but I might have gotten scared and backed off before he ran into those girls. It wasn't my fault."

"Doesn't matter," I said. "That's like saying you and a buddy walked into a bank intending to rob it, but you got scared and left in the middle of the robbery. You'd still be held responsible under the criminal law for bank robbery. And if the buddy you went into the bank with killed someone during the robbery after you left? You'd be held responsible for the killing too. This is the same thing. That's why they charged you, and that's why you're going to wind up in jail. They won't be able to convict you of murder, but you'll get convicted of vehicular homicide for the girl who died and aggravated assault for the girl who was burned. If she dies, you'll get convicted of two counts of vehicular homicide. You're going to prison. You might as well get used to the idea and start planning for it."

"But I didn't hit them! He hit them!"

"He'll get convicted and go to prison too, if it makes you feel any better."

He leaned forward on his elbows and started looking at me with what I perceived as a conspiratorial gleam in his eyes.

"What kind of money are we talking here?" he said. "How much will it take for you to get serious about this? Everybody has been telling me to get old Joe Dillard.

He's the baddest man around. He'll fight for you. He's not afraid of anything or anybody. He's a junkyard dog, that's what he is. He'll chew the state's witnesses up and spit them out all over the courtroom. That's what I need, Mr. Dillard. I need that junkyard dog. How much will it cost me?"

I stood and pushed the button on the wall to summon the guards. The words I'd spoken had absolutely no meaning to him.

"What are you doing?" he said.

"Leaving. I'm going home."

"What? Wait a minute! You'll take my case, won't you? I'll pay you two hundred thousand dollars, up front, cash on the barrel head."

There was a time in my life when two hundred thousand dollars would have enticed me to defend Jack the Ripper. But those days had passed. I'd made good money during my legal career, and I enjoyed the things money brought to me and to my family, but I was no longer interested in trading my conscience for a fat fee. I just wanted to be a good man, a good lawyer, a good husband and father. I wanted life to be simpler than it had been in the past.

This guy was guilty, and he'd already showed me he wasn't the least bit interested in the truth. He wanted to be free of responsibility for the death and pain he'd caused, and for two hundred thousand dollars, he would expect me to ensure both his freedom and his public absolution. And to be honest, for two hundred grand, I could have probably done it.

But I just didn't want to. The door buzzed and I pushed it open.

"So you're going to walk out on me?" he said. "Just like that? Didn't you kill five men not too long ago? Five men! Why aren't you in jail? What makes you any different from me?"

I stopped and turned to face him.

"I'm not any different from you, Mr. French," I said. "But I'm surprised nobody has ever taught you that life isn't fair sometimes. Good luck in prison."

CHAPTER TWO

The accusation Howard French hurled at me was true. It had been nearly a year since I'd ambushed and killed five men as they approached my home intending to kill me and every member of my family. I lay in wait for them, set traps for them, and I killed them exactly the way the United States Army had taught me to kill when I was still a teenager—efficiently and without passion.

The events that led up to that night were so perfectly arbitrary and chaotic that I'd often thought that perhaps something else was at play, something like fate or destiny, but I'd learned over the years that dwelling on the past was as useless as fretting over the future. In the aftermath of the "Gunfight at the OK Corral," as the media labeled it, I resigned my job as district attorney general and went back to private practice, albeit on a limited basis. My daughter had given birth to a baby boy back in May and had honored me by naming the child Joseph. My son was still pursuing his professional baseball career at the minor league level, and my wife's breast cancer was a painful, distant memory. I'd decided I wouldn't let what happened that night have any effect on me, and until French mentioned it at the jail, I hadn't thought about it in months. Once I walked out of his jail cell, I pushed it from my mind again.

Six days after my meeting with French, I learned of Lindsay Monroe's disappearance when I walked through the kitchen after mowing the lawn on a Saturday morning. My wife, Caroline, who had been sweeping the kitchen floor, was standing stone still, staring at a small television on the kitchen counter with a look of abject horror on her face. The weekend anchorman at the local CBS affiliate, a fresh-faced kid with a nasal voice and an accent that said, "Hi, I'm from nowhere," was doing his best to sound and look deadly serious. This is what he said:

"Police and a small group of volunteers are combing Tennessee's oldest town this morning in search of a six-year-old girl who was apparently taken from her bed last night. Lindsay Monroe of Jonesborough was reported missing shortly after 7:00 a.m. by her mother, Mary Monroe. Sources say Mrs. Monroe called 9-1-1 after going to Lindsay's room and finding the child's bed empty. Mrs. Monroe reportedly told the emergency dispatcher that a window in the second-floor bedroom was open and a screen had been removed. We go live now to News Twelve correspondent Nate Baldasano, who is outside the Monroe home."

"No," Caroline murmured. "Please, no."

The screen switched to a slim, mid-thirties, generic-looking man with black hair named Nate Baldasano. Baldasano had been a reporter for News Twelve for at least ten years. I'd been interviewed by him several times because I'd been involved in a lot of criminal cases both as a defense lawyer and later as a prosecutor. Ten years is a long time for a television reporter to stay in the Tri-Cities media market. It means one of two things: the reporter either lacks drive or lacks talent.

"There is a pall hanging over Jonesborough's National Historic District this morning," Baldasano said. "The police aren't releasing any information as of yet, but so far we know that a six-year-old first-grader, Lindsay Monroe, has gone missing. Her parents, Richard Monroe, a respected local businessman, and Mary Monroe are both inside the house at this time along with several police officers. Neighbors and friends of the Monroes have started a search of the immediate area."

The broadcast cut to a blonde woman. At the bottom of the screen was the caption, "Melissa Franklin, Neighbor."

"We're frantic," the woman said. "We've already printed hundreds of flyers and are going door-to-door passing them out and asking people to help us find Lindsay. Everyone around here knows her. She's such a sweet, lovely child."

A photo of the girl flashed onto the screen. I recognized her. She was dark-haired and blue-eyed, a beautiful little girl, grinning widely, missing a front tooth. The next shot was of the house. I recognized it too because it was smack in the middle of downtown Jonesborough, only a couple blocks from the old Washington County courthouse on Main Street. It was a large, two-story brick house that was built in the 1870s and was one of a dozen or so "historic homes" that the tourists liked to ogle from the sidewalk. I'd been inside it once, many years earlier, before the Monroes bought it. Caroline and I had been invited to a progressive dinner a week before Christmas—a dinner that starts with drinks at one home, then moves to another home for appetizers, then to another home for soup and salad, then to another home for the main course, that kind of thing—and the house where the Monroes now lived had been the last stop of the evening. At the time, it was owned by a retired liquor distributor named Lovelace. It had been updated and remodeled several times, and it was impressive. The interior reminded me of the Biltmore Estate in Asheville, North Carolina, all gleaming hardwood, expensive rugs, pristine antique furniture, and sparkling chandeliers.

"Sources tell me that an unknown perpetrator may have used a ladder to reach Lindsay's second-floor bedroom window," Baldasano said. "My information indicates that Lindsay was last seen around 10:00 p.m. last night when her mother put her to bed. One source, speaking on condition of anonymity, told me that a ransom note was left on Lindsay's pillow, although I have not been able to confirm that information."

The guy actually used the phrases "unknown perpetrator" and "my information indicates." He reported unconfirmed information about a ransom note. It was broadcast journalism at its finest. Caroline walked over to the television and turned it off.

"Let's go," she said.

"Where?"

"To Jonesborough. Lindsay is one of my girls. We're going to go help look for her."

Caroline had owned and operated a dance studio for more than twenty years. The relationships she formed with her students were deeper than those formed between most teachers and students. Typically, a teacher is involved with a student for a year, maybe two. Even high school coaches have kids for only a couple years before the athletes graduate and move on. But Caroline's girls, for the most part, came to her when they were three or four years old, and some of them stayed through their senior year in high school. Many of her students left dancing around the age of ten and moved on to things like cheerleading or gymnastics or volleyball or softball or swimming, but there were dozens of girls who had taken dance from Caroline for ten years or more. She watched them grow from babies to little girls to young girls to teenage girls to young women. She knew their families, their friends, their favorite colors, their birthdays, their favorite foods. She became an integral part of their lives.

I'm convinced that those young girls kept Caroline alive during the worst of her five-year battle with breast cancer. No matter how tired she was, no matter how sick she'd been, she always, always went to the studio to teach, and she would always come home rejuvenated. It was as if the enthusiasm and the optimism and the *life* in those young people transferred to her through some sort of spiritual osmosis and kept her going for one more day, one more week, one more month, one more year. It was a beautiful thing to behold.

Lindsay Monroe was a cute, feisty, spirited child, and had quickly become one of Caroline's favorites. Caroline often spoke of her when she returned home from the studio. She'd tell me stories about things Lindsay said or did. Caroline often affectionately described her as a "hot mess."

"They're already turning it into a circus," I said to Caroline. "Why don't we just let the police handle it? They're trained—"

"I'm going with you or without you," she said. She was standing at the door leading to the garage.

"At least let me change my shirt," I said. "I smell like a horse."

"Now," she said over her shoulder.

As I started after her, I felt a sinking sensation in my stomach. I'd defended one child murderer and prosecuted two others in my career. I'd been involved in dozens of other murder cases. I'd dealt with rape and robbery and violent assault, but I'd never, not once, had to endure a case that involved a young girl vanishing in the night. I had no idea what was going on, and I had no idea what would happen in the future, but the gnawing in my stomach told me that nothing good would come of this, nothing at all.

CHAPTER THREE

When Caroline and I arrived in Jonesborough around 10:30 a.m., we parked in the old courthouse lot and walked the three blocks to the Monroes'. There was a large group of people gathered on the sidewalk in front of the house and crime-scene tape had been stretched around the edge of the lot. Caroline ducked under the tape and started up the concrete sidewalk toward the front door. I went after her. We were met halfway up the walk by a young, uniformed Jonesborough policeman named Will Traynor. I knew Will from my time at the district attorney's office. He smiled, although it appeared to be a reluctant smile, as we approached.

"Mr. Dillard," he said as he reached out to shake my hand. "It's been awhile."

"Nice to see you, Will."

"I'd like to talk to Mary Monroe," Caroline said. "We're friends. Lindsay takes dance at my studio."

"I'm sorry, ma'am, but I can't let you go inside. It's a crime scene. I have strict orders not to let anyone past the tape."

"But I need to talk to her," Caroline said.

Traynor looked at me for help, and I took Caroline gently by the elbow.

"He's right," I said. "They'll skin him alive if he lets you in there."

"Sorry, Mr. Dillard," Traynor said.

"No need to apologize."

"Can you at least tell me if Lindsay is all right?" Caroline said. "Do you have any idea?"

Traynor looked around and lowered his eyes. "As far as I know, she's still missing," he said quietly. "We're doing everything we can."

"Thanks, Will," I said. "Good luck."

I turned Caroline around and we walked back under the yellow tape. Nate Baldasano immediately stuck a microphone in my face.

"What can you tell us, Mr. Dillard? Are you involved in this case?"

"No, I'm not involved and I can't tell you anything," I said. "Please get out of my way."

Caroline and I started walking back down the street in the direction of the courthouse, just to get away from the crowd.

"Is Lindsay the kind of kid that might wander off early in the morning?" I said.

"She's precocious and independent-minded, but I don't think she's reckless," Caroline said.

"Let's assume she wandered off, since we're here. Where would a little girl go?"

"She'd probably go into the backyard, but I'm sure they've searched it."

"But what could draw her away from the backyard? An animal, maybe? A stray dog or a cat?"

"Maybe. Kids like water. Maybe she came around front and went to play by the creek."

A small creek ran all the way through town about a half block from Main Street. It cut right through the Monroes' front yard.

"There are people all around the creek, Caroline. If she was there, somebody would have found her."

Not only were there people all around the creek, there were people everywhere. The news about Lindsay was out, and the street was quickly filling up. I could hear calls of "Lindsay!" "Lindsay Monroe!" coming from side streets and the alleys between the buildings, from the banks on either side of the creek, from the railroad tracks a block away. Several people had dogs on leashes, and almost everyone was carrying a cell phone.

"I don't think there's anything we can do here," I said.

She gave me that look of hers, the one where she sets her jaw and her eyes become lasers. It means, "Don't give me any trouble right now."

"What do you want to do?" I said.

"Look for her. Let's just look. Maybe we'll see something somebody missed."

We walked down Main Street to Fox and turned right toward the railroad tracks.

"Do you think there's really a ransom note?" Caroline said.

"I hope so," I said. "There's a lot better chance of catching him if he tries to pick up a ransom."

"Him? You're sure it's a him?"

"Women don't do ransom kidnappings. It's a man thing."

If you enjoyed the beginning of *Conflict of Interest*, you can purchase here via Amazon:

<u>Conflict of Interest</u>
Again, thank you for reading!

Scott